Hud

Hud

The Preacher's Sons 2

Mary E. Hanks

www.maryehanks.com

Suzanne D. Williams Cover Design
www.feelgoodromance.com

Cover photo:
Viorel Kurnosov @ shutterstock.com

Visit Mary's website:

www.maryehanks.com

You can write Mary at
maryhanks@maryehanks.com

To Sharyl

Thanks for loving my big brother and bringing so much joy and adventure into his life.

"Everything is possible for him who believes."

Mark 9:23

Chapter One

Three days before Lake's race

Hudson North slammed down the phone in his office and let out a low growl of frustration. Within minutes of each other, two of his company's four investors had withdrawn their financial support from his five-acre land development on the north side of Ketchikan, Alaska. Everyone experienced some setbacks in business. But this was catastrophic!

He pinched the bridge of his nose and shook his head, unable to believe his bad luck. Usually, he was better at convincing investors to see his vision. What had gone wrong with the North Dunmore project that would have provided six-month residencies for artisans and an apartment complex for locals?

If the other two investors heard about the fallout, they'd probably withdraw their support too. Just wait until his business partner heard about the collapse of their dreams. All their work and investment gone? How would Trista Dunmore, a mother of a young girl, cope with the loss? How would he?

The phone rang.

Momentarily frozen, he didn't even glance at it. If all the investors pulled out, that would ruin them. But even if he was in a terrible financial bind, he was a businessman who answered his calls. Unless it was Lake—he was not talking with that brother today!

A number he didn't recognize flashed across the screen. "Hello."

"Hud?" a female voice asked.

"Yeah."

"It's Irish."

He groaned. He didn't want to speak to Lake's fake bride, either. "This isn't a good time."

"I'm sorry, Hud." Her softly-spoken apology kept him from saying something disparaging or hanging up. "I'm partly to blame for you and Lake having a rift in your relationship."

"It's nothing personal," he muttered.

"I know what the argument is about." She took a breath. "I have a favor to ask you." She was apologizing and asking for a favor?

"What's that?" He glanced at his wristwatch.

"Lake is racing this weekend."

"And?"

"I wondered if you'd come to his race." She chuckled lightly. "I know it's short notice. But could you come and cheer him on? Then the two of you could talk and work things out. What do you say?"

"Not happening. Things are difficult enough here. Besides, why would I travel to Idaho to watch my brother do what I've seen him do many times before? I'm up to my ears in a business crisis while Lake plays with his dogs!" He sounded gruff and rude even to himself, but he wanted to end this call quickly.

Irish went silent. Had he been too opinionated? She probably wouldn't care to hear about his lousy day.

"Look," Irish said firmly. "I can't begin to understand the relationship between you and your eight brothers. Yes, Lake and I work with dogs, and that doesn't sound important to you. But to us, our dogs are our family. They're like our kids. They mean the world to us."

"Lake and I never saw eye to eye about that either."

"You mean the dogs or me?"

"Both," Hud wanted to say but didn't. Lake had married Irish to grab hold of their grandfather's wealth. In doing so, he went against everything he and Hud had agreed not to do—and against everything his brothers vowed never to do.

"You heard about him rescuing the dogs in the shelter, right?" Irish was obviously trying to appeal to his sense of decency or compassion, but it wasn't working. "He's given a bunch of animals, and therefore the people who will claim them as their family, a new lease on life!"

"Spare me the tears about pulling dogs from the jaws of death."

"That's exactly what he did! Some of the dogs were on a kill list."

"I don't see—"

"Look, you moron, open your eyes! Lake is a good and decent man who cares about God's creatures. He did something you wouldn't have done!"

Hud jumped to his feet, tension rippling up his neck and shoulders. "You look here. I don't know how you sank your claws into my brother's money." Irish gasped. "Call it compassion for animals if you want. I'd say it was a woman who knew what she was after—Richard Dupont's wealth—and she did what she had to do to get it!"

"I've never been so insulted in my life!"

"Welcome to the North family!" He stuck his finger beneath his tie and undid his top button.

Under normal circumstances, he wasn't quite so temperamental and snarky. Why did Irish act like he didn't care for others? Some would call his attempts to help artists altruistic. He did. So did his brother, Aiden, a struggling found-object sculptor living in an artists' community in Denver. Although, some of his brothers might disagree with his noble assessment of himself. Some might call him self-absorbed, standoffish, or even rude.

"Lake and I did marry to benefit a cause we believe in," Irish said in a hushed tone. "But we've fallen in love. We care deeply for one another."

"That's not what I've heard." He didn't try to subdue his annoyance.

"This informant doesn't happen to be Spur or Wilks, does it?"

He wasn't ratting out his younger brothers. He appreciated them keeping him in the loop, and he always took their calls.

"By your silence, my guess is correct."

"My silence means I'm ready for this phone call to be finished."

"You are hardheaded and offensive, just like I heard."

"Who told you that?"

"Someone who knows a lot about your family. About you," she said disapprovingly. "Suspicion goes both ways, brother."

Hud clenched his free hand tightly around a pen. If it were a pencil, he would have broken it in two.

"See you on race day?" She had some nerve!

"I doubt it."

"Did you know Lake is sending your parents on a cruise? *He* has a good heart. *He's* a nice person."

Her defending Lake surprised him. She almost sounded like she really cared for him. A cruise, huh? None of his brothers had mentioned that.

"I have to go." Hud ended the call and flung the pen across the room, hitting the wall.

Who in Thunder Ridge was telling Irish tales about him? Some brokenhearted female he'd never taken on a second date, no doubt.

What would Mom say about how rudely he'd spoken to the newest member of the North family? Never one to mince words, she'd tell him exactly what she thought of his unkindness. Then she would say she loved him, just like she'd done hundreds of times before.

Exhaling a breath of hot air, he wrote Irish a brief text. *Sorry. Crummy day. No excuse.*

Thanks, she texted him back. *I still hope you'll come to the race.*

He didn't respond.

Chapter Two

The call Hud had been dreading came an hour later while he was perusing some drawings and attempting to produce a lower cost estimate for the North Dunmore project. The third investor's withdrawal nailed another peg in his and Trista's financial coffin. With his jaw clenched, he listened to Harold Jorgenson complaining about the risks and low returns involved in the art-community concept. Even with the assurance of future profits from the apartment complex, he blamed Hud and Trista for not explaining their proposal better, while Hud silently berated him for not reading through his documentation before signing it!

"Who cares about the arts, anyway?" Harold demanded.

It took every ounce of internal strength Hud possessed not to yell, *"I care! My brother, Aiden, cares! Artists contribute to the beauty of the world we live in! Can you imagine the planet without paintings and sculptures in it?"* But what good would his explanation do? The man had given up on their project already.

Needing to rid himself of some stress and stir up whatever hope he had left, Hud exited his downtown office and trudged toward the docks lining the waterfront. He'd pick up a hot drink at his favorite coffee shop, then hike a mile, or four, however much it took to clear his head. Eventually, he'd head back to his office, call Trista, and face shutting down the place. Breaking the lease agreement would have undesirable consequences too. How was he going to pay for that? He groaned.

Had his first business venture really come to this? One investor remained who would, no doubt, catch wind of the others' decisions and bail, too. Hud had thrown all his savings into this undertaking, and so did Trista, each to the tune of fifty grand. He could barely think about their losses without feeling sick to his stomach.

He had been so determined to see this project through. Hadn't he bragged to Lake that he would do this alone and show them all? The proud, arrogant Hudson North could do anything he set his mind to, or so he'd thought. His grand idea had fizzled. A bitter taste roiled up in his throat. How had he lost all the money he'd worked so hard to save for fifteen years? All the toil of second and third part-time jobs? All the self-sacrifice of scrimping and saving every penny wasted? Gone?

He groaned again.

What if he lost his business investment and the waterfront condominium he loved? What if he went bankrupt? Tension spiraled up his spine and neck. How horrible to end up back in Thunder Ridge mooching off Mom and Dad like Spur and Wilks were doing!

No, that would not happen to him—not with his independent nature and his MBA! He'd get through this setback and start over somewhere else. He didn't know how or where, but he'd figure out a way.

Unfortunately, this financial disaster didn't affect only him. He had Trista to consider. He would do anything to keep her and her five-year-old daughter from suffering.

At the coffee shop, he placed his order and then stood at the side of the counter, awaiting his drink.

"Hudson?"

He tensed, recognizing his business partner's soft, feminine voice. Before turning toward Trista, he stiffened his back and lifted his chin so she wouldn't see his appalling emotional state.

"Tris—" The word died on his lips when he met her red-rimmed indigo eyes. Strands of dark chin-length hair protruded at odd angles from her head like she'd been thrusting her fingers through the strands. "What's wrong? Are you all right?"

She shrugged and her face crumpled. "Can we talk?"

"Sure."

Had she already heard about their deplorable business situation? He'd hoped to let her down easily after sorting things out in his own mind. She nodded toward a table for two in the back corner, where a to-go cup rested on the tabletop.

"I'll be right there." He waited for his mocha, dreading the inevitable conversation to come. A few minutes later, he sat down at Trista's table and sipped his hot drink. "What's going on?"

"I have an important question to ask you."

"Shoot." He set his cup down.

"Can I have my money back?"

The hairs on his neck stood up. She wanted her investment returned? When? In twenty years? She must not be aware of their current crisis. "When do you want your money back?" Drumming up fifty thousand dollars again would take him a long, long time.

"Today?" She grimaced.

"Uh. Sorry, Trista. That would be impossible!"

 "I'm in a desperate situation, Hudson."

"Aren't we all?" How in the world did she expect him to repay her share of the business today? Was she serious?

"What do you mean, 'Aren't we all?'" She pressed the back of her hand against her nose as if to stop it from running. "I put all my savings—my dad's life insurance money—into our company."

"We both took risks."

"I know." She thrust her fingers through her hair like he'd imagined her doing before. "But my mom is about to lose her house. I didn't know she was in such a bad financial situation. I suspected things weren't going well—just not at this level!" Trista's words ran over each other. "Layla and I have been staying with her since we moved back to Ketchikan. It's the only home my daughter has known. What will we do if Mom's house goes into foreclosure, and I don't have any savings to bail her out?" She pressed her fist against her front teeth and shook her head, tears flooding her eyes. "I'm sorry about asking for the money."

"If it were in my power to do anything—" He groaned. What a mess they were in! Trista's troubles moved him emotionally. She had the kid, which made her situation ten times worse than his. And, as she said, it was the money her dad had left her as his only beneficiary. But what could he do? He felt powerless. "I'd like to help you. Honestly, I would. But I don't have the money." He hated even saying this. "It's spent. You know that, right?"

Her dark blue eyes, sparkling with flecks of purple, shimmered with tears. "I thought you might be able to reimburse some of the funds—maybe enough to keep my mom afloat?"

When her lips trembled, his gaze latched onto the movement, mesmerized by it. He had to force himself to focus on her indigo irises, not on her puffy, kissable-looking lips. They were business partners and colleagues. Nothing more. But heaven help him, he'd been fighting an attraction to her for weeks. "I would do anything to help you. However, I'm stuck in this, also."

Groaning, she covered her face with both hands. "I'm sorry for breaking down. I'm not usually so emotional." Slowly, she lowered her hands and placed them around her cup. "I feel stupid for not knowing about Mom's finances sooner. I'm in business. I have a degree. I should have spotted her dilemma right off!"

Hud should have noticed Lake's dilemma sooner, too. Then he might have stopped him from making some of his terrible mistakes. Now he was in a disastrous economic crisis himself!

How could he even help Trista? He'd thrown all their money into the joint project. But their combined finances weren't enough to keep it afloat. That's why they were dependent on investors. For some reason, maybe due to the shaky economy, they'd pulled out one by one. What a wretched situation!

Granny Trish would tell him he ought to pray about it—and he probably should. But after walking away from Thunder Ridge and all it represented, how could he? Then again, how could he not? He was in such a dreadful jam. His dreams of forging an artists' community that would benefit Aiden and others like him were tanking. Unless—

No! A shudder rippled through him as if a dozen bees had stung him. Every muscle and sinew in his body tensed. Even briefly considering going against his brothers' pact and accepting his grandfather's vile inheritance twisted knots in his stomach and made his head ache. Lake had breached the despicable barrier, and Hud was still furious with him.

He wouldn't take the money!

Yet if he did—he couldn't believe he was even considering the idea—the legacy would solve his and Trista's financial losses. It would fix every monetary problem between them and pave the way for a more prosperous future for both! But at what cost? He took a swig of hot coffee, chasing down the bitter taste in his mouth.

"What's going on in your head? You had one of your ideas, didn't you? Have you considered a way to salvage my mother's house for Layla and me?" A tentative smile broke through Trista's sadness like she thought he might have the answer to all her troubles.

"No. It's worse than that." He stared out the window at the gray clouds mirroring his turbulent emotions.

"What could be worse than watching my mother and daughter thrown out on the street?"

He met her gaze. "Three of our investors pulled out today."

"Three? No. Hudson. That isn't possible!"

"It's the truth. That's why I have nothing to offer you." He pressed his fingers against his temples. "I planned to call and tell you to look for another job. We must close the office."

"This is unreal. I can't believe it." She slumped forward. "What will I tell Mom? How will I explain not having a home to my daughter? Not having food!" Tears flooded her eyes again.

"Look. I'll fix this," he said too quickly. How could he fix anything? The bank might loan him more funds. No, they absolutely would not! He'd maxed out all his resources. "Give me until tomorrow. By then, I'll either have some money to give you"—he gulped—"or else I'll have an answer to solve things for both of us."

"How will you do all that?" The doubt crossing her face said she didn't believe he was that capable, after all.

"I'll explain tomorrow." Yet he couldn't bear the thought of the *only* solution that came to mind. After the way he'd ridiculed Lake about marrying Irish to grab the inheritance money, how could he live with himself if he took the same course of action?

Yet if he walked away and left Trista and her daughter to suffer, how would he live with himself then?

Chapter Three

The next day, Trista's mom cried and bemoaned her situation, telling Trista how terribly sorry she was for letting things get so bad. Why hadn't she explained her indebtedness before now? Mom had been watching Layla when she could have gotten a job and possibly saved the house. Yet Trista knew she had been doing her best to help her and Layla, which added to her own sense of feeling responsible for everything that was going wrong.

She'd spent most of last night worrying and praying. At opposite ends of the spectrum, the two didn't mix well. But she was trying to wrap her thoughts around the business failures and the household losses—and attempting to trust God even when things looked bleak. The need to provide for her daughter and her mom weighed heavily upon her. Thus her worries. And more prayers.

Her phone chirped, and Hudson's name crossed the screen. "Hey."

"Can we meet?" He sounded tense.

"About?"

"What I mentioned yesterday. Will you meet me at the dock downtown?"

"The dock? Oh. I guess. When?"

"Thirty minutes."

"All right. I'll be there."

Then what? Clean out their office and say goodbye? If their partnership collapsed, would Hudson leave town? If so, she'd be reminded of their broken dreams and financial ruin whenever she drove by their old office or barely started land development. And he'd probably drum up another business scheme somewhere else—without her! Oh, she'd hate that!

Thirty minutes later, Trista stood on the large dock facing the choppy waters of the channel in front of downtown Ketchikan where gigantic cruise ships docked in the spring and summer. Today, the place looked like a ghost town. The dock was completely empty, other than her standing there with strong winds whipping against her. Her eyes watered from the breeze and the sting of saltwater in the air.

"Trista," Hudson spoke her name softly, barely distinguishable above the waves splashing against the pilings below. She hadn't heard him approaching. He held out a red rose. Why red? Was this his way of saying goodbye? She took the flower and turned it slowly in her hands.

"Thank you for all your hard work on our project." So this was goodbye! "It means the world to me that you believed in my ideas and joined forces with me." He gulped like he was having trouble swallowing. "That you trusted me."

Had she done that? She rarely trusted any man.

She plunged her other hand into her jacket pocket, shivering, waiting for him to say the words that would end their partnership. When Hudson turned silently toward the sea, rocking on his shoes like he was stalling or possibly feeling emotional, she asked, "What now?"

He shuddered as if he had a sudden chill. "We face the future."

"Without North Dunmore?" So much for her business degree helping provide a better future for Layla.

"Not without it. Perhaps altering it." He faced her with a strained look, his dark hair fluttering in the wind. He made a gulping noise. "What would you think of North and North?"

"I don't understand."

Grimacing slightly, Hudson knelt on one knee in front of her. Her jaw dropped *and* tingling sparks shot up her spine. Was he going to propose? Surely not! They weren't even romantic together! "Hudson, stand up!"

"Hear me out, okay?" He gazed up at her with a mournful expression.

"Get up, now, or so help me, I'm walking away."

"Fine." Groaning, he stood and dusted off the knees of his pants. That's when she noticed his greenish skin tone and how sickly he appeared. He barely met her gaze. "I was going to ask you to marry me, Trista."

"No, you were not! Don't mock the holy state of matrimony like that!" Even with those shooting tingles she'd felt, a marriage proposal between them was absurd!

Hudson tossed up his hands and walked a dozen feet from her. "Why did I think this might work between us?"

"I have no idea! What are you even talking about?" She stomped across the wooden dock until she stood in front of him. "Why did you get down on your knee like that? Have you been drinking?" She sniffed the air just in case.

"No! I had a stupid idea, that's all. One I thought might fix our dilemma and your mom's situation." He scraped his hand over his nearly-black hair and squinted toward the gray sky.

"Go on. I'm listening." Clutching the rose, she pursed her lips and tapped her foot.

Finally, he met her gaze. "Look, Trista. I don't love you."

"No kidding." She glared at him.

"I'm sure I'd fall for you in time."

"Thanks for the vote of confidence. I don't love you either! And I don't know that I ever could!"

"Wow." He went still. "A woman has never slapped me in the face with words before."

"It's about time, then. Why would you propose to me? Or think it would solve anything?"

Shaking his head like he was just as baffled as she was, he took a small box from his pocket and set it on his flat palm. She gulped, knowing the delicate box had to contain an engagement ring. But why would he ask her to marry him? When he opened the lid, a beautiful solitaire diamond engagement ring sparkled up at her. Had he bought it on credit since he said he was out of money?

"Why did you get this ring when we don't love each other?"

"I find you attractive."

"Hudson—"

"Hud," he corrected her. "You're pleasant to talk with when you aren't angry with me. We have common goals."

"At business. Not at life!"

"What's that supposed to mean?" His dark eyebrows furrowed.

"You are a player, that's what!"

He groaned and stuffed the ring box back in his pocket. "If we were to get married—"

"I'm not marrying you in a million years!"

"If we were to get married—notice I said 'if,' which implies we probably won't—I'd inherit enough money to back our current project, the next one, and pay off your mother's mortgage."

"What?" She staggered backward. "That isn't possible."

"Yes, it is. I'll have access to a substantial inheritance if I'm married by my thirty-fifth birthday. My brother, Lake, married someone he barely knew and took his half of the legacy. That's why I haven't spoken with him lately." He thrust out his hands. "Now

I'm in such a jam that I'm considering taking the detestable funds myself. But I loathe the idea of marrying someone to get the money!"

So he was serious about the proposal? Her limbs quaked. Her heart throbbed hard against her ribcage. Disbelief pulsed through her like a drumbeat. The idea of her and Hudson marrying was preposterous! Yet something compelled her to ask, "So if we married—not that I think we should, because I don't—you'd fall into a large sum?"

"Yes."

"And you must be married to obtain this money?" She still needed clarity.

"It was my grandfather's final way of manipulating Lake and me—or our mom since they were estranged." He let out a low growl of disgust or irritation. "Lake married the first woman who agreed with the conditions. I thought—"

"That I was like her?" Trista's volume escalated alongside her turbulent emotions. "That I would marry you for financial gain? Think again, Hudson North!"

He grimaced, showing his teeth between taut lips. "It would be a real marriage, eventually. I wouldn't want it any other way."

"*You* wouldn't want it any other way?" Heat rushed from her temples to her ankles. She'd never fainted. But she had the strongest desire to dissolve into the wooden boards of the dock and wake up with amnesia, forgetting this conversation ever happened. "Let's get one thing straight. I detest your suggestion!"

"Believe me, so do I." He glanced out toward the gray, churning waters with whitecaps flapping about like a multitude of tiny sailboats. "I promise I'd provide for you, Trista. Your daughter would never lack for anything. Nor your mom."

"How dare you insult me by bringing my family into this!"

"I didn't mean to insult you. I get that marriage to me is a jarring idea. But you should understand the benefits. The risks too." He shrugged. "I'm probably a difficult person to live with."

"Live with?"

"Would that be so awful?" He sounded more vulnerable and lacking in self-confidence than he usually did. "I am attracted to you, Trista. How do you feel about me?"

"You and I don't jive, Hudson. There's no chemistry or warmth." *Not much, anyway.* "If there were something between us, we would have—" She shook her head. "We didn't." Their relationship had only ever been about business. She'd never even flirted with him.

"Please—" He cleared his throat like he was having a difficult time speaking. "Will you consider marrying me for a cause beyond ourselves? For the artists we've been planning to help, the short-term residencies would mean the world to them—for my brother, too, who I hope will stay in one of our houses." His smile appeared forced. "I can get back on my knee and ask you properly if that would help."

"Please, don't!" She couldn't deny that Hudson was an attractive man with a great smile who could probably talk his way into any woman's affection. She'd gotten into trouble with one of those kinds of men before. She wouldn't let that happen again. "We work well together because we've been only coworkers."

"I agree. But I admitted to being attracted to you."

"Me and a hundred other women." How dare he put her in this position of having to discuss his love life!

"My mother raised me to be a gentleman."

"Would she approve of your proposal to marry me for money?"

He drew in a long breath. "For the good of providing for artists like Aiden and caring for your mom? Those are respectable reasons she'd understand."

Another gust of wind off the water blew against Trista, and she shivered. After Neil had left her pregnant and alone to fend for herself, her heart hardened to ever being in love again or trusting another man—especially someone like Hudson.

"The first time I saw you," he said huskily, "I was drawn to how you spoke with such conviction at the city council meeting. Then, when I approached you about my project, your blue eyes with the tiniest flashes of purple lit up like sparks of fire."

His mentioning the way they'd met and her eye colors stirred something within her—not attraction, but something warm and compelling. "You told me to find a need in the community and meet that need." She smiled at the memory.

"And now?" Hudson clasped her hand gently. She didn't pull away, intrigued by his glistening silver-black eyes staring pensively at her. "Are you ready to give up on your idea of service in the town you grew up in? To watch your mom's house get foreclosed?"

"You're playing dirty pool." She tugged her hand away. She shouldn't be letting him touch her. "I can't marry you—not even for a chance at your windfall that would make my life easier."

"Please, consider what I've said? Then we can talk again."

"I won't change my mind."

"Thanks for the warning." He smiled an infuriatingly handsome smile. He'd probably done that to the dozens of women he'd dated to get them to succumb to his wishes.

She didn't know how many people he'd gone out with recently. But when she first met Hudson seven months ago, he'd dated a different woman almost every night. She had been with a player like that before. She would never marry a man she didn't trust.

Chapter Four

On Sunday morning, Hud stood next to Irish at the finish line of the second day of racing in Priest Lake. He'd used his Frequent Flyer miles to come to North Idaho for the weekend to take care of two things. He'd accepted Irish's invitation to watch his brother's skijoring race. And on Monday morning, he planned to see Michael Peyton, the family lawyer who'd taken care of Lake's inheritance settlement. While he could have spoken to a lawyer in Ketchikan, he didn't want to muddy the financial waters of his personal and business life yet.

He was still contemplating the ramifications of possibly getting married and accepting the inheritance—and both were causing him a great deal of anxiety.

"Here he comes! Here he comes!" Irish pointed to a skier with two huskies pulling in front of him as if Hud didn't recognize Lake coming across the snow-covered trail toward them.

Hud wouldn't shout and cheer like Lake's wife was doing. She was undeniably enthusiastic! What were his brother's chances of winning if Irish had been racing this weekend? Spur and Finn had both informed him that she and her dogs were the faster competitors. Yet she stood there cheering for Lake and shouting encouragement as if her life depended on it. Was more going on between the newlyweds than Hud thought?

Pal and Ice charged across the finish line with Lake skiing strong behind them. Amid the applauding, Hud joined in the clapping too. "Good job, Lake!"

Irish ran through the snow to reach Lake and flung her arms around him. Their amorous kissing and hugging surprised Hud. According to Wilks, they acted emotionless toward each other. That didn't appear to be the case unless their affection was all for show. By Lake's wide grin and the way he held Irish closely to his side, that wasn't the case.

After offering congratulations to Lake and promising they'd meet up before he returned to Alaska, Hud left the event. He didn't want to explain the main reason why he was here yet. How could he confess to Lake that he might be accepting the inheritance? Even contemplating signing the documents made him want to return to Alaska without seeing the lawyer. But he'd promised Trista a solution. He had to set the groundwork for that, even if everything fell through.

Later that day, Gran asked him to attend the evening church service with her, and he reluctantly agreed. It was hard to say no to his grandmother.

Since he'd rented a high-end vehicle in Spokane, he offered to drive Gran and Mom to the church. They oohed and aahed over the car's leather scent and soft, comfy cushions. Thankfully, he'd had enough room on his credit card to afford this one last indulgence.

During the service, when the group stood to sing "Amazing Grace" and Hud remained seated, Gran nudged his knee. Just like when he was a kid, she wasn't letting him get away with that. Standing slowly, he met her gaze and nodded. He loved the dear woman and would do almost anything she asked.

Halfway into the second stanza, she tapped her hymnal, silently reminding him that she'd also like him to sing. He sang a few words to make her happy, but something about the lyrics stirred him emotionally, too. Of course, he recognized the familiar song that had been written by John Newton, a slave trader in the eighteenth century, whose life was transformed by God.

If the Lord could radically alter that man's heart, could he do the same for Hud's? Would God even listen to him after the years he'd ignored praying and reading the Bible? Would He forgive his past indiscretions? Guilt rose in his throat, nearly gagging him.

He mumbled the chorus of "Amazing Grace" and tried to focus on it, but his mind wandered. When he was young, Dad had told him stories about Hudson Taylor, a missionary called to China. Hud's birth parents had named him after his maternal grandfather. But when he and Aiden came to live with Aunt Liv's family, Smith said their names were also like some men of faith in history, just like his other sons were named after men of strong faith. Hud's role model was supposedly Hudson Taylor. Aiden's was A.W. Tozer, and Dad nicknamed him A.W.—a name that stuck.

At the time, being like Lake and having a name like someone Smith admired had deepened Hud's feelings about being a part of the North family. Only later, when he went through his difficult teenage years, did he resent the comparisons Smith made between him and the respected missionary.

The singing portion of the service finally ended, the congregation sat down, and Dad took his place behind the pulpit. He looked grayer these days and a little plumper around the waistline. When he smiled, his chin still dimpled as Coe's did.

"Aren't you the one with ants in your pants," Gran whispered in his ear. "Is God speaking to your heart? He's right here for you, my boy."

Hud put his finger to his mouth in a shushing gesture. Did the people in the pew behind them hear her?

"I love you. You know that, right?" Gran's wrinkle-lined eyes filled with tears.

He nodded. He knew she loved him and his brothers as if they were her own children. But her insistence on him turning his life around and trusting God anew made him want to stand up and run for the door.

During Dad's preaching, he tried not to fall asleep. If he did, Gran would probably elbow his side or whisper loudly in his ear again. But instead of dozing off, he found himself listening to the sermon.

For several minutes, Dad spoke about having a lasting faith through life's adversities—of staying strong in the most challenging times, even when the waves threatened to take down the ship. He talked about folks rising to do good for others despite any obstacles or hindrances they were experiencing. He could have been speaking directly to Hud—and maybe he was. But others in the congregation had to be going through tough times, too. He couldn't be the only one sidestepping the landmines of disbelief, anger, and despair.

Gran leaned into him, and her hand on his arm shook. Was she gently reminding him that if he needed prayer, she was here? Maybe prayer wasn't such a bad idea. He needed a miracle. Did God care about the horrible financial disaster he was in? He sighed and closed his eyes. Gran squeezed his arm tighter. His grandmother sitting beside him like old times was comforting. He felt loved, even if he was still in the valley of indecision.

Lord, help. It wasn't much of a prayer. But it might be a new beginning or a restart for him.

Hud imagined his spiritual heart needing jumper cables to ignite enough faith to trust God again. Perhaps Gran was the spiritual jumper cables he needed. He set his hand over her hand on his arm and listened to the rest of his father's sermon with a more tender attitude of gratefulness than when he walked into this old church building with all its memories, good and bad.

Chapter Five

On Monday morning, Hud had eaten a hearty breakfast with Mom and Dad, catching up on all the family news, and then spoke with the lawyer. Now he was driving his rental car out to Lake's property. His brother called earlier, wanting to show him something before he headed back to Alaska. Hud was glad for the opportunity to talk with him, despite the extra twenty miles there and back. He hoped to be transparent about possibly accepting the inheritance and marrying Trista, although that was a colossal assumption since she'd firmly said she would never marry him.

Talking with Lake wasn't going to be easy, either. Being completely honest meant swallowing more of his pride and doing a difficult thing—sincerely apologizing.

His discussion with Michael had gone better than he expected. The lawyer said the inheritance was still available if Hud acted quickly and followed the steps his grandfather laid out in his will. Mainly, he had to be married by his birthday—one week away. Was he seriously considering getting married in that short of time? He groaned.

Unlike Lake, who'd married Irish after knowing her personally for only a few days, Hud had known Trista as a business partner and friend for half a year. She was a beautiful woman and a loving mother. She had a strong work ethic. No doubt, she'd make a kind spouse, too.

But what about love? While he was attracted to her and cared for her as a coworker, they were a long way from being in love. Hud had agreed with his brothers' pledge never to marry outside of love—and he still agreed with that! Yet here he was contemplating marrying someone he wasn't romantically involved with and becoming an instant father? Anxiety crashed through him like waves crashing against the rocks. He knew nothing about raising a kid or being a good role model. Those were reasons enough for Trista not to marry him!

Her accusation about him having been with a hundred other women rang through his thoughts like a painful gong. Yes, he had dated a lot in the past. When he first met Trista, he was the type of man she'd accused him of being. But he wasn't that kind of man any longer. He hoped he was a better man now—at least he was trying to be.

Six months ago, he'd had a harsh reality check when he honestly looked at himself in the mirror and didn't like who he saw. Had God been speaking to his heart then? Was He, perhaps, wooing him back to a more meaningful life?

Just ahead, Lake stood at the side of the road waving his arms toward a different driveway than the one leading to his cabin. Hud lowered the window. "What's this?"

"Pull in, and I'll show you." Lake grinned.

Hud parked in a clearing where the snow had been scraped down to hard-packed ground. As soon as he stepped outside, Lake shook his hand. "Welcome to my future home and kennels." He gestured toward the clearing. A few tree stumps and chopped-off bushes remained at the edges. "This is where our house and garage will be."

"Doesn't seem very big." Hud tried imagining a house that Lake's money could afford.

"It's just Irish, me, and the dogs. We don't need anything fancy."

"What about all those little Lake and Irish kiddos?"

Lake rubbed his gloved hand over the back of his neck. "We're starting with a modest home—a place to bring the dogs in at night."

"I guess you can always add on later." Still, that didn't make sense. After Hud's visit with the lawyer, he knew how the inheritance payouts worked over time. But why wouldn't Lake build a grander house with the money he had right now?

"Come over here."

Hud followed his brother toward the far side of the clearing without pursuing the topic. Too bad he hadn't worn a warm hat. The air in Thunder Ridge was much colder than in Ketchikan, and his ears were already freezing.

Lake thrust out his arms. "This will be my pride and joy." Orange ribbons fluttered in the wind, creating a perimeter of some kind.

"What is it, exactly?"

"A building for kennels and a play yard for the dogs. North Kennels and Boarding. What do you think?"

Unable to envision the scene as Lake did, Hud related to the passion for the project that he heard in his voice. "It looks like you have everything planned out. Will there be a fence between the business and the house?"

"A flower bed will separate the residence from the kennels. We'll be housing animals, so we want a clear view of the kennels and yard from the front windows." Lake shrugged. "It's been a dream of mine for years to start a boarding business."

"I remember. Looks like Grandad's wealth is making your dreams come true." He tried to keep a sour tone from entering his voice. Even though he was considering taking the funds himself, he didn't like Lake marrying someone he didn't love to get the money. He hated that they were being controlled by their stern grandfather, even after his death! Why couldn't the man have been generous and distributed the funds without stipulations?

As Hud and Lake strode around the clearing, Lake explained various aspects of how the grounds would look and where he'd put two small separate buildings. One would be for Irish and her dogs to hang out. The other was for a guest cabin where Mom and Dad, Granny Trish, or even one of his brothers could stay if needed.

"Sounds like Mom and Dad may sell their house," Hud said, feeling a bit sentimental about it.

"Yeah. It's hard to picture them selling the place where we grew up. But things are changing for all of us." Lake stuffed his hands into his jacket pockets. "You want to head over to the cabin and have some coffee? I made pumpkin pie."

"Can't say no to pie." Hud still wanted to discuss something with Lake. Doing so might be easier over coffee and comfort food.

Once they were seated in the living room of Lake's tiny cabin, Hud ate his pie and tried not to worry about the conversation to come. "Great pie as always."

"Thanks. It's out of season, but I like pumpkin pie any time of the year."

"Me too."

With their plates empty, the men sat quietly as if neither knew how to broach what still needed to be said.

"So, you and Irish are—" Hud gulped, uncertain how to finish his thought.

"Falling for each other?" Lake grinned. "In love?"

"Yeah. Are you? I've heard rumors that it's a put-on for the brothers' benefit."

Lake guffawed. "How incredibly North of you to say!"

"Certain brothers may have baited me into believing you and your wife care nothing for each other. That it's all about the money."

"Would these be the same brothers who locked me in an empty room the night before my wedding?"

"I may have heard something about that practical joke." Hud chuckled self-consciously. "Our younger brothers learned their prank-pulling skills from the best!"

"Ah, yes. The influence of older siblings." Lake lifted his coffee mug in a toast.

"Hear. Hear." Hud did the same thing with his mug.

Lake's features grew sober. "Thanks for coming down for my race. I know Irish requested it. But I appreciate it, all the same."

"Sure." Hud fidgeted in his seat. "Can't say it's the only reason I'm here."

"I figured you came to see Dad and Mom after his announcement."

"There was that." Hud swallowed about five times. The cabin seemed too hot. Lake must have piled on the wood in the woodstove.

"So?" Lake peered at him. "Are you going to tell me the other reason you came to Thunder Ridge this weekend, just to turn around and go back?"

"Do you remember when you said you'd support me if I married a woman before we fell in love?" Hud coughed.

"Uh-huh." Lake's eyebrows quirked.

"I came here to talk with Michael."

"My lawyer? After all the guff you gave me, you're taking the money?"

"I'm considering accepting it to bail my partner and me out of a bad financial situation." Heat rushed up Hud's neck and face. "I know it sounds ludicrous."

"Not really." Lake lifted his hands, palms up. "But are things that bad?"

"Yes! Wretchedly so." Hud pressed his front teeth down hard on his lower lip. "It's difficult for me to admit, but—" He cleared his throat. "I, uh, man, this is hard. I need to apologize for the rude and abrasive things I said to you about marrying Irish. I'm so sorry. My comments were spiteful and mean and downright disrespectful." He raked his hand through his hair. "If it's working out for you, I'm thrilled. Honestly, I am. Now I'm in a dire predicament that makes the inheritance more tempting for me to take."

"Even if you have to marry someone you don't love to get it?"

"Yeah." Hud drew in a breath that hurt in his chest. "That's the other troubling part."

"Do you have someone in mind? You mentioned a woman you were interested in."

"Yeah. She's someone I admire and care about."

"What's the problem then?" Lake scooted forward in his chair, resting his elbows on his knees and clasping his hands. "I say, go for it!"

"She thinks I'm not the marrying kind."

"Ohhh. I see." Lake stroked his chin.

"Don't get all holier-than-thou on me."

"I'm not." Lake rolled his eyes. "She considers you a big flirt, huh?"

"She thinks I have a hundred women at my beck and call who I should propose to instead of her."

"Is she right?"

"No!" Hud nearly yelled.

"Then tell her that. Ask again."

"Just because your fiery redhead went along with a marriage of convenience doesn't mean other women would do the same thing." He gulped, realizing how rude that sounded.

"No, it doesn't." Sighing, Lake gazed toward the window. "I had marriage all worked out—how Laurie and I would build our lives together. Then my world fell apart. I didn't expect a second chance at happiness. But Irish and I are on a real journey together." A profound look of joy and satisfaction crossed Lake's face. "I'd marry her again in a heartbeat."

"Wow. Lake, that's amazing!" Whatever Hud came here expecting to hear, Lake being willing to marry Irish again wasn't one of them. He had a score to settle with Wilks. A bop on the nose would suffice for the myths he'd led him to believe.

"Is there anything I can do to help you?" Lake asked. "I mean, financially?"

"Nah." Hud would never beg for a handout from his brother. "It'll work out one way or another. I'll speak with Trista again. If the worst happens, I may need to live in one of those cabins you mentioned building."

"Of course. Is there any chance she's had a change of heart?"

"I doubt it." Hud recalled Gran praying for him last night. "Then again, didn't Gran tell us everything's possible if we believe?"

"About a million times!" Lake grinned, then quoted one of Gran's favorite verses, "Everything is possible for him who believes."

"Is she okay? She seems frailer than I remember."

"She's aging. She stopped dancing, hasn't been cooking much, and sticks close to home."

"Must be hard on her." Hud sighed, thinking his condo was awfully far from his family. "Let me know if she needs anything, okay?"

"Will do."

"I should hit the road. I have a plane to catch and a decision to make." Standing, Hud extended his hand. "No hard feelings?"

"None. I love you, man." Lake pulled him into a bear hug.

Embracing the brother he'd been annoyed with for too long felt right. Hud stepped back and patted Lake's shoulder. "Put Wilks in his place for me the next chance you get."

"Is he the one who told you the stuff about Irish and me?"

"Let's say he's due for a prank or ten to be pulled on him."

"I can't wait until he marries someone and the roles are reversed." Lake grinned.

"I'll make sure to be here for that one!" Hud headed outside into the cold. He had an hour-and-a-half drive and then two flights until he reached Trista and the beginning of their future together—*if* she'd have him.

Chapter Six

Trista padded into the kitchen barefoot and fixed a peanut butter and jelly sandwich after having spent the afternoon cleaning and sorting through Layla's and her bedrooms. She was trying to get their belongings whittled down to a minimum in case they had to move quickly.

Not that she had any idea where they would live. Mom wouldn't want to leave Ketchikan since the island town had been her home for her whole life. And her sister, Fanny, still lived here. But affordable three-bedroom rentals were difficult to find. Maybe Mom could move in with Fanny or her friend, Lucille, for a while. What would Trista and Layla do then?

Trista was heading back upstairs, eating her sandwich, when a knock at the door made her pause. She glanced down at her grubby sweatshirt, holey leggings, and bare feet, and groaned. Quickly swallowing the food in her mouth, she called, "Coming!"

When she opened the door, Hudson stood there with a pink carnation outstretched in his hand. "I didn't expect to see you today." She wiped the back of her hand across her lips.

"I just got back in town." He handed her the flower, and his gaze skimmed her clothes, ending at her brightly colored toenails. A smile crossed his mouth.

"Layla loves hot pink"—she felt the need to explain.

"So do I. Especially on your cute toes."

"Hudson—"

"Seriously, Trista. I'm a man. Do you have to fault me for thinking your toes are cute?"

"Not if I thought you were serious—which you aren't! So, yes. I fault you for not being sincere!"

"Ouch. I hoped your heart might have softened toward me." His eyebrows lifted like he'd asked a question.

"In three days? Hardly!" Did he really hope her heart had softened toward him? Or was he just saying that to try to win her over to his financial scheme?

"Are you ready to discuss my proposal?" He pressed his hands together in a begging pose.

"My answer is still the same."

He heaved a sigh and leaned against the doorframe. "May I come in for a few minutes?"

"So you can pressure me into marrying you?"

"No, I—"

"Who's that, Trista?" Mom called from the living room. "Who wants to marry you?"

Trista shot Hudson a warning glare to be quiet.

"It's me, Mrs. Dunmore!"

"Shhhhh." All she needed was for Mom to get involved in their discussion.

"I'd like to come in and talk with you and Trista." Hudson winked at her. "But she doesn't want to speak with me."

She was tempted to pelt him with the carnation—or a kitchen utensil!

Mom strode into the room. "We don't usually keep people from speaking with us unless they're dangerous. Are you a menace to our safety, Mr. North?"

"Not in the least." He grinned charmingly at her. "I'm here to discuss an idea that would ensure your ability to stay in your home for as long as you want."

"Well, well. Let's invite the man in and hear him out, shall we, honey bear?"

"What if we don't like his idea?" Trista already didn't like it.

Despite her objections, a few minutes later, the three sat around the kitchen table piled with bills, paperwork, and old magazines. They each held a steaming coffee cup. Mom placed a plate of homemade oatmeal cookies next to Hudson. "Now what's this about?" She tipped her head, peering curiously at him.

"I want to marry your daughter, Mrs. Dunmore."

"Hudson—"

"I'm sorry, Trista." His face hued crimson. "I'm not trying to force my way in here. I want you to feel free to say no."

"Then, no! A hundred times no!"

"Trista!" Mom exclaimed.

"That's okay. Your daughter and I disagree about some things." He picked up a cookie and fingered it. "I'm not sold on the idea of a quick marriage myself."

"Then why are you suggesting it?" Trista demanded.

Hudson gazed at her as if begging her to understand. "If we meet the conditions, I can access an inheritance that would solve all of our financial troubles, including bailing out our company."

"Bailing out—" Mom turned a shocked gaze on Trista.

"Hudson, so help me!" Trista hadn't even explained their financial predicament to her mother. Whenever she emptied her desk, that would be soon enough to tell her about their grim situation. Taking a breath, she faced Mom. "All but one of our investors pulled out of our North Dunmore project."

"And he pulled out today." Hudson grimaced.

"What?" He should have led with that unwelcome news!

"Your company is failing?" Mom's face paled. "What about the savings you put into the project?"

"We'll lose Trista's money and mine if we don't act quickly. That's why I asked her to marry me," Hudson spoke softly. "To access the funds, I must be married and stay married for five years."

"Which would be five years too many!"

"Honey bear, are you considering this?" Mom gazed hopefully at her.

"No!"

"With the inheritance money," Hudson continued as if she hadn't said anything, "I'd bail out our company, pay back Trista's investment, and settle the mortgage on your house."

"You'd do all that?" Mom sounded in awe of him.

"I'm not marrying him, Mom!"

"I'm still hoping to change her mind." He grinned like his manly smile alone might change her mind.

"Of course, she should consider it."

"Mom!" Why couldn't Hudson accept her decision not to marry him and leave it at that?

"Tell me some more about this inheritance." Mom leaned forward, her arms crossed over the table's edge like she was preparing for a long story.

"My grandfather left a large sum of money to me and my brother, Lake, the oldest sons of his two children. Per his legacy, we must be married by our thirty-fifth birthday." He rubbed his knuckles together. "My window is closing. I vowed never to take the money—as did my brother. But when Lake married quickly and accessed the funds, I saw how it might work for Trista and me. How we could marry, then fall in love later."

"Like you can plan all that! You manage property and money—you can't manage me!" Trista shoved away from the table and marched to the sink. She ran the water hard, scrubbing her hands beneath the stream and washing away thoughts of what being married to Hudson might be like—of what him kissing her as a husband might be like. Blood rushed to her face. She didn't want him kissing her! And she didn't want to be his wife!

"You're saying you'd pay off my whole mortgage?" Mom asked in a bewildered tone.

"Yes. And cover whatever medical bills you have in the future."

Trista shut off the water and spun around. "It's bribery, Mom. Don't listen to a word he says!"

"I'm not bribing her. I'm explaining what I would do for my mother-in-law if you were my wife."

Wife? Trista's thoughts leaped back to picturing him kissing her. She couldn't break their visual connection—or her imaginings—for several seconds. "What about Layla?" She gritted her teeth, frustrated at herself for even asking the question. Still, she pursued an answer. "What will the great Hudson North provide for his wife's daughter?"

He gave her the sweetest smile that caused tremors to radiate down her limbs. Her heart palpitated. Her mouth felt parched like her tongue had adhered to the back of her teeth. If the man's smile affected her that much, how would it be if they kissed? She groaned at her brain's stubborn refusal to let that mental image go.

"I'd set up a college fund for her and provide for whatever she needs in the future." He sagged against his chair like the conversation was exhausting. "Is she legally available to be adopted?"

"Yes," Trista whispered and sat down again.

"I would do that too. I was adopted. Officially becoming part of the North brothers was a huge deal for my kid brother and me."

"What do you think?" Mom clasped her hands together and peered at Trista.

After Neil had walked away from her and Layla, Trista vowed never to fall for any man like him. She never wanted to be with someone who could convince a woman he loved her one second, then drop her from his life the next. How could she trust Hudson not to do the same thing when she already deemed him untrustworthy regarding women?

"Will you consider my proposal? I want to head out to the property and check on some things tomorrow." He gave her a softly compelling smile. "Would you mind going out there with me, and we can discuss this some more?"

Mom stared at her with such trusting, hopeful eyes. Trista had promised to take care of her. What if she declined Hudson's offer, and her mom lost the house, and the loss plunged her into depression or some horrible health crisis?

"Fine. I'll go out to the property with you." They were still business partners, for now. "Then I'll tell you what I think of your phony marriage proposal!"

"Trista," Mom said in a scolding tone.

"She's right. I'm sorry for my lousy proposal. I can do better." Hudson met her gaze for a long moment. Then he left quietly, leaving Trista to deal with her churning thoughts.

Chapter Seven

Less than twenty-four hours after returning to Ketchikan, Hud was driving his truck toward Trista's and his intended development site, knowing they needed to have a serious discussion. However, initiating that conversation was difficult since Trista had hardly spoken to him since he picked her up.

He didn't blame her for not wanting to marry him. A few days ago, the thought of marrying anyone outside of love had been repugnant to him, too. It still was truth be told. Yet if he were going to marry anyone, he'd choose Trista. At least they were already friends and coworkers. Couldn't that develop into something more in time?

He stole a glance at her, but she didn't look his way. He could show her the prenup and the adoption papers Michael had drawn up. If that didn't convince her to marry him, he'd propose more sincerely. If she still refused his marriage offer, that would be the end of it. He respected Trista and wouldn't keep pestering her. They'd have to empty the office and go their separate ways. Although never seeing her again tugged heavily on his thoughts, too.

If, by some miracle, she agreed to his proposal, how long would it take for them to fall in love? Or for them to feel like a real married couple? What if that never happened? The gravity of such a possibility tightened his shoulder and neck muscles until he physically ached. Anxiety spiraled up his middle. Determinedly, he tried to relax and not jump headlong into thinking the worst. But considering taking the marital plunge and waiting for Trista's final answer to his proposal had him tied in knots.

He glanced at her again. She stared out the side window, the back of her head facing him—not talking about their business or about her daughter like she would have before he proposed. He'd caused this rift. Even if she said yes to marrying him, they'd start out with weird, unsettled feelings between them. And since his birthday was only five days away, they would have to marry quickly. It was hardly enough time to discuss issues a normal couple would have already worked out.

One thing was obvious—Trista's silence and how she was avoiding looking at him proclaimed loud and clear that she didn't want to marry him.

"Looks like more rain," she finally said.

"Sure does." Heavy raindrops hit the windshield, and Hud flipped on the wipers.

"My mom warned me to wear my rain hat like I was still a kid." At least she was speaking to him.

"Moms and grandmothers are like that, no matter how old we get." He sighed as he pulled into the property for which he and Trista had paid a hefty price.

The truck bounced over a deep rut. He clutched the steering wheel tighter and veered around another hole. The ground felt soggy and uneven due to all the recent rains. He parked the vehicle near the tiny gray outbuilding that housed tools and would be a welcome shelter for them to get out of the downpour. He grimaced toward the dark clouds clinging to the mountainous area behind the property. Those ominous clouds had to mean more rain was coming.

Trista put on a yellow rain hat that matched her raincoat. "We'll have to run to dodge those raindrops."

"I guess." Too bad Hud hadn't remembered to wear a hat. He wasn't wearing boots, either. "You want to wait here for a few minutes?"

"For what?" she asked suspiciously.

"To wait out the worst of it. What else?"

"Nothing." She rolled her eyes and opened the cab door. What was with the look?

Before he could ask her about it, Trista climbed out and was trudging around a wide puddle en route to the outbuilding. Wishing he'd worn more weather-appropriate outerwear, he opened his door and followed her. His shoes were like sponges soaking up the muddy water. Already shivering, he stepped inside the shelter that appeared even tinier on the inside and shut the door.

Trista turned on a battery-powered lantern, and a soft glow filled the space. "We won't be able to walk around the property until this rain lets up."

"I didn't expect it to be so bad." He wiped raindrops off his face. "I didn't check the weather report."

"In Ketchikan, it's safe to say there will be a chance of rain. But today's deluge is worse than usual. Although it's been pretty bad for a few days now." She removed her yellow hat, exposing her dark hair pressed against her head.

Just then, a thunderous roar crackled in the air.

"What was that?" Hud's heart rate shot up.

"I don't know."

The ground shook beneath them. The lantern crashed to the floor.

"Hudson—"

"Tris—"

They reached for each other and lunged beneath the wooden counter along the wall. He wrapped his arms around her, holding her close to him. She pressed her cheek against his chest as a roar of what sounded like mud, bushes, and water pounded against the sides of the small structure. The whole building shuddered. With all the scraping and shaking, would the roof hold, or would the shed collapse? Hud held his breath, waiting for the worst of it to pass—and silently praying it would pass safely. Trista's body trembled in his arms, her cool lips brushing against his neck as she prayed or mumbled something.

Were they going to get swept away in the landslide or flood? Would they survive whatever was going on outside the shed? Neither spoke aloud as they waited for the eerie, threatening sounds and shaking to cease. The noise continued for about ninety seconds but felt more like an hour.

When all was silent other than the rain pelting the roof, Trista scooted quickly away from him and reached for the lantern. She flipped the switch, but it didn't work. She shook the lantern. Nothing happened. The dim light coming through the filthy narrow window revealed tools and blueprints scattered across the floor. The doors of a storage unit had opened, and items were heaped in front of it.

"Was that a mudslide?" Hud asked shakily.

"I think so."

They stood and peered through the small window into the murky grayness, their cheeks almost touching.

"I don't believe it!" Trista exclaimed.

"No kidding!"

They didn't have a full view of the property, but a river of mud, branches, rocks, and trees had skidded past them, tearing up the land. A perilous mound of earth, bushes, and upended trees stood outside the door. His truck wasn't in sight. It must have been propelled somewhere downhill. Thank God they hadn't stayed in the cab as he suggested.

"It came so close." Trista shivered, and Hud wanted to pull her into his arms again.

"But we're alive."

"Uh-huh." She didn't meet his gaze. Was she uncomfortable with how closely they had waited out the mudslide? He didn't feel the least bit uncomfortable about it. He'd enjoyed Trista's nearness, the scent of warm vanilla in her hair, and the soft way her body melted against his while he held her.

"Maybe we should go out and see what's happened." He moved toward the door.

"Let's wait. This slide might trigger another one."

"I should check on the truck."

Her palm landed on his arm. "It's too dangerous, Hudson. Just wait, okay?"

"All right. But how will we get back to town?" They'd driven about seven miles from her mother's house to the property on the north side.

"I'm sure a rescue crew will start working on mud removal soon." She returned to the window, peering out. "This has happened before."

"Here?" His voice shot up as if he had no control over it.

"Not here. Elsewhere on the island." She pulled her cell phone out of her back pocket and tapped the screen. "Mom? There's been a mudslide on Hudson's and my property."

"Oh, no! Honey bear, are you okay?" Mrs. Dunmore said loud enough for him to hear.

"Yes. But it may take some time for us to get back." Trista met Hud's gaze with a wary look. "Possibly all night."

"What?" He raked his fingers through his hair. All night? He'd brought her out here, hoping to convince her to marry him, not for disaster to strike and for them to fall into each other's arms out of desperation. But that's what had happened. And he'd discovered just how much he enjoyed holding Trista close. He'd liked the way she clung to him, too.

"Love you, Mom. Give Layla a big kiss for me." She ended the call.

"All night? Seriously?"

"It's possible. No doubt the road is blocked. The situation is too precarious for us to walk back to town." She smoothed her hands over her hair, then her face. "I'm worried about not getting back to Layla, but Mom will take care of her."

"You think we'll have to stay here without heat?"

"As I said, another slide may still happen." She shrugged. "This shed doesn't seem safe. But it's the best we've got."

"Thankfully, we were in here. Not in the truck or outside."

"Amen to that." She waved her hand toward the area beneath the table. "Thanks for what you did to protect me."

"Of course." Now wasn't the time to tell her how much he had enjoyed feeling her heart beating against his chest and how he liked her lips pressed into his neck. He'd never been so fearful for his life or so at peace with a woman in his arms before.

"God watched out for us. If the mud and trees hurtling down the mountainside had directly hit this building, we wouldn't be here talking about it."

"You're right." A shudder trembled through him. He'd felt strong holding Trista and keeping harm away from her. But he hadn't been the only one protecting her. Humbleness came over him, followed by relief, and then thankfulness. If God saved them and kept them alive during a freak act of nature, did He possibly have a plan for their lives together? *God?* Hud cleared his throat. "What do you think we should do now?"

"Wait here. Someone will come to our rescue, eventually." She peered out the window again. "The land looks like a bulldozer went over it at top speeds, scraping everything into garish mounds of earth and foliage."

"At least we didn't build anything here yet." Their investors would have gone crazy over this disaster—if they had any investors left.

Trista scooted onto the wooden counter and wrapped her arms around her knees. "It may be a long night."

"Lots of time for us to talk, then."

"Perfect," she muttered.

He would have commented, but suddenly, the rumbling came again. Without talking, they lunged under the counter. Trista didn't resist his efforts when he wrapped his arms around her again. She clung to him as much as he held her while another pile of mud and debris rumbled past the shed. The noise and shaking were just as severe as before.

Would they survive a second onslaught?

Chapter Eight

Hudson's thundering heart beat loudly beneath Trista's ear. His arms were still wrapped around her even though the terrifying sounds of mud and debris scraping against the shed had stopped. She felt bewildered—not only from the mudslide, but from how calm and cared for she felt in Hudson's arms. She'd never known how gentle her business partner could be or how comforting his musky scent of aftershave and warm skin were.

"It's okay, Tris," he'd whispered several times during the mudslide. "We're going to be all right." She thought he'd mumbled some prayers too.

Picturing her and Hudson getting smashed beneath the mud, rocks, and trees cascading down the sloping hill behind them had been a shocking wake-up call. In a flash, she'd pondered what she wanted in life. She wanted to see Layla grow up. She hoped to have more children. And she wanted a life of her own—not one where she felt pressured to go along with a fake marriage!

Earlier, she'd stared out the window of the truck all the way out to the property, contemplating the things she'd like to say to Hudson. *"If you were the last male on the planet, I wouldn't marry you! You date women and toss them aside like yesterday's newspaper. You'll marry someone one day and divorce them the next. I don't trust you! You are not husband material!*

However, huddled together beneath the old counter that would have been useless if a mudslide had directly hit the shelter, she felt less sure about him not being a good husband for her. Although, she was scared and probably wasn't thinking clearly—that's why Hudson's comforting embrace and the scent of his deodorant and bodily warmth made her want to stay in his arms.

"Is it over?" His voice was low and soft.

"Hard to say." She backed away from him a couple of inches. In his dark gaze, she saw worry … and something else. Attraction? Longing? Were her eyes giving away her tender feelings toward him, too? Although her emotions were caused by the panic she felt about the mudslide, right?

Waiting underneath the wide shelf and fearing for her life, she'd felt like the mudslide had scraped away the world. As if she and Hudson were the only two people left on the island, their uncertain emotions scraped away, too. All that remained was a tenderness toward him that she couldn't fathom. Outside, everything was still except for the rain pelting the tin roof above them. Inside, her heart pounded like a loud drum beating an unfamiliar rhythm in her ears.

Their gazes locked in the dim light coming through the dirty window. She gulped and didn't glance away. He leaned toward her slowly, his dark, shiny eyes compelling her to come closer, too. He paused a breath away from her mouth as if asking if it was okay if he kissed her but not saying the words.

Did she nod slightly? She must have since his warm lips touched hers in a bare breath of movement, like an expression of gratitude for their survival. Of the two of them having gone through a terrifying experience and living to tell about it.

Then the kiss changed in intensity, going from soft and sweet to intense and passionate. For a few moments, she felt connected to him in a way she'd never felt with anyone else before. He pulled her closer, and she wrapped her arms around his shoulders, clinging to him. He hungrily brushed his mouth against hers, deepening the kiss, his lips searching hers and hers his in an exploration of emotions and desire. His kisses took her breath away. One of his hands smoothed gently over her cheek. Her fingers roved through his hair, caressing the soft strands. She loved kissing Hudson! Had she subconsciously wished for this to happen all along?

Abruptly, he set her away from him. Dazed by their kissing and all that came before it, the finality of the movement surprised her—followed by a rush of embarrassment. Why did she let things get so romantic? Why did she kiss him with such abandonment?

"That was very nice, Tris," he said huskily.

"It was the mudslide. The fear." She tried explaining away her heated reaction to him.

"If so, let the mudslides keep coming." He smiled warmly, holding her gaze. It wasn't an off-handed expression of a womanizing male. His lingering gaze and soft smile said he felt something emotional and endearing for her. That's why she smiled back at him, almost inviting him to kiss her again.

Hudson stroked her hair, ticklishly tucking some strands behind her ears. He gazed into her eyes so deeply and intently, she nearly leaped back into his arms. She couldn't believe how drawn she was to him. Thankfully, he'd had the decency to put on the brakes—something she might not have done after the unexpected intensity of their kissing.

"We should, uh, check through the window again. See what's happened." Her words came out breathily.

"Let's wait a few more minutes, just in case."

"Okay." She scooted back a couple of inches.

"I liked holding and kissing you, Trista."

"Yet you stopped." She shivered due to the cold creeping through the walls—not because she'd been warm in his arms and was left feeling chilled.

"Believe me. I didn't want to stop."

"Forget I said anything."

"I stopped because—"

"No reason to explain." She felt embarrassed enough.

"I want a real relationship with you, Trista. Not a fling. Not throwing caution to the wind because we nearly succumbed to a mudslide's evil intent."

She sighed, mostly relieved at his admission. She didn't want a fling either.

"I care for you."

"Is that how you kiss women you care about?" Her worries about the bazillion women he'd dated came back to taunt her.

"I kissed you because I care about you, and I'm attracted to you." He stroked her hair again, reminding her of their tender kisses and embrace.

She groaned and crawled out from under the counter. She needed some space. As soon as she cleared the wooden legs, he stood also. They looked out the mud-streaked window, side by side. Their five acres looked like a disaster zone. Mounds of mud and trees littered the property. Thick, muddy water flowed around the piles and down the slope. Was the ground even stable? Would there be a third slide?

Hud crossed the space to the door in two strides.

"Watch out! Open it carefully," she said, concerned for his safety.

Glancing at her, he nodded and opened the door two inches. She followed and peered around him. The mudslide had formed a wall of trees, bushes, and mud. Yet the building hadn't been destroyed. "Thank God!" he said reverently.

"Yes. He protected us again."

Hud closed the door and faced her. "Shall we climb out?"

Her phone vibrated. She pulled it from her pocket and checked the screen. Mom. "Hello?"

"Are you okay, honey bear?" Mom asked in a panicky tone. "I heard on the radio there was a second slide as bad as the first."

"That's true."

"Are you okay? When are you coming home?"

"I'm okay. I don't know when we'll get back." She met Hudson's gaze. Spending the night here with him wouldn't be a horrible idea. But after the way they kissed, things could get out of hand if she let down her guard even once. Not that Hudson would force anything to happen between them. But her own emotions and romantic desires were flip-flopping—no denying that! "I'll call later when I have more information. Love you. Kiss Layla for me."

"Will do. Stay safe."

Trista ended the call, then tapped into the local emergency information group on Facebook. After reading several posts, she said, "Others in the area are trapped or trying to dig out of their homes."

"Where?"

"Up the road. Not far."

"Shall we go and help?" It was nice that his first thought was to help others in a crisis. "As long as it's safe, that is. I wouldn't want to put you in any more danger."

Their gazes held, and she saw another side of Hudson North she hadn't known before. It seemed he really cared about her. Perhaps caring was a good starting place for them.

"Sure. We have shovels here." She grabbed two from the floor where tools and miscellaneous items lay scattered. "It's still raining out." She pulled on her rain hat.

Hud made a face and moved toward the door. "Guess I'll get soaked, then."

"Hudson?"

"Do you mind calling me Hud, especially since we're kissing now?" He grinned and winked at her. "No one calls me Hudson other than my mom and grandmother when I'm in trouble."

Calling him Hud sounded too personal or too soon in their altered relationship. But he was right—they had kissed. And what a kiss it had been! However, calling him Hudson would be a better way for her to keep their business persona present in her thoughts tonight.

"Or you could always come up with a sweeter name to call me."

"Such as?"

"Sweetheart. Darling."

Oh, he was pushing it. "We'd better get going, *Hudson*."

"Yep. Sounds like I'm in trouble."

Why had she let him kiss her? And why had she kissed him back so ardently? Kissing changed everything between them!

Chapter Nine

For the next few hours, Hud worked alongside the owner of the house adjacent to their property, two other volunteers, and Trista, digging out the front entrance of the dwelling. Rain poured down his hair and cheeks in rivulets. Mud and grime had worked their way down his shirt and into his underwear. His shoes were full of sticky, wet muck. Trista, who was laboring as hard as he was, looked rain and mud speckled, too.

He shoveled five scoops of mud and debris, tossing it onto a pile behind him. Heart pounding and muscles aching at the unaccustomed exertion, he paused with the shovel's tip in the mud and rested his arm on the handle.

Trista was also resting. Their gazes met, and she smiled sweetly at him. Was she thinking of their kisses like he was? What he wouldn't give to be back at the outbuilding cuddled up with her, kissing the night away. He took a slow breath. *Steady, North.* He was helping their neighbors. He and Trista weren't at a place of kissing through the night, either. He told her he didn't want a fling—and he meant it. Still, feeling cold, wet, and miserable, he let thoughts of holding her and getting warm together linger in his mind for a few more moments.

Then, sighing, he continued shoveling, working closer to the house's entrance where the front porch had been ripped off the structure. Part of the home's corner was gone too. The five of them kept digging and moving mud and rocks. Eventually, they cleared a wide enough path for the occupants to come and go through the front door safely.

Silently, the volunteers tromped across a field of torn-up land, going around the worst of the trees lying in muddy graves. They joined another group who were already shoveling mud and rocks at the next house.

An older woman offered the workers water bottles and packaged cookies. She said she'd been saving up for a disaster. Even though the treats were a tad stale, Hud was hungry, and he was grateful for the sustenance.

Unaware of how much time had passed, darkness overcame them. Someone started up generator-powered lights, making the area visible to the volunteers. Otherwise, they would have had to stop working.

"I'm going to call Mom," Trista said tiredly. "She's called a couple of times. I should touch base with her."

"Sure." He lowered his voice. "You were right. We'll have to stay out here tonight."

"I know." She gave him a long look, then turned away to make her call.

Was she silently reminding him that she mistrusted him? Her complaint about him being a player was a tough one to dispel. Even her doubts about him saying he cared for her, as if that wasn't strong enough language, troubled him. How could he convince her that he honestly cared about her and was serious when he kissed her back at the outbuilding? That he hadn't been affectionate with her just so she'd marry him!

He sighed. He was tired and overthinking everything.

Lord, help Trista and me figure out what to do. The whole getting married thing was a crazy idea, wasn't it?

It had been a while since he spontaneously prayed—other than during the mudslide. But ever since Granny Trish prayed with him at the church service in Thunder Ridge, he'd been more open to praying—more willing to face his failings, too. Why had he strayed from faith and living in the honorable way he'd been raised to do? Was his wandering just young adult rebellion? Resisting what his parents and Gran fervently pushed him toward all those years?

More raindrops dripped down his back, and he shuddered. He dug more shovelfuls of mud, flinging them onto the growing pile.

When Trista finished talking on the phone, she rejoined him. By her drooping shoulders, slow movements, and the grayish pallor of her skin, she was totally exhausted.

"Do you mind if we head back to the shed?" he asked, not bringing attention to her fatigue.

"That would be great. I am beat."

"Me too."

He said goodbye to the workers who'd removed enough mud to reach where the porch used to stand. Using the flashlight app on his phone that wouldn't last much longer, he shined the light before Trista and him, directing their way back toward the shed.

As they walked through thick mud and around rocks and tree limbs, he thought about his failed proposal and what not accepting the inheritance would mean for them. Without the funds from the legacy, they'd lose their property, financial investment, and their dream of creating an artisan community. Trista's mom would lose her house, which meant Trista and her daughter might become homeless. He'd probably have to walk away from Trista, too. Even though he could already imagine himself falling in love with her, he couldn't push her into marrying him or wanting to be with him.

Marriage was a lifelong commitment. He wouldn't enter such a commitment lightly, and neither should she.

Chapter Ten

More tired than she'd ever been, Trista slowly removed her raincoat and hat, then dropped them on the shed floor. Both items were so filthy she might never wear them again. Her wet, muddy pants clung to her skin. Her boots were full of muck and silt. Groaning, she slid to the floor next to the wall and tugged off her boots, which were challenging to remove.

She felt achy and drenched clear through. The scent of stagnant mud clung to her clothes and skin. All she wanted to do was get warm and dry and fall asleep. But where and how was that going to happen?

Hudson groaned on the other side of the small space and pried his mud-covered shoes from his feet. Then he peeled off his muddy socks. This was the first time she'd seen his feet bare—or anything bare. She gulped and focused on getting her own dripping socks off.

They'd labored side by side all afternoon and evening in terrible conditions. She admired Hudson, er, Hud, for his work for the people hit by the mudslide. She'd never forget the gritty determination on his face as he shoveled mud and rocks to reach those people's doors. Even now, muddy rainwater had left grayish streaks running down his face—but he'd never looked more handsome or heroic to her.

She caught him watching her through the scant light coming through the window. The rain had let up, and the moon was peeking through the clouds, giving them glints of light. He met her gaze with a look of male appreciation or attraction, causing her heart to pound harder. Shivering, she crossed her arms over her wet clothes.

Hud removed his dripping coat and dropped it to the floor. He stood barefoot, shuffling back and forth as if trying to get the blood circulating to his toes. Filthy water dripped off his pant legs, leaving rivulets on the floor. His right knee was exposed through a foot-long rip in his pants.

They'd have to find a way to keep warm through the night—other than cuddling up together. But standing in this cold shed and shivering for eight hours would probably end with both getting pneumonia or worse.

Seeking a solution, Trista riffled through the items that had fallen from the large metal shelving unit. Not finding anything useful, she dug through the things inside. Her fingers latched onto something plasticky. "I found something!" She grabbed a stiff, crinkly tarp and pulled it out.

"That's good." Hud's teeth chattered. "It should hold our heat in if we wrap it around us snuggly."

Their gazes met again. How much snuggling would be needed to find the warmth they required? She shuddered with cold and her imaginings. She peered back into the shelving unit and spotted some fabric.

"Here's something else!" She tugged out a dirty, oversized sweat-shirt. "It's your lucky day." She tossed the article of clothing at him.

He held up the grease-stained shirt and scowled. "This won't fit me."

"But it will be warm."

"You wear it, then." He extended it to her. "Ladies first."

"I'm not wearing that! It would fall off my shoulders."

One of his eyebrows quirked, but he didn't comment.

Squatting down, she foraged in the bottom of the storage unit. When she glanced over her shoulder, Hud had removed his shirt and T-shirt. Their gazes met longer this time. By necessity, they'd have to stay close together tonight, sharing whatever warmth their bodies and the tarp provided. But their kissing earlier made every glance between them ignite her thoughts with imagery of where those kisses might lead if she allowed them free rein.

Which, of course, she wouldn't! She'd promised herself she would never again take that route outside of marriage. Now, she wanted to make wiser decisions and be more sensitive to following Jesus's ways. And, hopefully, Hudson would respect her boundaries.

He shrugged into the dirty sweatshirt, and it hung sloppily over his shoulders. It was dirty and stained—she needed to focus on that, not on how handsome he was. Yet her thoughts leaped to his good looks and how happy she'd felt in his arms. The gentle way his lips had moved against hers still affected her hours later, making her want to experience more of a romantic connection with him.

Only, she couldn't. She needed to keep her thoughts centered on surviving this night—not on any passionate encounters with this man who'd asked her to marry him on a lark. Even if he kissed her like a fairytale prince kissing his princess and turned her insides to mush with his slightest gaze, she was keeping her distance from his lips tonight!

Before closing the doors of the storage structure, the dim light on her cell revealed another piece of fabric. She tugged on it. "It's an old towel!" Feeling like she'd found a prize, she held up the soiled material. "I think I'll make a shirt out of it."

"Aren't you industrious?"

"I guess I am." With her remaining light, she spotted a small saw and cut a hole in the center of the towel big enough to slip her head through. Still shivering, she tested it. The fabric didn't stretch over her head, so she ripped it a little. There. "Turn around," she ordered.

"Yes, ma'am." Hud turned his back toward her.

Trista swiveled around and yanked off her wet shirt and underthings. She put the dirty towel over her head. Needing one more thing, she dug through the heap of items and located a length of rope to tie around her middle. The towel was big enough to drape over her arms and reach her waist, providing modest coverage. "Okay. I'm dressed."

Hud grabbed the tarp and arranged it under the counter without glancing at her. "We'll have to sit close through the night. I hope you don't mind."

"We'll be fine if you don't try anything."

"Me?" He asked in an innocent tone. "Do you trust me so little?"

"I want to trust you."

"Then, do. Our pants are soaking wet. What if we—"

"Our pants are staying on!"

"But Trista—"

"No!"

"Fine." He groaned. "Then we'll have to stay wrapped together in the tarp like enchiladas. Just for warmth—I promise."

"Sitting up. Side by side."

"That should work." He waved his hands toward the tarp.

Trista crawled under the wooden work shelf. Their shoulders bumped into each other's as they tried to get situated.

"Sorry." Hud wrapped the plastic sheet around her and tucked it beneath her feet. The tarp was stiff and cold and didn't conform easily to their bodies.

Her cell light flickered a couple of times. "Hurry. I have to turn off my phone and conserve battery power to text Mom in the morning."

"Okay." He put his arm over her shoulder.

She lurched forward and glared at him, even though she couldn't see his features well. "What are you doing?"

"We have to sit close."

"Not that close."

"I promise to act gentlemanly. I'll put my arm around you and—"

"No! Side to side," she said through gritted teeth.

Sighing loudly, he lowered his arm and overlapped the edges of the tarp in front of them. "I never knew how stubborn you could be."

"Get used to it." She pressed the power button on her phone.

In nearly total darkness, their shivering sounds and teeth chattering grew louder. Trista's wet pants felt icy and uncomfortable, but she wasn't removing them even with Hud's promise of being gentlemanly. She wouldn't put herself in any compromising situation.

"Trista?" His breath brushed her cheek. "I liked kissing you earlier." Why did he have to bring that up in the pitch dark?

"Let's not discuss it." Not when she was sitting beside him, experiencing the slight heat radiating from his torso. She still shook uncontrollably, so talking would be better than sitting in the darkness imagining them freezing to death. "Hud?"

"I like it when you say my name like that."

"Hudson."

He sighed. "Yeah?"

"We should talk about the marriage you proposed yesterday."

"You want to discuss that now?"

"Isn't that why you brought me out here?" She saw a faint glistening of his eyes in the dark.

"Seems a lifetime ago."

"Are you taking the proposal back?"

"Maybe."

"Really?"

"Why don't you want to marry me?" He turned a question on her. By his warm breath on her cheek, he was looking right at her.

Because you date women and cast them aside like TV dinners. Inwardly, she groaned at how harshly she judged a man who had shoveled for hours to help others. The way he got filthy with rainwater and mud streaming down his face yet kept shoveling muck without complaining had been endearing. Pastor Chad would probably tell her to have more grace and willingness to give a fellow human being a chance. And she should, right?

Hud had taken a risk in developing a low-income property for struggling artisans like his brother. Doing so revealed a kind and compassionate side of Hudson North that Trista had admired for the last six months. But that didn't mean she wanted to marry him!

On the other hand, his kisses had the power to make her think he might be a perfect match for her. Kissing him for a lifetime could turn out to be the best dream come true she'd ever imagined. But then she pictured the gazillion women he'd dated, and her romantic feelings cooled right down.

"Trista?"

"There's no reason for me to marry you because you can pick someone else in your lineup of women who wants you for a husband more than I do." His cool fingers touched her cheek in the dark, reminding her of his gentle touch when he'd kissed her. "Hud—"

"Sorry." He pulled his hand away. "Earlier, you fell into my arms and kissed me as eagerly as I kissed you." Why did he have to keep bringing that up? Why did she have to keep thinking about kissing him every time their gazes met?

"So I got carried away." Her cheeks flushed hot, and he chuckled. "What?" She elbowed him, and he let out a soft "oomph."

"You won't admit you liked kissing me? Maybe wanted more?"

"Hudson North! I don't deny that kissing you was exciting and dreamy."

"Tris?" he said softly.

"No. I'm not going to flirt with you tonight. So watch out, or you will be sleeping on the other side of the room—without a tarp!"

"I promise I'll behave."

"You'd better." She crossed her arms over the towel covering her upper torso, trying to still her shaking and warm herself.

"For the record, I don't have a lineup of women who want to marry me." He shuffled beside her like he was trying to get more comfortable. "Honestly, I haven't dated in six months. I would have asked you out, but we were coworkers."

"Still are until we dissolve our business."

"I proposed to you to solve that problem. I'm sorry it was such a crummy proposal. It was one of the weirdest things I've ever done." He released a long sigh. "I hope you'll still consider marriage to me as an honorable solution to our problems. And your mom's."

"Please don't bring her into this."

"I'm not going to push you about marrying me. It's too big of a commitment." He touched her hand beneath the tarp. "Regardless of what happens, I hope we can stay friends."

Friends? After the way they kissed? How was that even possible?

Chapter Eleven

When Trista shivered in spasms, Hud knew she needed more warmth. "May I sit closer so we can stay warm? I'm worried about you being too cold."

"I'm fine." Her shivering proved she wasn't anywhere near being fine.

"You said, 'side to side.' May I be nearer to your side?" Thirty seconds of silence passed. "Hypothermia is a concern for both of us. For our survival, can we sit closer together?"

She shivered almost violently. "All right. Just for survival."

"Thank you." He scooted closer and pulled the plastic sheet farther over her. Then he set his hands on his stomach, avoiding touching Trista as she leaned against his arm, still shivering. Needing a distraction from the cold and their closeness, he said, "When we were kids, my brothers and I made a pact that we'd never marry outside of love as our parents did."

"Why are you considering it, then? You proposed to me—a woman who doesn't love you."

He didn't love her either, yet her words stung. "After Lake married to get the inheritance, I was really upset with him. But then, everything flip-flopped financially for me." He drew in a breath, then exhaled slowly, trying to relax his own shivering. "I found myself facing a tempting monetary solution—with strings attached that I, too, found repulsive. However, when I seriously considered how it could fix things for both of us, I proposed to you."

"A marriage of convenience? Really, Hud?"

"It does seem wrong, doesn't it?"

"Yes!"

With the darkness thick around them, he explained how his parents had met and a little of their story. "They found love through laughter and baking." He took a chance and said, "If I could win your heart through baking, I would."

"My heart isn't won that easily." Was she being honest or flirting with him?

"How can a man who wants to win your heart prove himself to you?" Probably due to the dangers they'd faced, and because of their kissing, he felt like being more vulnerable with her.

"I don't know." She shuffled slightly. "I respect who you are as a businessman. I like how you want to put your money into helping others. You showed that you're a caring human by helping the neighbors in a crisis tonight."

"But?"

"But you're a player. I was with that kind of man before." Her shoulder leaning against his tightened. "I promised myself I'd never fall for a guy like that again!"

He bit back a groan. "I have dated casually, and sometimes, not very seriously. But that's all in the past." He wanted to be truthful and put her concerns about him to rest. "I would be a faithful husband, Tris. Those days of dating random women are over. I want something real and lasting with a wife. With you, if possible."

She didn't say a word, and the silence was maddening.

"You would never have to worry about me flirting with anyone else." More silence. "I would be one hundred percent committed to you and our family." Still, no response. "My dad is a preacher. My mom was a homemaker in a household of twelve. I respect both and the loving example of marriage they portrayed to us kids."

"Yet all nine of you made a pact never to marry as they did? Why?" She turned like she was looking at him. "There must have been a flaw you saw in their relationship. What was it?"

Light sparkles from her eyes shimmered in the darkness, tempting him to lean toward her and touch her lips with his. He didn't. He'd promised her gentlemanly behavior, and he would keep his word. "My brothers and I thought our large family, and Mom and Dad's unusual marital beginning that was common knowledge in our church group, made us freakishly weird. You know how cruel kids can be? We had to endure some nasty comments growing up."

"So you were embarrassed about your parents' marriage?"

"Uh, well. Sort of? Some bullies taunted us. Then Lake and I overheard some gossiping ladies in the church label us trouble-makers." Some of their comments still bugged him to this day. "They said we were going to turn out as derelicts and end up in marriages of convenience because 'nobody on earth would want them otherwise!'"

"Rough for kids to hear."

"No kidding. The barb stuck with me. So did the determination not to let their assessment of us come true."

"So you made a pact with your brothers based on the words of a few mean kids and some grumpy old gossips?"

"Yeah. It sounds foolish now." Back then, having the pact had been a game changer, helping Hud forge a strong bond with his brothers, especially with him and Lake. "The guys and I used to talk about having a perfect wife too."

"Good luck with that!"

"Just teenager talk." He chuckled. "Gran squelched most of it. She told us when the right woman came along, she would be perfect for us—like her husband had been perfect for her and Liv was perfectly right for Smith."

"Did you ever ponder what would have happened if your folks hadn't married?"

"That came later. So did an appreciation for the parents we had." He thought of Mom's loving attitude and how she'd always accepted him as one of her own—even when he was a knucklehead. "I don't remember all that much about my birth mom. However, Liv has been my mom since I was eight. She's always treated me the same as Lake and Coe."

"I can't wait to meet her—I mean, if I ever meet her."

"You will. May I put my arm around you?"

"I don't know, Hudson."

"Hud."

"Hud," she whispered. "I'm not going to play with fire."

"You think I'm fire?" A grin spread across his mouth, and he didn't try to subdue it.

"I kissed you, didn't I?"

"You sure did." He'd like her to do that again. "May I put my arm around you and help us stay warm?"

At least a minute of silence passed. Finally, she moved forward a tad, allowing him to put his arm around her. When she leaned into him, he immediately felt her warmth. Hopefully, she was taking in some of his too. "How are your feet?"

"No man has ever asked me that before."

"Good. I'm the first. Are they still freezing?"

"Yeah, they are." She sighed.

"If you want, put them closer to mine."

"Hud—"

"You don't want to play with fire. But we're talking about icy feet getting warm—that's it."

"Fine." She bumped her feet against his ankles.

"You weren't kidding. Your feet are icicles!"

"I told you so." She pulled them away.

"Come on, Tris. It's okay. Put your icicles back over here. I'm a tough guy."

"Then stop complaining!" She set her feet next to his. "Don't get any ideas, either."

"With those freezing appendages? I won't!" He nestled her feet snugly against his lower limbs. "How's that?"

"Better. Thank you."

"Of course." He leaned his head against hers. "I like you, Trista Dunmore."

"Too bad you want to marry me just to get your inheritance."

"That plays into it." He wouldn't act like it didn't. "But when we kissed earlier, it was amazing and felt real. I'm sure we could make a go of a marriage."

"Sounds like a business arrangement."

"In the beginning, perhaps. I never thought I'd ask someone to marry me who I didn't love."

"I don't love you either."

"So you said." When her warm breath brushed against his chin, he longed to kiss her and try to change her mind. "Will you marry me, Tris?" he asked softly, trying to sound sincere and honest, even though they were sitting on a concrete slab in the dark with a plastic tarp wrapped around them. "I will do my best to make you happy."

She let out a long, weary-sounding sigh without giving him an answer.

Chapter Twelve

Trista awoke to a loud banging on the shed door. Slowly, she uncurled from her position against Hud's chest with his arms still surrounding her. Stiff and achy from sleeping on the hard floor, at least she was warm. Even her toes were warm! She met his gaze in the dim morning light and whispered, "Yes. I will marry you."

A lazy smile crossed his lips.

The banging came again. "Anyone in there?" Was that Pastor Chad's voice?

"Yes! We're here!" Trista crawled out from the snuggly-wrapped tarp and felt instantly chilled.

The door opened and light flooded the room. Pastor Chad rushed in. "Trista? Are you all right?"

"I'm fine." She accepted his one-arm hug. "What are you doing here?"

Pastor Chad, dressed in a hooded raincoat, squinted at Hud as he crawled out from beneath the table. "I'm part of the rescue team, making sure everyone is all right."

"This is our business property. Hud's truck got swept away by the mudslides," she explained. "We had to spend the night here."

"I see."

Hud extended his hand. "Hello. I'm Hud North. Trista's—"

"Fiancé." She clasped his other hand tightly.

Hud met her gaze and smiled. "That's right. Fiancé."

"I'm Chad Gray." The minister shook Hud's hand, glancing back and forth between them. "You're getting married?"

"Yes!" The heat of another blush spread up her face.

"Congratulations! Why haven't I heard of this before now?"

"I agreed to Hud's proposal this morning. We are going to get married quickly."

"Quickly?" Pastor Chad's eyebrows shot up.

"We, just, well—" What must he be thinking? "It's a long story."

"I'm happy for you." He shook her hand, then Hud's again. "May the Lord bless your marriage with longevity and peace."

"Amen," Hud said quietly.

"Now, what can I do to help? Do you need water? Breakfast bars?"

"Both would be great, thanks," Trista said.

"I'll be right back. I left my backpack outside." Pastor Chad strode out the door.

Hud turned toward her. "You're sure you want to marry me?"

"In the night, I prayed and felt at peace about taking that step with you." She leaned up and kissed his rough cheek. "I'm hoping love will knit our hearts together in time."

"That sounds good to me." He gave her one of those smiles she already loved.

Pastor Chad returned and handed them each a water bottle and a couple of prepackaged breakfast bars. "These should sustain you for a while."

"Thank you." Trista unscrewed the lid, then guzzled a long drink.

"Yeah, thanks." Hud drank from his water bottle.

"There's a relay bus at the south end of the mudslide. It will take you to another checkpoint two miles south." Pastor Chad set his hand on Trista's shoulder. "I'm glad you are safe. Your mom has been worried."

"I did call her last night."

"That's good." He glanced at Hud. "You'll make sure she gets safely to the bus?"

"Absolutely."

"All right. I have to move on to the next residence." Pastor Chad waved and exited, leaving the door ajar.

As soon as Trista heard his footsteps fading, she groaned. "You know what he thinks, don't you?"

"Yeah. Are you going to set him straight?"

"I will. It was too embarrassing to explain right now."

Hud clasped both of her hands. "Thank you for saying yes about marrying me."

His tender smile made her want to lean up and kiss his soft lips. But she determinedly stepped back. "Let's hurry and catch the bus." She picked up the tarp that had kept them warm enough to sleep during the night and tried folding it.

Hud put his hands over hers, stilling her movements. "May I kiss you?"

"You may kiss me at the altar."

He stared at her for a long moment. "Okay. Until then, I'll eagerly await the chance to kiss you again."

"And Hud? We'll wait until we're falling in love for the rest to happen between us, okay?" She wouldn't make the same mistake twice. She wouldn't stay in his bedroom before she knew beyond any doubt that he'd be faithful to her and stick with her beyond the five-year contract. "Do you agree to that?"

He swallowed. "I agree."

"So help me, if you try anything—"

"I'll be a complete gentleman." He held up his right hand like he was promising to tell the truth in court. "I will abide by whatever makes you feel comfortable in our marriage. I will be faithful to you, regardless of our sleeping arrangements. And I promise to do my best to fall in love with you."

"You'll do your best to fall for me? Can't you come up with something better than that?"

Smiling softly, he pulled her to him for a quick hug. "I look forward to falling in love with you, Trista. I hope to make you so happy and in love with me that you'll want to kiss me all night long."

"Hudson!" She shoved away from him. "That isn't helping me stay away from the fire."

"You asked me to do better at my promise." He kissed her once on the cheek. "Now, let's head for the bus. We have a wedding to plan!"

Chapter Thirteen

"You're what?" Mom pressed both palms against her chest.

"Hud and I are getting married!" Trista grinned, then grimaced.

"Oh, honey bear!" Mom hugged her. "My dear girl, I wish you great joy and happiness!"

"I wish for that, too." Trista raked her fingers through her messy hair. She still hadn't showered or changed out of the jacket a volunteer at the bus stop had given her. "I can't guarantee we'll have a real marriage or happiness, but I hope we will."

"You don't think you love him?"

"No. I don't love Hud!"

"Not even a little?" Mom asked woefully.

"Mom, no! We are doing this for reasons other than love." Their heated kisses and how eagerly she'd responded to his affection after the mudslides flashed through her thoughts. But she shoved those memories out of her mind as determinedly as she shoveled mud away from the neighbor's house last night.

"I saw the way he looks at you." Mom fluttered her hands and paced from the kitchen table to the sink and back again. "Even so, I don't want you marrying him so that I can keep this house. I would never encourage you to marry someone for money or to make my life easier."

"Thanks. But I've made my decision."

"What will Pastor Chad say?" Mom asked nervously. "Will he perform the ceremony?"

"Hard to say. He found us together."

Mom gasped. "Found you how?"

"We were just waking up."

"Trista!"

"We had to stay wrapped together in a tarp all night to keep warm. Otherwise, we might have succumbed to hypothermia."

"And Pastor saw you like that with Hudson?" Mom's mouth dropped open, her face turning pale.

"Yes. He may assume the worst. But I told him we're getting married."

"Oh, Trista." Mom shook her head.

"Nothing happened. I will explain it all to him."

"What if he refuses to perform the ceremony, considering the circumstances?"

"Then we'll go before a judge." She hugged Mom. "I know it isn't what you want to hear. But I won't pretend that Hud and I love each other in front of you. You should know the truth about us from the start."

"I wish for more for you."

"Believe me, so do I."

"Layla will be taken care of?"

"Hud says he'll adopt her." Trista ran the faucet and filled a glass of water. "I won't let that happen unless I'm sure the marriage will stick."

"You doubt already? Don't marry him, then! Don't make yourself or Hudson miserable."

"Mom, I already explained that I'm not in love with him." She took a quick drink of water. "We'll work it out as we go."

"I can't believe it's come to this." Groaning, Mom covered her face with her hands. "Oh, Lord, help us!"

Trista hadn't imagined her mother taking the news so badly. Wasn't she the one who urged her to consider Hud's proposal? Did she think they'd fall for each other instantly?

"I'm going to take a bath. Hud's gone home to clean up and call his lawyer."

"When will you get married?"

"In three days if we submit our application for a marriage license today."

"Three days," Mom said glumly. "I'm sorry about the problems with the house. If I hadn't fallen behind so badly, you wouldn't be in this terrible predicament."

"It's not your fault." Trista patted her shoulder. "Hud's generosity will provide stability for our family for a long time."

"But without the hope of love?"

"I didn't say there wasn't any hope of love." She smiled and kissed Mom's cheek. "We need to have a little faith, that's all. Isn't that what you often tell me?"

"Oh, honey bear."

"It'll be okay, Mom."

After taking a long, hot bubble bath, Trista chose a slim-fitting pair of slacks and a fuchsia-colored sweater that brought out the purple highlights in her eyes, or so she'd been told. Today her eyes looked tired. It was hard to cover up the effects of a rough night's sleep with eye shadow and black mascara, but she was determined to try.

When her cell phone chirped, she found two texts from Hud. *I spoke with the lawyer.* Then—*Are you still in?* So he was uncertain?

Maybe she'd let him squirm a little. *I'm having some doubts.*

I don't blame you.
My mom says not to do it.
Really?
She wants me to wait for true love.
Is that what you want?

Did she hope for true love between her and Hud? This texting was getting too personal when she wanted to make him squirm—not her. *Are you ready to fill out the marriage license application?*

Yes. If you're still game to marry me.

This was her chance to send him a resounding note of finality. Instead, she let her fingers fly over the keyboard app. *If you are brave enough to marry me, I'm in.* She wasn't backing out. She'd felt peace about her decision last night. She would cling to that peace and hope for good things in their marriage in the future. *I'll fill out my part of the license application. Then fax it over for you to do your part.*

"Brave enough" sounds like a challenge, he responded.

Take it how you like!

Chapter Fourteen

After filling out his part of the marriage license application and faxing it to the Bureau of Vital Statistics in Juneau, Hud had one more bit of business to complete—e-signing the form for accepting the inheritance. For ten minutes, he'd been staring at the spot on the computer screen where he needed to sign. The final e-signature would be required after he married Trista in three days. But signing this document made him feel like his chest had been cut open and he was giving up one of his ribs.

Another cup of coffee might help. Or he could call Lake and ask if he'd felt such misery when he signed. And if so, what had he done to overcome it?

Hud groaned. He needed to face this step like a man—like a North, like one of the preacher's sons. He lifted his chin, feeling some pride in his heritage. Yet, despite his internal pep talk, he still didn't type his name.

He let his mind wander to earlier when Pastor Chad had stormed into the outbuilding. He'd looked so shocked and something else—judgmental or assuming—to find Trista alone with Hud. He hated that anyone might judge Trista harshly because the two of them had been together overnight.

But people were bound to talk—wasn't that how gossip typically spread? As a pastor and his wife, some of Dad and Mom's life had been on display for the congregation to observe and comment on. Some had remarked about it within Hud and Lake's hearing. However, that wasn't their parents' fault! *No, it wasn't.* Hud exhaled, letting some of his previous bitterness and grievances go.

People couldn't help but be curious about others. However, a measure of grace and understanding from Dad's parishioners would have gone a long way in alleviating some of his youthful resentments. Still, he couldn't blame anyone else for how seriously he'd taken the mean comments and allowed them to fester in his spirit for years.

God, I'm sorry.

Starting today, he wanted to have more grace in his heart for others—and more toward himself for messing up so many times in the past. He wanted to live with more thankfulness, too, starting with appreciating the step Trista was willing to take with him. He thanked God for it!

What would his family say about him marrying quickly and not inviting them? Mom, Dad, and Gran would surely understand. His brothers? Not so much. One good thing about him and Trista marrying in Alaska was his siblings wouldn't be around to pull any of their pre-wedding shenanigans.

Enough stalling. Sign the document and be done with it!

By signing, he was agreeing to accept the money. He was also agreeing to marry Trista and for them to stay married for at least five years, preferably for their whole lives.

He would be entering into an arrangement he'd vowed never to participate in. But why had he made that vow, anyway? Wasn't Mom and Dad's marriage admirable? Enviable, even? They'd had a long-lasting relationship filled with love for each other and their family. Who cared how it started? Most people in Thunder Ridge probably respected them and looked up to them as an example of a godly marriage.

Even Coe had mentioned something along those lines the day Hud tried to get him to persuade Lake not to marry Irish. Only Hud had stubbornly opposed Lake marrying and getting the inheritance. Now here he was planning to do the same thing! The harsh reality of his past opinions colliding with what he was about to do twisted a tight knot of anxiety and remorse inside him. He didn't regret marrying Trista, but he regretted some of his previous actions and opinions. Some past behavior had been downright deplorable. He groaned and raked his fingers through his hair.

Sign the document!

Would he and Trista ever find true love? What he'd experienced kissing her was amazing. He looked forward to more of that. A lifetime of simmering passion between them would be nothing short of incredible.

Sign already!

It was a good thing they were friends and business associates. He was thankful not to be jumping into marriage with a stranger. And while he couldn't claim purity, whenever he told Trista he loved her, it would be the first time he said those words to any woman besides Mom and Gran. He wouldn't say them to Trista lightly or until he meant them, either, however long it took.

Did you finish the pre-signing? Trista texted him.

No.

Stalling?

Something like that.

He took a deep breath, exhaled, then swallowed hard. He hovered the mouse icon over the signing line for a few more seconds. *Lord, help me.*

Click.

It's done.

Chapter Fifteen

Mid-morning the next day, Trista and Hud sat across from Pastor Chad, discussing wedding plans and explaining why they were getting married quickly. With his right leg crossed over his other knee, Hud appeared calm. But his slip-on shoe swinging back and forth in agitated movements told a different story.

Trista tried to sound reassuring when she told Pastor Chad that even though they were getting married before they fell for each other, they believed love would come later. Considering the frown on his face, he wasn't convinced.

"Your mother is okay with this kind of marriage?"

"She understands why we're doing it. I don't know that she's okay with it."

"What about your parents?" Pastor Chad tipped his head toward Hud.

"Mom and Dad had an unusual beginning to their marriage, but they've been together for thirty-five years. I'm sure they'll understand our situation and trust God for the best in our lives."

"I see." Pastor Chad smoothed his palm over his chin. "I believe in striving for a strong marriage and family, making it a priority from the beginning. Do you agree?"

"Sure. I have eight siblings. We had strong parenting and love despite much wrestling and prank-pulling." Hud was obviously trying to keep things light.

Pastor Chad chuckled. "Sounds admirable. What about children? Have you two discussed having a family of your own?"

"Uh. Not yet." Hud briefly met Trista's gaze, his cheeks darkening. Had his thoughts leaped to what it meant for them to have babies like hers had?

"I have Layla," she said. "But I want more kids."

"You do?" Hud's eyes widened.

Why the surprised look? He came from a large family. Didn't he want kids? They hadn't discussed many personal topics, but she assumed he wanted to have children.

"I'd like Layla to have siblings someday." She tried to gauge Hud's reactions. His shoe swayed back and forth faster. He gnawed on his lower lip. His shoulders bunched up like his muscles were tight. What was with him? Was he having second thoughts about their marriage? Or did he really not want kids?

"Hud?" the pastor asked.

"I haven't given it much thought."

Why not?—Trista wanted to ask but kept the question to herself. They should have discussed this topic before coming here, probably before she agreed to marry him.

"There was a time when I didn't want to have children." Pastor Chad grimaced like he'd eaten something sour. "I kept my plans not to have kids away from my wife. That was a bad decision."

Hud squirmed in his seat. Why was he acting so uncomfortable about this subject?

"You must have changed your mind since you have three darling boys." Trista nodded toward a picture of Pastor Chad, April, and their sons on his bookshelf.

"I sure did." He glanced at the photo, a soft expression crossing his face. "I nearly lost my wife over my stubbornness and secrecy. I'm thankful God changed my heart." He leaned forward, his gaze intent on Hud. "If you are at odds about having children, talk it over before you get married. If you can't agree, put on the brakes. Seek counseling. Wait for love?"

Trista agreed. Even with the inheritance stipulations, she couldn't marry someone who didn't want a family.

"Do you have any regrets about having those kids?" Hud lifted his chin toward the photograph. "You must have had reasons for not wanting to be a parent."

Tension rippled through Trista.

The pastor smiled. "I have zero regrets about us having our boys. Nor about doing everything in my power to mend things with my wife. I love my family more than anything … other than Jesus."

"I sense a 'but' coming."

"But I had a lousy dad—an overly busy pastor who didn't have time for a son. I feared I'd turn out exactly like him."

Tears flooded Hud's eyes. He wiped them away with the back of his hand. A warm tenderness for him oozed into Trista's emotions. She didn't understand his sensitive response, however, she wanted to clasp his hand and comfort him. Instead, she remained still, hoping to better understand the man she'd agreed to marry.

"What makes you hesitant about having children?" Pastor Chad asked in a gentle voice.

Hud's brow furrowed like he was pondering something deeply. "The thought of bringing kids into this world and then not being around for them nearly kills me."

"Oh, Hud." Trista gripped his hand, then, compassion making her heart ache for him. He was thinking about his birth mom and dad and how they died in a car accident when he was a kid, wasn't he? About them not being around for him and his brother all these years? He squeezed her hand back but didn't meet her gaze.

"None of us have the assurance of being here for our families like we hope to be." Pastor Chad folded his hands over his desk. "Did your family go through a tragedy when you were young?"

"Yeah." Hud glanced upward, blinking fast. "My parents died when I was eight and my kid brother was two."

"I'm so sorry."

"It turns my stomach when I think about the possibility of leaving my kids without a dad."

Oh, Hud.

Pastor Chad nodded. "I understand."

So did Trista. A heaviness settled in her middle. Was Hud's opinion on the matter going to be a deal breaker between them? "Are you saying you never want to have children?"

Their gazes met and held. His eyes were moist, and she could see he still carried internal wounds from losing his parents. Recognizing that about him and seeing he wasn't quite the tough guy he usually portrayed made her care for him even more.

"It's something we'd have to talk about." Hud released a long sigh. "I thought we would be so busy with our building projects, and with you already having Layla, that our lives would be full enough."

"They probably will be." Trista glanced between him and Pastor Chad. This was a conversation they should have had by themselves. But they came here to discuss marriage. "However, I hope you will be open to having kids in the future. You'd make a great dad."

"Based on what?" A rare look of insecurity crossed his features.

"Based on how you promised to take care of Layla and adopt her, providing stability. And the way you said you'd pay for my mom's mortgage. Even how you leaped in and helped the neighbors after the mudslide." She patted his arm. "I was proud of you, Hud. You are a generous, caring man."

"You think so?"

"I do," she said solemnly as if she were making a vow. "Any children of ours, including Layla, would be lucky to have you for a dad."

He sighed and gazed downward, staring at their clasped hands.

"What I'm hearing is Trista wants assurance that you'll keep an open mind about having kids." Pastor Chad said in a moderator's voice. "Right?"

"Yes. And that we'll keep talking about it."

"Hud?" Pastor Chad prompted.

"Sure. Absolutely. We can revisit the topic whenever Trista wants to." A mischievous grin crossed Hud's mouth. "It's not like I hate the idea of making babies with you, Tris."

"Hud!" Heat bled from the roots of her hair to her feet. She released his hand.

"Sorry. Just trying to lighten the mood."

Pastor Chad cleared his throat. "Perhaps while you're waiting for your marriage license to be approved, you can both make sure you're prepared for a future together. Now, let's discuss money, shall we?"

After talking about babies and Hud confessing his feelings about fatherhood, any other subject seemed mundane. Trista caught him staring at her intensely a couple of times. Did he already wish they were falling for each other? Or was he questioning them getting married at all?

Chapter Sixteen

One of the calls Hud dreaded came that night. He knew he was in trouble when Granny Trish's name crossed his phone screen. He didn't want to discuss his upcoming marriage with her. But he wouldn't lie about it, either. "Hey, Gran."

"My sweet boy, I hope I didn't wake you."

"Nah. It's only eight o'clock here." He glanced around the dark condo where he'd collapsed onto the couch a couple of hours ago, eating pizza and watching a TV show, then dozing off. "What's up?"

Why was Gran calling? Did Lake blab about what he had been doing in Thunder Ridge a few days ago?

"Hud, I love you like my next breath."

"I know you do." His heart thudded an irregular beat, and he braced himself emotionally. His grandmother was notorious for meddling in his and his brothers' lives. What was she going to pry into his life about today?

"The Lord has put a heavy burden on my heart for you."

"Is that right?"

"I had a dream about you last night." There was foreboding in her tone. "I've been so worried about you."

"I'm okay, Gran." Hud set his stocking feet on the floor and scooted forward on the couch cushion.

"What's going on with you?" she asked softly.

"Uh, well. Why don't you tell me what your dream was about?" Did she receive a warning from God that he shouldn't do whatever he was about to do? His gulp sounded loud in his ears.

"I pray for you boys constantly. Your names are on my breath all through the day."

A tenderness toward his grandmother spread through him, overriding his apprehension of whatever she was about to tell him. "I appreciate your devotion to praying for us, Gran. I'm sure Lake and the others are grateful too." Other than Stone—but he wouldn't mention his rogue brother, whom he hadn't heard from in a year.

"Last night, I prayed for you before I went to sleep. Then I dreamed that I made an apple pie just the way you like it."

"I've always loved your apple pies."

"I miss making them for you." Gran's sigh carried a weary note. "In my dream, you weren't hungry and refused to eat my pie. It seemed you were sickly from worrying or fretting." She took in a slow draw of breath. "Are you worried about something, Hud?"

"I have been under a lot of stress. Some financial stuff fell through, and I've been dealing with it." That was the truth, but not the whole story.

"I have a little savings set aside. It's yours if you need it."

"Ah, Gran, you're the sweetest to offer. But I must work this out by myself."

"And with the Lord's help?"

"Sure. However, I am used to depending on myself." God knew his thoughts. If He had given Gran a dream about him, the Lord already knew his sorry situation—no reason to pretend otherwise. "I am trying to pray more. I've been thinking about my upbringing. And you."

"Aw, sweetie. I'm always here for you. Love you forever. God loves you too—even more than me, your mom, and dad combined." She had always told him affirming things about God and his parents loving him. He appreciated that about her, even when it made him uncomfortable sometimes. "What about not being hungry? Does that sound familiar?"

"I wolfed down most of a pizza by myself a while ago."

"I mean spiritually."

"Oh. Right."

"Are you hungry for the things of God? Do you want Him in your life, guiding you toward making the right decisions?"

Her questions hung like hot air balloons dangling over a city. How could he answer the highly personal yet loving queries? "I want to be."

"That's a great starting place."

"I'm glad you're praying for me. I'm thankful to have you in my life." He couldn't imagine his world without Granny Trish in it. He pinched the bridge of his nose. "I've made some decisions that might be startling and may irritate some family members."

"Oh?"

"In a few days, I'll be in Thunder Ridge and explain everything." He let go of pinching his nose. "There's someone I want you to meet."

"You're bringing a woman home?"

"Yes. But don't tell Mom and Dad, okay?" Since Gran had been worried and called, he wanted to share a little something with her. He still had to figure out how to tell the others about his plans.

"I won't mention anything. It's your story to share. I can't wait to meet your mystery woman."

"She's lovely."

"I'll be praying for you and trusting God to guide you."

"Thanks for caring enough to call, Gran."

After goodbyes, Hud closed his eyes and sighed. Had God given his grandmother a dream about him as a warning to pray for him? Was spiritual hunger the thing he lacked?

He stretched back out on the couch, trying to be honest and authentic with God. *Am I starving spiritually? I want to make my way back to You. I want to be a good husband for Trista. A loving dad to Layla, too. Help me, Lord Jesus.*

A faint peacefulness swept through him as he dozed off again. Maybe Gran's prayers were working already.

Chapter Seventeen

Trista stood in front of her bedroom mirror, smoothing her hands down the knee-length lacy white wedding dress she'd chosen. Hud told her not to worry about the costs of the wedding—that he'd take care of everything. But she'd only invited Mom, Aunt Fanny, and a few close friends, and none of his family members were coming, so there wasn't any reason to spend a fortune on a dress she'd wear once. Still, it was a lovely dress.

This morning, she'd enjoyed a quiet pre-wedding breakfast with Hud, where they discussed the life-changing steps they were about to take. He asked her if she was confident they were doing the right thing. Confident? How could anyone know for sure that they were making the right decision? Wasn't it too late to change course, anyway?

The last task before donning wedding attire had been picking up their marriage license at the local Bureau of Vital Statistics office. With that task accomplished, everything was set for her to become Mrs. Hudson North.

"Trista North," she tested the name.

Just then, Layla skipped and danced into the bedroom in her light blue taffeta dress and white shoes. Thanks to Mom's handiwork, her hair was braided with a ring of daisies fashioned like a crown.

"Mommy! Look what Grammie did! Isn't it pretty?" She twirled in a circle, smiling widely.

"You are so adorable!" Trista clutched her daughter to herself in a hug. "You will be the best flower girl ever!"

Layla giggled, and her green eyes, which looked so much like her father's, sparkled brightly. After today, her beautiful irises would have to remind Trista of the Northern Lights or a forest of trees with moonbeams shining on them—anything other than the eyes of the man who'd refused to accept his fatherhood responsibilities and made her mistrustful of other men.

Now she was marrying a man who'd promised to adopt Layla, give her a college fund, and provide for her. That was sweet of him, but would Hud ever love Layla as a father? Would he love her as a wife? She gulped over thoughts of what she hoped marriage with him would eventually entail—a tender closeness and sharing in intimacies of mind, heart, and body. But would she ever find a way to fully trust him? To fully love him?

"Grammie says it's almost time to go to the church!" Layla skipped out of the room, dancing and twirling the way she came in.

Trista glanced around her bedroom, which had been her refuge for a long time. Tonight, she'd be staying at Hud's condominium. Even though she was going to sleep in his guest room, they'd agreed to begin their journey as a married couple under the same roof.

She and Hud would be flying into Spokane tomorrow, and then driving to Thunder Ridge so she could meet his family, while Layla would be staying with Mom. Last night, Trista had tried to carefully explain about the wedding and her quick trip away with Hud. But her daughter's emotional crying and pouting left her troubled about what the days ahead might hold.

Trista pivoted on her white heels and checked the back of her dress and hair, then took a deep breath. It was time for her to fulfill her side of the agreement with Hud.

Lord, please help our marriage become more than a financial arrangement. Help us love each other and grow into a married couple and family. Thank You in advance for blessing us with a sweet love story—I'm counting on one being out there for us!

From the narrow space between the two closed doors at the back of the church, Trista watched Layla skipping down the aisle to a romantic classical tune. She tossed red rose petals into the air with abandonment, like she was born for such a moment. Tears slipped down Trista's cheeks as tender emotions cascaded through her. Even though she wasn't in love with Hud, this was her wedding day—her *actual* wedding day.

The music volume increased, which was her cue to walk down the aisle. She took a moment to breathe and collect herself, then she moved into the chapel. If her dad were alive, he would have walked beside her today. Even Mom offered to accompany her, but Trista wanted to do this part alone. Somehow, walking on her own toward Hud seemed symbolic of their solitary lives joining together. Halfway down the aisle, she lifted her gaze to meet her groom's. He smiled broadly like he was inviting her to come closer to him, and her heart flip-flopped.

Hud looked so handsome! A gray tux complemented his dark hair and eyes. A ruby-colored tie adorned his neck and brought out the rosy color in his cheeks. Was he blushing? The lower half of his face had that shadowed look she loved. She melted a little inside as she gazed at the man she was about to marry, tempted to whistle to show her approval. But her mother would frown on such casual behavior during a wedding ceremony—even in a marriage like Trista and Hud were having.

When she reached him, he clasped her hand and drew her to his side. "You look amazing, Tris."

"Thank you. You look pretty spectacular also."

"Beats the mud and grime you saw me wearing a couple of days ago."

She chuckled at the memory. Although she never wanted to forget how he'd looked digging out the neighbor's front yard. His tender humanity during the crisis had made her think twice about there being more to Hudson North than the tough, savvy businessman she'd worked with for the last six months. But this moment with him all dressed up in a tux smiling at her? She didn't want to forget this either.

"Are you guys ready?" Pastor Chad asked.

"I am." Trista met Hud's gaze again and smiled.

He nodded solemnly. "I am too. For better or for worse."

"Oh, you had to mention that!" She nudged his arm.

Pastor Chad glanced toward the audience and smiled at someone. Trista peeked over her shoulder and spotted April grinning back at him. Seeing them exchanging loving expressions gave her a renewed sense of hope. Since God had helped Chad and April find their way back to each other and love, couldn't He also help Trista and Hud find their way to a loving relationship?

She focused on the pastor's opening remarks about love, devotion, and a companionship that would survive the decades. *Lord, please let it be so.*

Trista and Hud recited traditional vows to each other and finally reached the part she'd been looking forward to with some eagerness. They hadn't discussed the wedding kiss, but she'd been anticipating kissing Hud again ever since their momentous kiss in the shed. She moistened her lips and prayed Layla wouldn't make any childish comments. Even Cinderella's kiss with Prince Charming usually got exclamations of "yuck" and "that's gross" when she watched the movie.

"You may kiss your bride," Pastor Chad said.

Hud leaned toward her. "May I kiss you, Tris?" Did he recall her telling him he couldn't kiss her until they were at the altar?

"You may."

Gently, he took her in his arms. With his gaze locked on hers, he stroked some strands of hair from her cheek and tucked them behind her ear. "I've been looking forward to this part all day."

Me too.

His lips met hers, and electrical sparks zinged up her spine. He took his time with the kiss as if it were their first one. Then he trailed butterfly kisses across her cheek. "You are a beautiful bride, Trista. I will never forget this moment. I hope you never do either." His lips brushed hers again like he was sealing his words with a soft kiss.

"Mommy! Stop kissing him!"

Trista pulled away from Hud, heat rushing up her cheeks.

The small crowd laughed.

"Are you going to be mushy with him all the time?"

"I certainly hope so!" Hud leaned over and kissed Trista lightly again.

"Yuck!"

"Layla." Trista shook her head at her daughter.

"Do you want to walk down the aisle with your mom and me?" Hud held out his arm toward Layla.

Turning up her nose at him as only a five-year-old could, she clutched Trista's arm. Hud didn't seem to mind the rebuff. Smiling at Trista, he linked his arm with hers, and the three of them walked down the aisle together.

Chapter Eighteen

"I have something to tell you." Hud stroked his fingertips over the back of Trista's hand, resting on the divider between their seats during the plane's approach into Spokane.

"What's that?"

He should have confessed this to her before now, but he'd had a lot on his mind lately. With the wedding plans, trying to hold the business together, preparing the guest room for Trista, and e-signing the inheritance documents, he'd almost forgotten about it. "I, uh, didn't tell my parents." He swallowed hard, wishing he had mentioned this while they were sitting in his living room last night, reminiscing about their wedding ceremony.

"Tell them about what?" Trista's sparkling flecks of purple in her dark blue eyes glimmered in his direction.

"Us. I didn't explain about the wedding."

Her mouth dropped open. Then she made a choking sound. "You didn't tell your parents that we were getting married?"

A woman on the other side of the aisle leaned forward, scowling at him.

"No. I wanted it to be a surprise."

"Oh, Hud, bringing a wife home will be quite the surprise! How could you do this to me?" Trista glared at him. "How could you do this to your mom?"

"I tried explaining it to her in an email, but I couldn't tell her I was getting married that way."

"Of course you couldn't! But you should have called her."

"I'll say," the woman across the aisle muttered.

"I know. You're right." He sighed and stroked his hand across his forehead. He should have called Mom and Dad. Gran, too. But he didn't, and now they would have to face his family as a newly married couple.

After the jet landed and was taxiing toward the terminal building, Trista asked, "Won't Liv resent not being invited to her son's wedding?"

"Possibly. But I hope she'll be happy for us and not feel slighted."

"I want her to like me! I can't believe you didn't tell her about us. That was just—"

"Thoughtless? Insensitive? I'm sorry." After another sigh, he said, "Look, Trista, my mom will absolutely love you. You don't have to worry about that." His parents would forgive his omission and love him and Trista, no matter what—he knew that much about them and their belief in extending grace to everyone. "Everything will be fine. I promise."

"Fine?" She glowered at him as the noisy plane came to a stop. "Is your grandmother going to hate me?"

"It's not in Granny Trish's DNA to hate anyone."

"The powerful emotions mothers and grandmothers have toward their children and grandchildren might surprise you!" She stared at the jet's ceiling, mumbling about him throwing her into the lion's den.

"If Gran could love nine rapscallion children and make us all feel like she loved us best, she'll love you as a granddaughter, too."

"I don't appreciate your not telling them. It seems like you're ashamed of what we did." She eyed him suspiciously.

Suddenly, he felt a little too warm even with the jet's cool air blowing toward him. He tugged at his shirt's neckline. Was he ashamed of marrying Trista and accepting the inheritance he'd despised for so long? Had he acted dishonorably by not coming clean with his parents?

"Are you embarrassed about us, Hud?"

"Absolutely not." He swallowed with some difficulty. "I mentioned to Granny Trish that I was bringing a woman to Thunder Ridge."

"A woman?"

"I meant you. She's looking forward to meeting you."

Trista groaned and shook her head.

Another sigh emerged from deep inside him. Mom and Dad might be disappointed about not being invited to the wedding—Trista was right about that. And they'd wonder why he and Trista married quickly. But he was most concerned about his brothers' reactions to him going against their pact. After all he'd said about Lake doing the unthinkable, how could he face them? Would they take their grudges to another level by pulling some annoying wedding prank?

Two hours later, Hud parked the rental car in Mom and Dad's driveway and turned off the engine. The North's dinnertime had always been at five-thirty sharp, so he'd timed their arrival perfectly. "Are you ready for this?"

"If I say no, will you drive me back to the airport? I'd feel better if your mom was expecting us." Trista's voice shook. "Do you see what you've done? How nervous you've made me feel?"

"I'm sorry, Trista. I didn't mean to make you feel uncomfortable about meeting my family. But I think it will go better than you imagine." He tapped his fingers against the steering wheel. "Be fore-warned. There might be some commotion at the beginning."

"Like they'll throw tomatoes at me?"

"No. Mom and Dad will engulf us in giant bear hugs and make a big fuss, especially since it's my birthday."

"Some birthday." She opened her door. "Let's go. The sooner we face them, the sooner we can return to the airport."

Chapter Nineteen

Hud opened the front door of his parents' house as quietly as possible without knocking. The boisterous talking and laughter at the dinner table warmed his heart and reminded him of what he'd been missing since he moved away. He drew Trista into the dining room quickly, pulling her to his side. "Surprise, everyone!"

The chatter ceased. Mom, Dad, Gran, Spur, and Wilks turned startled, drop-jawed expressions in their direction. Then chaos broke loose.

"Hud!" Mom jumped up and ran to him, hugging him tightly. "What a surprise! Happy birthday!" She hugged Trista, too, even though she didn't know who she was yet. Right behind her, Dad joined the hugs and cheerful greetings.

Spur and Wilks shook their hands and joked about Hud having a woman in his life for his birthday. If only they knew!

Trista giggled nervously.

"Mom, Dad, everyone," Hud said as hugs and greetings subsided. He settled his arm over Trista's shoulder. "This is Trista, my wife."

"Your wife?" Mom gasped.

"What did you do, bro?" Spur demanded.

"Now, everyone. Let's hear him out," Gran said. "He must have had his reasons." Hud met her gaze and nodded once in thanks.

Mom returned to Trista and hugged her again. "Trista, welcome to our family. I'm Liv. Or Mom." She grabbed Hud by the shoulders. "You got married? Why didn't you tell me?"

"I wanted to surprise you."

"You did that, all right." She hugged him again. But when she backed away, her eyes were filled with tears.

A gnawing ache crept through him, and he deeply regretted not calling her and telling her the truth. Mom deserved to know about their wedding and the reasons why they'd married as they did.

Dad shook his hand and clapped him on the back. "Congratulations, son." He hugged Trista again, too. "Welcome to the family. Come and sit down. Tell us all about it."

"Have you had dinner?" Mom sniffed and discreetly brushed her fingers beneath her eyes.

"Yes. We picked up sandwiches at the airport." Hud led Trista over to his grandmother. "Gran, this is Trista."

She opened her arms wide. "Welcome, dear. I'm Granny Trish. Or Trish."

"I'm glad to meet you." Trista leaned down and hugged her.

Hud hugged Gran and whispered, "Thanks for keeping our secret."

"Of course, my boy." She patted his cheek. "You didn't tell me you were marrying the girl!"

"Sorry."

"That's okay. God knew."

Hud gulped and nodded.

Once they sat down, and Spur and Wilks were stuffing their mouths with food again, Mom asked, "How did you two meet? Why did you get married without telling us?"

"I'm sorry, Mom. We decided to get married quickly. But I wish you could have been there."

A softer look crossed her face. "Me too. Having another daughter-in-law in the family is a wonderful surprise and a blessing!" Mom smiled at Trista, warmth filling her gaze. "Of course, I would have wanted the wedding to be here or for me to be there. But it's great to meet you now."

"Thank you," Trista said softly.

"We would have wanted it to be here, too." Spur's reddish eyebrows rocked. "Hud just didn't want to deal with his brothers at his bachelor party."

"That's the truth!" Hud nodded.

"What's with the practical jokes?" Trista asked. "Hud warned me about you guys."

"As well he should! When you least expect it, the North brothers show up." Wilks rocked his thumb between himself and Spur.

"Did you hear what we did to Lake the night before his nuptials?" Laughing, Spur bumped Wilks's elbow with his. "We locked him in his guest room without any furniture. He'll never forget the night before he wed Irish."

"I still can't believe you did that." Mom shook her head.

"Since your arrival surprised us, we don't have anything up our sleeves *yet*." Wilks winked at Trista. "We'll start working on it right away."

"Wilks—" Hud squinted a warning toward his brothers.

"Now, fellows," Dad said. "We don't want to scare Trista off or make her think our family isn't polite."

"No, sir. We want her to feel right at home like a true North!" Spur grinned, and his freckles spread across his face.

"Spur," Hud said gruffly, "one of these days, you're going to bring a girl home. Then you'd better watch out!"

"Yeah, yeah."

"Trista, how did you meet our Hudson?" Gran's eyes sparkled toward her.

"We spoke with each other at a city council meeting. Now we're partners in a business venture that's—"

"Showing a lot of promise." Hud shook his head slightly at Trista, hoping she read his meaning. He'd tell Mom, Dad, and Gran about accepting the legacy later. For Trista's sake, it was better if his brothers assumed their marriage was authentic.

Spur glanced back and forth between them as if he was analyzing their relationship. Could he tell by how they were behaving toward each other that they weren't spouses in the traditional sense? Hud stroked some hair off Trista's cheek and gave her a tender look, mostly to put Spur's suspicions to rest. But when he touched her face and felt her warmth, he enjoyed the sensation of his fingertips against her skin so much he was tempted to lean in and kiss her like a husband who already loved his wife.

"Was there some trouble with the business before?" Mom moved some food around on her plate.

"Uh, yes. There was." Hud cleared his throat. "But it's taken care of now."

"Is that right?" Mom squinted at him.

"You see, there was a terrible mudslide," Trista said.

"Oh, my dear." Gran patted her palm against her chest. "Were you there?"

"Yes." Hud rested his arm over the back of Trista's chair. "We both were."

"You should have seen Hud, Mrs. North." A hint of pride rose in her voice.

"Liv, please."

"Liv, you would have been so proud of Hud's empathy and goodwill efforts toward the people caught in the mudslide's path."

Mom turned a glowing gaze in his direction. "Hud has always been honorable and helpful."

He squirmed under her praise, aware that he hadn't always been honorable. "I did what anyone would have done. What other neighbors and responders did."

"We spent the night in an old outbuilding on the property we were, *are*, purchasing." Trista swallowed hard as if realizing what she'd almost said.

"You mean you spent the night alone together before you said, 'I do?'"

"Spur—" Dad said warningly.

Still, five curious gazes turned in Hud and Trista's direction.

"Hud was a complete gentleman." Trista folded her hands in her lap.

Spur coughed forcefully.

"So, Spur, what's this about you moving to Hawaii?" Hud veered the conversation away from Trista and him.

"Yeah, Spur." Wilks elbowed him. "When are you finally leaving?"

Spur's jovial expression wilted. "In two weeks."

"You don't sound too thrilled. Aren't sunny beaches and long-haired hula dancers alluring enough for you?"

"On the contrary. I can't wait to meet a Hawaiian girl."

"Then, what?"

"I found out about a mandatory training I have to take."

"What kind of training might that be?" Hud studied his brother's slumped shoulders, crossed arms, and deep frown.

"A boot camp for 'spiritual reshaping.'" He made air quotes with his fingers.

"It's an internship," Dad said. "Nothing unusual about that."

"Yeah, but it's like school," Spur said grimly. "You know how well that turned out for me."

"Do you feel called to this mission?" Trista asked.

Gran patted her hand. "Of course, he does, dear. He just doesn't know it yet." She smiled across the table at Spur. "We love you,

Spurgeon! We're cheering you on wherever God leads you. Your trip to Hawaii will be such a blessing!"

"That's right." Mom nodded. "A golden opportunity."

Groaning, Spur wiped his hand across his chin and didn't comment.

The conversation transitioned to Mom asking Trista questions about her life in Alaska. When Trista mentioned having a five-year-old daughter, Mom grinned and clapped. "I can't wait to meet her! I'll finally get to be a grandma! I mean, if it's okay for me to call myself that."

"Of course! Layla will love having another grandma. Maybe she'll join us on our next trip south."

"That would be wonderful!" Mom stood. "Now, I'm going to get a room ready for you two. You are staying with us, aren't you?"

Hud met Trista's gaze, and she nodded. "Sure. That would be great, Mom."

Trista stood also. "May I help you?"

"Certainly. Thank you."

The ladies were heading up the stairs before Hud realized what he'd agreed to. Since they were newlyweds, Mom would prepare only one guest room. How was Trista going to feel about that?

"So, big brother, are you and Trista hitched in the same way Lake and Irish got hitched?" Wilks grinned widely. "Or is this an honest-to-goodness marriage?"

Hud clenched his jaw, stopping himself from telling Wilks to take a hike—or some other dismissive comment.

"You boys have carried the teasing far enough," Dad said while assisting Granny Trish with standing. "Let's all pitch in with cleanup. Then we'll call it an early night."

Hud was grateful for his father's interference, however, he knew he'd have to face the music with these two brothers tomorrow.

Chapter Twenty

Trista sat on the edge of the bed, smoothing her hands over the peach-hued quilt, waiting for Hud to bring up her suitcase. Surely the bed was wide enough for them to sleep at the far edges and still get a good night's sleep without bumping into each other. Or maybe they could pile up some pillows in the middle. There was nothing to worry about. So why was she sitting here fretting?

When they made the bed, she didn't have the heart to ask Liv if a second bedroom was available for Hud. She didn't want to expose their lack of marital intimacy to her mother-in-law. How embarrassing! Trista covered her face with her hands and groaned. But now what? She wasn't ready to share a bed with Hud, even if they were sleeping on opposite sides of the mattress.

Footsteps sounded on the stairway and Trista tensed. Hud entered, carrying their two small travel bags. "Are you okay?"

"I'm all right." She barely met his gaze.

Hud had told her about his big family and how the guys were rowdy and enjoyed teasing each other. But she'd felt a little overwhelmed at the table. She didn't have siblings, so the brothers' jovial laughter and camaraderie were foreign to her, especially the part about them liking to pull practical jokes.

Then, when Liv kindly made up the bed, chatting about the room like it was their honeymoon suite, Trista's heart nearly broke. How was she supposed to pretend she and Hud were a loving couple in front of her in-laws?

She wanted to head back to Ketchikan and the comfort of home and be with Layla. She'd barely wrapped her brain around being married to Hud. Now she was supposed to sleep in the same room with him?

He sat down on the bed next to her without touching her. "Sorry about this. Do you want me to talk to my mom? I'm sure there's a spare bed in one of the other rooms."

"No. Let's not bring attention to our lack of—" She clenched her hands together.

"Are you sure?" he asked softly.

"It's not a perfect situation. But yes."

"Want me to sleep on the floor?" A slight grin crossed his mouth.

"Would you mind?"

His smile faded. "Sure. That'll be fine."

It would be better than attempting to sleep at the edge of the bed all night. Better than waking up and finding herself accidentally curled up in Hud's arms—perish the thought! "Are you going to tell them about our marriage being in name only?"

"I don't know." He stood and rummaged in a large armoire, then pulled out a thick comforter and pillow. "This ought to work." While he unfolded the blanket, she opened her bag and dug out a long-sleeved T-shirt and leggings. "Turn around," he said gruffly.

"Why?"

"I'm giving you fair warning." He unbuttoned his shirt.

"Wait." She turned her back to him. "All right." Tempted to glance over her shoulder, she resisted. She expected him not to peek while she was changing—she'd do the same.

He dropped noisily onto the floor. Hopefully, no one downstairs heard the thud. "I'll keep my eyes closed."

"You'd better." Even with his assurance, she shut off the light and went to the other side of the bed before undressing and getting into her sleeping apparel. She quickly slid under the covers. "Good night."

"Good night, honey."

She snickered. "My mom already calls me honey bear. So you'll have to come up with a different cutesy name." She was glad for the cover of darkness to talk about endearments.

"What will you call me to convince my family we're madly in love with each other?"

"Do we have to pretend that much?"

"If not, my brothers will suspect our marriage lacks genuine affection." He sighed. "I already read doubt in their expressions and questions."

"Okay. How about sweetie pie?"

"Sounds like something Gran called me as a kid."

"Darling?" she said, relaxing against the soft pillow.

"I could get used to 'darling.'" Suddenly, Hud's voice came from somewhere close to her. His warm breath smelled of mint.

"Hud? What are you doing?"

"Don't worry. I'm not getting on the bed." He stroked her cheek in the darkness.

"Hud—"

"Shhh." He kissed her forehead. "Good night, sweetheart."

She gulped. "Good night, my darling."

"I like it when you call me sweet names." He touched her cheek once more, then shuffled back to his comforter on the floor. "You sure about this?"

"About you sleeping on the floor?"

"Mmhmm."

"Uh, yes. I'm sure."

He dropped onto the floor with an even noisier thud. Someone surely heard that!

Chapter Twenty-one

When Hud returned from showering the following day, Trista was already dressed and had folded his bedding and put it all back in the closet. "Good morning. Thanks for hiding the evidence." He pointed to where his bed had been on the floor.

"No problem. Can we find some coffee?"

"Absolutely."

"The bed was comfortable, but I never sleep well in a new place. Thus my need for coffee—like right now."

"All right." He chuckled. His back and shoulders had been stiff and achy from the hard floor when he woke up. Thankfully, the hot shower eased some of the pain. But coffee sounded great to him, too.

He led Trista down the stairs, keeping his tread soft. Hopefully Spur wouldn't start the day by pestering him about married life. He didn't mind explaining to his parents what led to his marrying Trista. Spur and Wilks? Not a chance!

Since Hud had urged them to harass Lake about his decision to marry Irish, he deserved his share of guff—not Trista! He didn't want them pulling any tricks on her.

He knew his way around the kitchen, so he quickly prepared a single-serve coffee with a splash of vanilla creamer for Trista. She sipped from her cup, then sighed contentedly and walked into the living room. After fixing his brew, he followed her and sat down on the couch beside her.

They drank their coffee in silence, and he assumed Trista enjoyed the early morning calm in the house as much as he did. He appreciated that she wasn't overly talkative in the mornings. He'd been around enough people—namely some of his brothers—who yakked and made excessive noise when they first woke up.

"Good morning!" Spur leaned around the wall from the kitchen, grinning. Hud groaned. "You two are awake early! Not quite how I imagine newlyweds behaving on their honeymoon."

Trista tensed. "Yesterday was a long travel day. I couldn't wait to load up on caffeine."

"Uh-huh. Better that than Hud's romancing, huh?" Spur smirked.

"Get out of here!" Hud threw a couch pillow at him.

Spur ducked back into the kitchen, laughing.

"Don't let him get to you." Hud took a couple of swallows of his hot coffee.

"Do you think he suspects something?"

"He's fishing, that's all."

"Follow my lead," she whispered. "So, my darling"—she used a louder tone of voice and nodded toward the kitchen—"what are we going to do for our honeymoon today?"

"Well, sweetie pie, I don't know."

"Sweetie pie?" she hissed. "I thought you said that was childish!"

"Sorry. It just popped out."

Spur strode into the room with a steaming cup of coffee between his hands and plopped down on a chair, his gaze dancing between Hud and Trista. "Did you hear Mom and Gran are throwing a big bash in your honor? Mom even mentioned a mock wedding."

"What?" Hud barked.

"Another fake wedding, huh?"

"We had a real wedding ceremony, Spur." Trista sounded annoyed with him.

"I'm sure you did. But is it a real marriage?"

"Spur!" Hud gritted his teeth. "You don't know anything about our situation."

"Maybe not. But I can tell when two people aren't acting like lovey-dovey newlyweds."

"Trista and I are—" The lie he almost perpetrated didn't exit his lips as easily as it would have in the past. Not with his wife sitting beside him. And not with the way he was trying to listen to God's voice in his heart. "Just lay off."

"You took the inheritance, didn't you? Guilt's written all over your face."

"Spur—"

Trista clasped the crook of Hud's arm. "You might as well get it over with and tell him."

Hud sighed. "All right. But this stays between us." He squinted at his brother. "Yes. I took the inheritance. I had my reasons. And it's no one else's business, including yours."

"She's a lovely reason—I'll give you that." Spur lifted his chin toward Trista.

"So help me. If you are planning even one rude thing to say or do to her, you will deal with me." Hud clenched his fist.

"Does anyone else in the family suspect your marriage isn't genuine?"

"Lake knows the truth about our relationship."

Shoulders back, chest out, Spur said, "Your secret is safe with me, for now." He strode toward the kitchen as if he were on an important mission, then paused. "In exchange for my silence, I'd like you to do something for me."

"What's that?"

"Convince Dad to let me bail out of the Hawaii gig." A serious expression crossed Spur's face.

"Why don't you talk to him yourself?"

"I've tried. You know how determined Dad is when he gets something in his head."

Hud followed him into the kitchen for a more private discussion. "Why have you let it go this far? You said you're leaving in two weeks."

"That's what my ticket says, but I'm having second thoughts."

"You hate the idea of going to Hawaii that much?"

"A vacation there sounds out of this world." Spur set his cup in the dishwasher. "Not a month of spiritual training! I want to sunbathe on the beaches. Surf. Babe watch."

"Spur, Spur, Spur." Hud shook his head. This brother needed to grow up and face life as an adult. He was going on thirty! But would a stint of serving in Hawaii do that for him? "It's good to care about something. Or someone."

"Looks like you found someone to care about, if it lasts. Why isn't she your real wife?" Spur snorted. "She's beautiful. Kind. Seems to like you, although I can't understand why!"

"I'm not discussing my private life with you!"

"Okay. You have your secrets. I have mine."

"Do you have a secret keeping you from wanting to go to Hawaii?"

The broad smile that crossed Spur's mouth made him look more jovial. "Just talk to Dad and tell him I've reconsidered. Agreed?"

"I can't guarantee it will help anything."

"Try your best, and I'll go easy on—"

"Spurgeon!"

"All right." Chuckling, Spur strode out the door.

His smug demeanor made Hud nervous. Even if he spoke with Dad, did his younger brother have something annoying up his sleeve? What kind of practical joke might he and Wilks pull?

Chapter Twenty-two

Liv, Smith, Spur, and Wilks worked together on a breakfast of pancakes, bacon, and scrambled eggs. They even corralled Hud into chopping and frying potatoes, and soon he was helping in the kitchen and bantering with his brothers and Smith. Trista enjoyed watching him acting lighthearted and joyful in the house where he grew up and with the people he loved. It gave her another glimpse of her husband's personality that differed from his business persona.

When Liv asked her to chop some fruit, Trista jumped at the chance to participate in the family dynamics, too. The assembly-line production helped her imagine what it was like when the North family prepared meals for twelve people. Her life with Layla and Mom was so much simpler. Mom usually cooked for the three of them, and Trista cleaned up afterward.

She and Hud would have to work out their own system for sharing cooking and housecleaning responsibilities. So far, they hadn't even discussed where they would live. His place had a spectacular waterfront view but only two bedrooms. Mom's three-bedroom house allowed her and Layla to each have a room—something Trista appreciated. Would Hud be willing to let his condominium go and get a bigger apartment so the three of them could live together? Rentals were scarce in Ketchikan, but it might be worth looking into.

Throughout the meal, the group was noisy and talkative. Trista took in all the conversation quietly. Everyone was polite to her, but she noticed some inquisitive expressions being sent her way from her brothers-in-law. A few elbow jabs and winks passed between them. Did that mean they were conspiring to play a prank on Hud and her like Wilks had implied last night?

"What do you say, Trista?" Liv asked.

"Oh. What? Sorry. I must have been distracted."

"Do you mind if we have a small gathering later today? A birthday dinner for Hud and a wedding reception to celebrate your marriage?"

"Uh, sure. I guess that's okay."

"Lake and Irish will be here. I wish Aiden could fly in." Liv gave Hud a soft smile. "It's too short of notice, but he misses you terribly."

"I try to keep tabs on him."

"That's a nice big-brotherly thing for you to do." Liv patted his shoulder, then turned toward Trista. "I hope I get to meet Layla soon. With nine grown boys, I'm hoping for a lot of grandbabies."

Trista's cheeks flushed at the implication of her and Hud having kids. While she hoped they did have children together someday, considering their circumstances and Hud's reluctance about fatherhood, she didn't want to discuss it with Liv. "Is there anything you want me to do for dinner?"

"Oh, no. This is a celebration for you and Hud!"

"How about a veil and a wedding dress?" Spur asked.

"I don't need—"

"And vows. They should recite real vows to each other."

Hud set his fork down noisily. "Trista and I already said real vows to each other, Spur."

"Aww, Hud." Liv pressed her palms together pleadingly. "I'd love to hear you and Trista recite your wedding vows. Would you mind doing it again for Granny Trish and me? Please?"

Hud sent a glare in Spur's direction. "I don't know, Mom."

"Gran, what do you think?" Liv asked.

"I'd say it's up to the newlyweds." Gran smiled at Hud and Trista. "I'd love to hear the two of them reciting their vows. But I'm pleased as punch to have met Hud's beautiful bride. Her name being so close to mine—Trish and Trista—makes me feel closer to her already."

"Thank you." Reaching in front of Hud, Trista clasped his grandmother's hand. Then she settled back in her chair and whispered to him, "It's okay with me if we recite our vows again. If it means that much to Liv and Trish, what's the harm?"

He sighed. "I guess I don't mind either."

"Hurray!" Liv clapped. "I can't wait!"

Wilks nudged Spur's arm, and a look passed between them.

"So, Dad," Hud addressed his father. "Mind if we have a chat after breakfast?"

"I'd like that, son."

Was he going to talk with his dad about Spur's request? Trista glanced at the redheaded brother whose smirk seemed like a forewarning of trouble. But what did she know about these North brothers?

Chapter Twenty-three

Hud sat across from Dad in his small study off the living room, hoping his brothers wouldn't overhear them. He'd left Trista chatting with Mom and Gran in the dining room. He was thankful the three of them were hitting it off so well.

"What's this about, son?" Dad smoothed his hand over his chin, which looked freshly shaved. "Everything going okay with you and Trista?"

"Uh, sure. Fine." Should he tell Dad the truth about their reason for marrying? Had he already guessed? "I want to discuss Spur."

"Oh?" Dad crossed his arms over his chest. "What's this about?"

"He asked me to talk with you about his upcoming trip." Inwardly, Hud groaned. What was he doing bringing up this subject? He had more important matters to discuss with Dad than challenging him about letting Spur lead his own life. His younger brother could fight his own battles! Why was Spur making an issue about Hud talking to Dad about his situation anyway?

"Spur must have you in an emotional chokehold for you to go to bat for him." A tight smile crossed Dad's face. "What is it this time?"

Hud stifled a groan. "You aren't forcing him into helping your Hawaiian pal, are you?"

"Forcing? Is that what he told you?"

"Something along those lines."

"I'd say your brother is playing you a mile a minute. Hud, listen." Dad ran his hand over his partially graying hair. "Spur's been footloose for most of his adult life. I'd like to see him get involved in something greater than himself. Something outside of Thunder Ridge, if possible. Spur told me he's fine with going to Hawaii."

"Apparently, he isn't fine with it now." Unless Spur was playing him, as Dad said. What if he was waiting for Hud to be away from Trista and then sprang something mischievous on her? He'd better hurry this conversation along. "So there wouldn't be a problem if Spur has a change of heart about going to Hawaii?"

"Not a one. If he didn't want to go, he wouldn't be going. I think your brother is pulling a fast one on you." Hud groaned, tempted to race into the other room and remain by Trista's side until tonight's event ended. "But while you're here, why don't you tell me about you and your bride? Why did your marriage happen so quickly?"

"Why do you think it happened?" Hud asked tensely, still worried about what Spur might be up to.

"Well, you might have married Trista to obtain your grandfather's inheritance." Dad's Adam's apple bobbed. "Did you?"

Hud wished he could say he loved Trista wholeheartedly already, and that was the only reason he'd married her. But he wouldn't lie to Dad, even to get out of an uncomfortable conversation. "I wish it hadn't come to that, but it did."

"No condemnation, son."

"I honestly care for Trista."

"I'm sure you do."

"We aren't in love yet." Hud clasped his hands together tightly. "However, I hope and pray we'll find a lasting love like you and Mom did."

"I'll be praying for that, too." Nodding slowly, Dad stared at something on the shelf across from him. "Mom and I only want what's best for you boys. We didn't want you to start out on the wrong footing in marriage."

"Like you guys did?" Dad's jaw dropped, and Hud wilted inside at how easily he'd reverted to acting like a rebellious teenager instead of a grown man. "Hey. I'm sorry. That was uncalled for. You and Mom have done nothing but shown me love and grace, even in the most challenging times."

"It's okay. We butted heads a few times in your teenage and young adult years."

"I was determined to find my own way."

"And have you … found your way?"

"I hope so."

"Trista seems like a nice woman." Dad folded his hands on the desk, his expression serene.

"She's the best. I don't deserve her."

Dad's eyebrows pulsed high on his forehead. "Why would you say that? You deserve happiness and good things in your life. You've treated her like a gentleman, haven't you?"

"I've tried."

"Good. And because of the urgency in accepting the inheritance before your birthday, you probably proposed to someone you knew and were attracted to?"

"That's right. I've been interested in Trista for a while." Hud let out a long sigh. "But we were business partners, so I didn't act on my feelings."

"And you were friends?"

"Yes."

"That's a wonderful place to begin. Mom and I formed a friendship before love came, too." Dad stood and held out his hand. "I wish you both the best in marriage and life. Mom and I will be praying for you every day. I mean that."

"Thanks, Dad." Hud stood and shook his hand.

"Thanks for chatting with me." Dad pulled him into a hug. "Now go and keep a watch on your bride. Spur might have a trick up his sleeve since he got you to come in here and champion his cause."

"I should have known better."

"You boys always liked pulling your pranks."

"Yeah, we did. Thanks, Dad." Hud dashed out of his father's office in search of Trista.

Chapter Twenty-four

Trista had enjoyed her visit with Liv and Trish so much. Both women had included her in their conversations and asked questions about her interests and opinions. They'd easily transitioned from discussing gardening to Hud's growing-up years to verses about God's love and mercy. They acted thrilled when Trista told them about growing up with a mom who believed in Jesus and ensured she was in church every Sunday. Any worry over them being upset about Hud's and her wedding vanished with the warm interactions and her feelings of acceptance. She helped Liv clean up the kitchen, and then the ladies went their separate ways.

Trista donned her coat and headed outside to find a quiet place to call Layla. She strolled down the snow-lined walkway and tapped Mom's number.

"Hey, honey bear. Are you enjoying your honeymoon?"

She chuckled at her mother's assumption that she was on her honeymoon. In what universe did a newlywed bride make her husband sleep on the floor?

"I'm here to meet Hud's family. Trying to keep all their names straight is my biggest challenge."

"You'll do fine. Any family would gladly embrace you as their daughter and sister."

"Thanks, Mom. Is Layla nearby?"

"That she is." Mom's voice turned tender as she addressed her granddaughter. "Here you go, ladybug. It's your mama."

"Mommy?"

"Hey, sweet pea. How are you doing?"

"Fine. Are you coming home today?"

"Tomorrow."

"Tomorrow takes forever to get here," Layla whined.

"Sometimes it feels that way. One more sleep and I'll be with you."

"I miss you."

"Miss you too. Are you and Grammie doing anything fun today?"

Layla moaned. "She says we have to go to the store, but I don't want to."

"Try to be a good helper for your grandmother, okay?"

"All right." Layla huffed. "Hurry home!"

"I will get there as soon as I can. Promise."

"Mommy? Grammie says we aren't going to live with her much longer. She's wrong, isn't she?" Layla's voice got louder and higher pitched.

"Sweet pea, Hud and I are married. We will move in with him eventually."

"I want to stay here with Grammie." She sniffled like she was close to crying. "I'm staying with her! Not with Hud!"

This wasn't an argument they should be having on the phone. "Let's not worry about it right now, okay? Thanks for telling me how you feel. Here's a big kiss." Trista kissed the air in front of the phone. "Love you."

"Love you too." Sniff, sniff.

Gulping down her own tender emotions, Trista ended the call. She'd rarely been away from Layla overnight and hearing her sniffling and sounding upset tugged on her mama's heart. She blinked at the tears welling in her eyes.

"Trista?"

She spun around, wiping moisture off her cheeks. Spur stood right behind her. "Yes?"

A noisy vehicle pulled up on the road next to her. Wilks leaned out the driver's window and waved. "Hey, Trista. Wanna go for a ride?"

"Oh. Not really."

"How about grabbing some coffee with Wilks and me?" Smiling widely, Spur rocked his thumb toward the car. "Seems like you could use a coffee break. See some sights?"

"I should wait for Hud." She stepped back from Spur. Was this about them pulling some practical joke? If so, she should go back into the house and stay as far away from them as possible.

"Hud and Dad are still yakking. It'll take an hour or more for them to solve the world's problems." Spur shrugged deeply. "Hud won't even know you're missing."

"Missing?" The word came out like a yelp.

"I meant gone. You know, going with us to get coffee," he said smoothly. "You'd like a cup of gourmet coffee, right? I bet you're a mocha or a latte kind of woman."

"I suppose I am." A creamy vanilla-flavored coffee sounded delicious. She could use something comforting, since she was feeling melancholy after her talk with Layla. She envisioned sitting in a coffee shop in Thunder Ridge, enjoying the small-town ambiance. What could be the harm in going for coffee with Hud's brothers? It would be in a public place. Even if their invitation was about a prank, what were they going to do? Pour salt in her drink?

"Will you come and chat with two of your new brothers? Find some delicious coffee with us?" Spur held out his arm toward her invitingly.

Did she dare go with them? "Shouldn't we wait for Hud?"

"Wilks and I would like the three of us to visit. Please?" He held her gaze without any appearance of malice.

She took a breath. "I suppose … I could go with you."

"Yes!" Spur linked their arms as if they were already friends and strode with her to the car. He opened the backseat door and swayed his hand gallantly toward the inside.

Suddenly, she felt another urge to head back to the house and keep her distance from Hud's brothers. Just a silly, unfounded notion, right? Or was it something more? "I need to come right back here," she said firmly.

"After we have coffee, we'll bring you back. I promise."

"Okay. Good." Trista forced herself to breathe normally and relax. She didn't have siblings to gauge the nuances between the North brothers by, but surely there was a code of honor among them. They might pull pranks on each other, but not on their wives or girlfriends, right?

As soon as she buckled up, Wilks gunned the gas. The car jerked forward as if the gas pedal had been stuck. Spur glanced back and shrugged apologetically, still grinning affably.

But fifteen minutes later, Trista knew they weren't in Thunder Ridge or Sandpoint any longer! "Where are you guys taking me?"

"For a scenic ride."

"I thought you were bringing me to a coffee shop."

"Oh, we are!" Spur pointed toward the stretch of road ahead of them. "We know where all the best coffee joints in North Idaho are. Don't we, Wilks?"

"That we do. Even some in Spokane!"

"I'm not going that far for a cup of coffee!" It had been a long drive from the airport on the west side of Spokane, then up through the panhandle of Idaho to get to Thunder Ridge. "Please take me back to your parents' house. I don't want coffee that badly."

"We'll head back shortly." Spur cast her another one of his easy smiles. "Want to listen to some music?"

"No! Take me back now!" She yanked her cell phone out of her jacket pocket. Whatever these guys were up to, she didn't want any part of their schemes. She'd call Hud and—

Spur plucked the phone from her hands. "Sorry."

"Give that back!"

"We don't mean you any harm, Trista." He lifted his right hand, palm out. "This is just a teeny-tiny payback for some of Hud's past pranks toward Wilks and me."

"You should have seen how he and Lake threw me fully dressed into Lake Pend Oreille when I turned twenty-one!" Wilks laughed. "Or the time—"

"I don't care about any of that foolishness. I want to go back to your parents' house!" She thrust out her hand. "Give me my phone!"

"How about if I text Hud and explain that we're taking you for coffee and a nice drive?"

"No! Turn this decrepit vehicle around before I start screaming and don't let up until you do as I say!" All she had to do was imagine one of Layla's meltdowns, all her screaming and ear-piercing shrieks, and replicate it. Hud's brothers might mean this escapade in fun, but she didn't care for it at all! She hardly knew these two. Now they were pulling a stunt like this? She wasn't putting up with it for another minute!

Spur tapped her phone. "There. I sent Hud a text."

"What did you say?"

"That we were going for coffee."

"He'll be so angry about this."

"I'm counting on that." Spur chuckled. "Our older brothers used to play all sorts of pranks on us younger kids. Now it's up to Wilks and me to continue the tradition."

"How about growing up and behaving like men?" She glared at him, then at the back of Wilks's head. "How about putting childish ways behind you? Maybe even respecting the godly way your parents raised you?"

"Now you sound like Mom or Gran," Spur said sullenly.

"Good! You need a wake-up call." Trista had agreed to go for coffee with them. But not an hour away. And not like this! "Turn the car around," she said sternly. Her phone vibrated. "Aren't you going to answer it?"

"Nah."

"Answer it now, or so help me, I will scream loud enough to break your eardrums!" Spur didn't do as she said. "Fine." Trista inhaled a huge breath and blasted out the most ear-piercing scream she could muster. Both men gawked at her with nearly identical, shocked expressions. "You thought I'd take this practical joke silently? Think again!" She took a deep breath and let out another high-pitched scream.

"Cut it out!" Spur yelled and covered his ears.

"Stop! Stop!" Wilks jerked the car to the side of the road. "Man. She's got a set of lungs."

Trista gulped in ragged breaths. "Take me back to your parents' house—or I'll scream again and again. If you turn this car around now, I'll *try* to forget you pulled such a horrible stunt on a sister-in-law you just met! Otherwise, I might have to press kidnapping charges against both of you!"

Wilks's eyes widened like silver dollars. "We didn't mean it like that."

"No, we didn't." Spur squinted at her as if trying to read the validity of her threat.

"Then turn this car around, now, and prove you have a conscience!" She glared hard at Wilks, then Spur. "I'm sure your parents raised you better than this."

"Yeah, they did." Wilks gunned the car and made a sharp U-turn that made the tires squeal.

"This didn't turn out as I planned," Spur muttered.

The phone vibrated again.

"Answer the stupid phone!" Trista yelled. Spur tossed her cell phone onto the seat, and she lunged for it. "Hello?"

"Are you all right?" Hud asked in a panicky tone. "Where are you? What have those morons done?"

"I'm fine." She gritted her teeth. "I don't know where I am. Your brothers thought they'd have some fun at my expense."

"I'll kill them!"

"Get in line!" She squinted at Wilks in the rearview mirror. "We had a little misunderstanding, but it's resolved now. We should be back at the house in fifteen minutes."

"But you're okay?"

"Let's say I have everything under control."

"I'm impressed you stood up to my brothers—whatever they did."

"They aren't as impressed." She pinned her gaze on Wilks's reflection in the mirror all the way back to the North's residence. If she were a betting person, she'd wager that Hud's brothers would never pull another prank on her.

Chapter Twenty-five

Throughout the afternoon, Hud stayed close to Trista, making sure his brothers didn't attempt any more pranks. He hadn't spoken with them about their stunt *yet*. Even though Trista had begged him to let the incident go, insisting she took care of it in her way, he was biding his time until he had the opportunity to chat with Spur and Wilks himself. He planned to corral Lake at tonight's event, and the two of them would speak some big-brother wisdom over the two troublemakers.

Mom had ordered a stack of pizzas for the party and made a giant chocolate cake with "Congratulations, Hud & Trista!" and "Happy birthday, Hud!" written on top. The decorations around the dining room were festive with balloons, red hearts, and bride-and-groom decals. A bouquet of daisies and carnations made a pretty centerpiece on the long table.

When Lake and Irish arrived, she carried a cute husky puppy in her arms, who she introduced as Little Dipper. While the ladies chatted and laughed over the puppy's frolicking, Hud took Lake aside and explained what Spur and Wilks had done with Trista and what he had in mind for them.

"Count me in!" Lake laughed. "I have a score of my own to settle with them!"

"Excellent. I'll let you know when I'm ready."

Several times during the evening, Hud observed the affectionate way Lake set his arm over Irish's shoulder and how the two of them gazed adoringly into each other's eyes. Seeing his brother and sister-in-law acting so happy together gave Hud hope that he and Trista might also find a close relationship with each other.

"How are you doing?" Mom linked her arm with his.

"I'm okay. This is a nice get-together you planned. Thanks for doing all this for Trista and me."

"Sure thing, honey. I'm thrilled to have met your wife. She's adorable. I'm eager to meet her daughter, too." She grinned and leaned her cheek against his arm. "I finally get to be a grandma!"

"I thought you'd like that." He met Trista's gaze across the room, and tenderness for her rushed through him.

"You care for her, don't you?" Mom stepped back and gazed into his eyes. He knew she was asking about love, even though she didn't use the word. He'd always been able to talk straight with her about stuff. What made him hesitate now? "Long pause there, son. I was hoping—" She shrugged. "Never mind. I love you so much, Hud."

"Love you too."

Mom glanced at Lake and Irish, and a shadow briefly crossed her features. Was she worried about something? She turned back to Hud. "Everything will work out for you in time. God is going to bless you and Trista with a long, satisfying marriage—I'm certain of it." She gave him a one-arm hug.

"Thanks, Mom." Her positivity and love encouraged him to speak more openly with her. He drew her over to the window, away from where anyone else might hear. "You know, don't you?"

"That your marriage is similar to how Dad's and mine started?" Her eyes glistened with unshed tears.

He nodded, a gulp hitching in his throat. "Does it upset you?"

"Not really. I'm surprised you went that route—although I understand."

"You wanted more for us, right?"

"Sure. For you and Lake." She sighed, and Hud felt a pang of regret for disappointing her. "But it worked out okay for Dad and me." Mom drew in a long breath. "I'm guessing you took your grandfather's inheritance?"

"Yes. I was afraid to tell you. I tried writing several times." He gritted his teeth. "I fought taking it. Man, I fought it."

"I'm sure you did. It's okay, Hud." She smoothed her palm over his arm. "You and Lake battled conflicting opinions and your own hearts to reach your decisions. I respect you both for following the Lord's leading and letting Him guide you."

Had he done all that? Most of the time, Hud didn't think he even recognized God's leading. It was nice to hear Mom speaking so confidently about him. "You don't hate me for getting the money?"

"Never! No matter what your decisions are or how you choose to live, I will always love you, Hudson North." She put her hands on his shoulders and looked him in the eye. "Why wouldn't I? You are the son of my heart." She hugged him, and for a moment, he clung to her.

"I am sorry for not calling you about the wedding," he said as soon as they stepped back from the embrace.

"Ah, Hud. I'm glad you're here now, letting us share in the wedding festivities." Sniffing like she was near tears, her smile wobbled. "Did your business need a shot in the arm?"

"Desperately. Trista's savings was going down with the ship. She has a daughter and a mom to take care of. They were going to lose everything. I couldn't let that happen."

"Of course, you couldn't. You are a man of honor." She patted his cheek gently. "I'm proud of you."

He gulped, feeling like a boy of eight gazing trustingly into his mom's eyes. He had been afraid of letting her down by accepting the money she was denied—and because of getting married as he did. He hoped one day he would return to Thunder Ridge and tell her she was right about him and Trista having a long, satisfying marriage.

They exchanged hugs again, and Mom wished him a happy birthday. Then he returned to the bantering group in the living room. Trista was laughing as Irish placed a lacy curtain over her dark hair. Hearing her laughter and seeing her gorgeous sparkling eyes, he felt a familiar stirring of attraction for her. It felt like he already had deeper feelings for her than he did six days ago when they first kissed.

"In the spirit of fun and a mock wedding, here are your accessories." Lake wrapped a foil cummerbund around Hud's waist and tucked a folded dish towel into the neck of his shirt for a tie.

Wilks held up his phone with some hip-hop wedding music playing. Sunday dragged Hud to one side of the room to stand beside Dad.

"Do we have to do all this?" Hud complained.

"Yes, you *get* to do all this." Sunday chuckled.

The rest of the family formed two lines, creating a faux aisleway for Trista to walk down. Being the good sport she was, she sashayed down the row, holding the bouquet from the table and grinning at Hud.

His bride was lovely, inside and out. She was becoming more special to him by the hour. Even her not being enraged at Spur and Wilks's obnoxious prank earlier spoke highly of her tolerance for his brothers. Although he appreciated that, he still planned to have it out with them. But he couldn't dwell on their actions now, or he would be scowling at them instead of smiling at Trista.

She reached his side and linked her arm with his. "Are you okay?"

"I'm blessed to have you as my wife. I mean that."

"Thanks, Hud."

He wished they were alone so he could tell her he looked forward to falling in love with her. Hopefully their mock wedding vows included him kissing the bride!

"Dearly beloved," Dad said in his preacher's voice.

Since it was a mock ceremony and in a relaxed atmosphere, the group cheered or whistled at various points. Gran said, "Amen," during a few serious moments.

Hud and Trista recited traditional vows and then chuckled through the extra ones someone must have coerced Dad into saying. "Do you promise to wash Hud's socks and clean up after him from this day forward?"

"Sorry. I can't promise any manual labor. Might break a nail." Trista winked at Hud. "I promise to tell him to do those things himself."

He grinned. "Until death do us part."

Dad cleared his throat. "Hud, do you promise to make Trista pancakes every morning if she wants them?"

"I promise." He hoped and prayed for many breakfasts to cook for his wife.

"I gladly accept." Trista made a cute face.

"You may kiss your bride," Dad said amid cheers from the audience.

Finally! Hud leaned near Trista's ear and whispered what he had at their actual wedding. "May I kiss you?"

"You may." She let out a huff. "Make it quick."

"Not too quick." Pushing her lacy veil back, he smoothed his fingers down her cheeks. Then he did what he had been dying to do since they flew into Spokane. He tipped her back and kissed her warm lips. His heart pounded a wild, raging beat as she kissed him back as if she'd anticipated this part of the ceremony as much as he had. He prolonged the kiss even though they stood before his family, who continued cheering and clapping. After he set her on her feet, they grinned at each other.

"I present to you, Mr. and Mrs. Hudson North!" Dad said jubilantly.

Catcalls and whistles resounded from the group.

Hud clasped Trista's hand and dashed with her through the aisle of well-wishers. Sparkling confetti fell over their heads and shoulders. Trista laughed and wiped small pieces of paper from her face. He couldn't resist helping her get a few dots off her nose and eyelashes. "Thanks for marrying me again, Tris."

"It was worth it for that kiss." She blushed a rosy color.

"We can reenact our wedding vows any time you'd like." He smiled tenderly at her.

"Good to know." She smiled back at him and winked.

Claps on the back and hugs from his family kept his mind from drumming up an excuse for Trista and him to head upstairs and practice their vows some more. Their mock wedding ceremony had stirred up some longings for real tenderness and love to happen between them. But he recalled what he still planned to do tonight—get revenge on Spur and Wilks—and that cooled his amorous feelings.

He met Lake's gaze and nodded discreetly. A few years had passed since he and Lake took matters with their brothers into their own hands. But this was going to be one of those times.

Chapter Twenty-six

Hud strode outside into the snowy backyard and stood behind the trunk of a large cedar—far enough from the kitchen window so no one would see him. As prearranged, Lake coaxed Spur and Wilks outside to tend to the puppy. Who could resist a cute pup, right?

"What do you need us to do?" Spur asked. "I hear leftover pizza calling me."

"Tromp down some snow and make a place for our future racing champion to relieve himself, will you?" Lake pointed to a pile of snow.

"I'm not your dog handler," Spur grumbled. "That's Finn's job now."

"Just do it."

"What's your problem?" Spur kicked at the two feet of snow, making an indentation.

"Who's out there?" Wilks peered into the darkness toward the tree. Had he spotted Hud watching them from his concealed position?

Lake set the dog in the snow where Spur trampled down a circle. Then, in a fast move, he grabbed Wilks from behind, pulling him to the ground in a headlock.

"Hey! What are you—" Wilks kicked and fought him.

Hud dashed out from behind the tree and charged at Spur.

"What's going on?" Spur shouted.

Hud grabbed him around the waist and knocked him down. Despite Spur thrashing and kicking, Hud washed his face roughly with a large handful of snow.

"What's—" Spur sputtered. "Stop! Hud—"

Hud and Spur wrestled and rolled in the snow. Hud repeatedly scrubbed his brother's face in the icy wetness. Spur fought against him the whole time. "It was a joke! We didn't hurt her. Just wedding fun!"

"You were the only ones having any fun." Hud was seeing red for more reasons than Spur's ruddy cheeks. Pinning him with one arm across his chest, he pulsed his gloved finger toward Spur's nose. "Don't ever mess with my wife again, you hear me? Never!"

Spur shoved his weight against Hud. "Now you know what it feels like to get pranked and be powerless."

"What does that have to do with anything?"

They wrestled and rolled in the snow again. Not full-on fighting, but with the powerful wave of fury Hud was feeling, it could have easily transitioned into a punching brawl. He wouldn't let that happen. But putting Spur in his place? He'd keep at this until he yelled, "Uncle!" or apologized for what he did to Trista.

With loud grunts and groans, Lake and Wilks wrestled in the snow a short distance from Hud and Spur. And this wasn't even Lake's fight!

"Hey, hey, hey!" Dad called gruffly from the back porch. "Stop that! You guys are grown men. Enough!"

Hud groaned and pulled back. He'd hoped Dad wouldn't find out about their scuffle. While he was distracted, Spur retaliated with a solid shove. Hud toppled backward, landing hard on his rear. Spur shoved a handful of snow in his face and smeared it across his cheeks, the ice searing his skin. "Two can play your game, big brother. You aren't the only one with muscles around here anymore."

Hud itched to slug Spur. He deserved one good punch.

"Hud! Spur!" Dad yelled, tromping through the snow toward them. "Stop, now!"

Lake and Wilks were bent over on the other side of Dad, both breathing hard. The puppy ran around Lake's feet, yapping.

Hud blew out a harsh breath. He didn't want to stop fighting. He wanted to continue until his punk brother learned his lesson and said he was sorry—and meant it!

"What's this about?" Dad set his fists on his hips.

Spur stood slowly. "Hud's just mad because—"

"Shut up!" Hud ordered. "Don't ever try anything with my wife again! Your prank-playing days where she and I are concerned are over."

"The same goes for Irish and me!" Lake said sternly and slightly out of breath.

"Spur?" Dad turned to him with a frown. "Want to tell me what this is about?"

"No, sir." Spur dusted off his coat and pants, then stomped into the house, grumbling about the day being ruined.

After Dad and Wilks followed him inside, Hud trudged back to the tree he'd previously hid behind, his fists and arms shaking with the need to punch something. He'd only gotten more riled during the wrestling match in the snow.

"You okay?" Lake trailed him, holding his puppy.

"Still furious, is all."

"I would be too. Although I heard Dad telling Wilks for him and Spur to meet him in his office in five minutes." Lake's snicker reminded Hud of the old days when they were glad for Spur to be sent to Dad's office instead of them. "You know what that means."

"A long lecture?"

"Yep."

"Too bad he can't ground them for three months, too." Hud felt an ache in his shoulder from where he'd rolled over a hard piece of ice or a stick. "Did we do this to them?"

"What's that?" Lake shuffled the puppy in his arms, and the dog snuggled his nose into Lake's coat.

"Did we train Spur and Wilks in the art of mischief? Spur said something along those lines."

"Could be. But taking those guys down again felt like a million bucks. Might hurt a little, though." Wincing, Lake rubbed his whiskered chin. "Nothing like a snow wrestling match to cool some tempers."

"Not nearly enough." Hud took a deep breath, then expelled it noisily. "Spur convincing Trista to get in a car and driving off with her? That made me want to do more than rub his face in the snow. However, he didn't call 'Uncle' like he used to. And he fought me *almost* equally."

"I guess we aren't the tough big brothers we once thought we were." Lake chuckled. "Is middle age making us wimpier?"

"Speak for yourself!"

"Hud?" Trista called softly from the doorway. "Are you okay?"

"I'm all right." He grimaced at the soreness in his cheek. "I'll be in shortly."

"I wanted to check and make sure."

"Thanks." He waited until she went back inside, then shook Lake's hand. "Thanks for the assistance tonight."

"Any time our brothers need some advice, I'm in!" Lake nodded toward the house. "So you're leaving tomorrow?"

"That's the plan. We must return to our obligations and the reasons why we joined forces in matrimony."

"I hope things turn out well for you and Trista."

"Me too." Hud walked beside his brother toward the house. "Seeing you and Irish together has been encouraging. It seems like you two are genuinely in love."

"We are." Lake sounded in awe of the fact. "It became real for us faster than I imagined. Irish is amazing. Being in love with her is beyond anything I ever dreamed of or felt."

"Even with Laurie?"

"Even with her." Lake took a deep breath. "I thank God daily for bringing us together.""

Hud petted the puppy. "I'm happy for you, bro. I wish you all the best."

"Thanks. Good luck with the housing project." Lake grinned like he couldn't resist a parting shot. "And in the husband department."

Hud play-punched his shoulder. "When that happens, I'll stop regretting taking the money. Until then, guilt still churns in my gut."

"I know what you mean. But remember what Gran used to tell us? Everything works out for good in the end."

"I remember. I just hope that doesn't take too long to happen!"

Chapter Twenty-seven

A week after returning to Ketchikan, Trista was still curious about what Hud and Lake had done to Spur and Wilks on their last night in Thunder Ridge. Some sort of snow scuffle, she'd surmised. But when she questioned Hud about his red scratched cheeks, he said he didn't want to discuss it. Since both of his younger brothers came to her separately and apologized, whatever their intervention was, it must have been successful. Spur said he hoped she and Hud had a happy life together. Wilks simply said he was sorry. She hugged both.

On the day they got back, Hud shrugged and nodded when Trista told him she'd be staying at Mom's house for a while longer. It was only a temporary situation—although a week had passed. But with the way Layla kept fussing and crying about the move and having to be away from her grandmother, Trista hated dragging her to Hud's, kicking and screaming. Even though she couldn't give in to her theatrics every time, she didn't want to make a crisis of them becoming a family, either.

She finished the email she was working on to a potential investor in Fairbanks. The man's past philanthropic giving had been focused on the arts and providing for artists. It seemed like a perfect match with Hud's and her plans to support artists for six-month residencies.

They were already discussing moving on to another place with a similar blueprint once their current project was completed. Hud mentioned Kalispell, Montana, or Joseph, Oregon, as a potential destination. But Trista wasn't eager to uproot Layla and traipse off to another state. If her daughter hated the idea of moving a half a mile away from her grandmother's house to live at Hud's, she would be furious about relocating a long distance. Maybe they could start another art residency somewhere closer, like Wrangell or Petersburg. That way Layla could see her grandmother more often, and Mom wouldn't always have to be alone.

"Hey, Tris." Hud entered their office carrying a pastry box.

"Are you trying to fatten me up?" He'd been arriving with treats and desserts almost daily.

"Not quite." He looked her over appreciatively. "I like you as you are. But I thought you might enjoy something sweet today."

The heat of a blush crept up her cheeks. "I'll have one of whatever you're offering."

"Is that right?" He grinned like he was thinking of something romantic instead of pastries.

"Oh. I didn't mean—"

"Right. Sorry." He held out the box to her. "Apple fritters and maple bars."

"My weakness." She opened the box, eyeing the delicacies. "What's your favorite?"

"You."

"I meant the pastries, silly." Still, his flirting got to her and left her wanting to fall into his arms and kiss him like she hadn't done since their mock wedding. Too bad they were at the office where anyone could walk in on them. "Are you a maple bar or an apple fritter sort of man?"

"Maple bar. I like my treats very sweet." He winked at her.

Was he saying he thought she was sweet? Biting her lower lip to stop a grin, she set out two maple bars on napkins while he poured each of them fresh coffee.

"Did you get the banking business squared away?" Trista took a few bites of the pastry, then picked up the napkin and wiped her lips free of maple frosting.

His gaze seemed to follow her every move. "It went great." He stuffed the last bite of his maple bar in his mouth. A crumb resting on his upper lip made her want to reach over and brush it away … or kiss it away. But they weren't at the place in their relationship of walking over and kissing each other whenever they wanted. Even so, the desire was there to get to know her husband better. "The land is ours. Weather permitting, clearing the debris and leveling the ground will be finished in a few days. Then it's on to the next phase."

"That's great!" She tasted her coffee and sighed. "How do we ensure that a mudslide never happens again?"

"I've already hired an engineering firm to inspect the area. It was a freak act of nature and probably won't happen again, but it's good to be proactive where safety is concerned." He took a sip of his hot drink. "I imagine the recommendation will be to build a retaining wall. Also, the loan officer asked what we'll be calling our development now that our last names are the same."

"Other than North Dunmore?"

"Yes. North and North? Or just North?" Hud clasped her hand. "Do you regret anything?"

"Such as?"

"Marrying me. Jumping into a relationship—"

"For the money?" She moaned. "No regrets, Hud. Just some uncertainties."

"I'd like to think it was for a good cause."

"Me too. But we are in a weird situation. Married, yet not married. Sharing our lives, yet living separately."

"I hope that changes soon." He smiled warmly at her. "Thanks for taking this risk with me when you don't love me."

"I don't hate you, either." Hadn't she been imagining kissing him a few minutes ago? Not that she'd admit that to him!

"I'm glad to hear it." He played with her fingers, slowly twirling her slim gold wedding band and engagement ring. "What can I do to help us get through the awkwardness?"

"You feel it too?"

"Sure do." He released her hand and stood.

"I thought I might be the only one."

"You aren't." He picked up their napkins and tossed them into the trash. She stood and found herself standing quite close to him. In a smooth move, he took her in his arms and gazed into her eyes like he was searching their depths for something. Attraction? Permission to kiss her? She could barely breathe for a few heartbeats. "I care about you, Tris. I want you to know that."

"I care about you too."

"Do you want more between us?" His warm breath smelled of coffee and sweetness.

"More as in—?"

"More romance. More building a marriage relationship that will last."

"In time I do."

"What about now? What do you want right this second?" His tone was softly compelling, and his mouth was oh, so close to hers.

"I don't know what I want, Hud," she whispered.

"Are you sure?" His lips touched hers gently, soft as silky butter smoothing across her mouth. He kissed her with ultimate tenderness, like a man who wanted to get to know a woman he didn't have the foggiest idea of how to be romantic with or woo.

She kissed him back tentatively. But then something altered between them. The air felt electrified with sparks of romance and a desire for closeness, and she kissed him with all the longings she'd been holding back. Hud was her husband! She was immensely attracted to him! Why shouldn't she kiss him the way she wanted to?

She smoothed her palms across his cheeks, touching the scruffiness of his face, familiarizing herself with him. She strummed her fingers through his soft hair, giving herself to their kiss and his embrace, even though they were in their place of business.

Hud broke away first but didn't let her go. His slightly rough cheek brushed against her face. "Tris?"

"Hmm?"

"We've only been married for ten days, but I think I'm falling for you already." The low rumble of his voice and how he was being emotionally vulnerable with her made her smile. "I'm not saying that just so you'll say it back. Is it okay that I said I'm falling for you?"

"Of course, it's okay." She kissed his cheek. "We're married, Hud. Things will progress as they progress. I want us to be open and honest about everything, including how we feel about each other."

"When you're ready, you'll tell me, right?" He stroked her hair back behind her ears, the ticklish sensation of his fingers touching her ear lobes unnerving her. He met her gaze, his eyes sparkling with moisture or emotion.

"Ready to say I'm falling for you?"

He smiled. "Yes, that, too."

"Ohhh. You mean sharing a bedroom?"

"Yes." He whispered the word that had the power to change everything between them.

She stepped back, physically and emotionally creating some space between them. "This relationship of us being married before we're in love is unusual. I hope and pray we truly fall in love with each other. But allowing myself to have these feelings for you—"

"Wait. Allowing yourself?"

"We're at work. There are rules about these things."

"Ah. Rules." Sighing, Hud raked his hand over his hair, messing it up. Maybe she should straighten the strands for him and kiss him some more—anything to bring back that softer look in his eyes. But what if a client entered the office while they were kissing? She was grateful that hadn't happened moments ago. "We're married, so workplace rules don't apply to us, Tris."

"I don't think that's how it works." Otherwise, how would she ever get any work accomplished? "I have some more emails to answer. I should probably get busy." She glanced toward her computer station. Could she even concentrate on her tasks after those dreamy kisses and what Hud had asked her?

"You said you were allowing these feelings for me. Does that mean you had feelings for me before? Perhaps all along?" A smile spread across his lips again.

She felt caught in a web. If she said yes, then he'd say they should move forward with a real marriage. If she said no, there was the slightest chance she'd be telling a falsehood. "I'm unsure. But I'm more confused than ever when we kiss like we just did." She dropped onto her chair in front of her computer and stared at the screen without really focusing on it.

A minute later, she glanced over her shoulder and found Hud still watching her, a thoughtful expression on his face. Their gazes tangled like they were already dancing to the rhythm of their hearts. If he kept meeting her gaze with so much warmth and tenderness, and his eyes kept shining at her so adoringly, falling head over heels for him would not be a problem.

Chapter Twenty-eight

Hud and Trista arrived at their acreage the next day to check on the cleanup process. Bulldozer operators were pushing the remaining debris, uprooted trees, and large rocks into giant stacks. A front-end loader grabbed chunks from a pile and dropped them into a dump truck. Other dozers were leveling out some areas where houses would eventually be built. The combined engine sounds were loud in the otherwise quiet setting.

Seeing all the machines in motion, Hud was grateful for another chance to make a go of the project he and Trista had envisioned seven months ago. It had taken him going against his internal instincts not to accept the money his grandfather left for him—and being willing to marry a woman he wasn't in love with first. But despite the occasional awkwardness between him and Trista, he never again wanted to contemplate whether he'd made a mistake in marrying her.

When she was in his arms, and especially when they were kissing, he was completely besotted and enamored with her. He thought asking her to marry him may have been the best decision he'd ever made in his life! He had stronger feelings for her than any woman he'd ever dated. He wanted to be with her more. Spend all his waking hours with her. Now if only he could convince Trista of his devotion to her and their marriage, they might be able to make a real go of their relationship. That thought gave him a burst of hope and he silently prayed for their future.

"Wow." Trista nudged his arm. "What a difference a week makes, huh?"

"Yeah. It looks promising." He pointed toward the dozers leveling out the ground. At this rate, they'd be marking out the lines for the streets soon.

"Looks like we have some streets to name!" She grinned.

"Just what I was thinking. Do you have any in mind?"

"I spoke to Layla about it last night. She suggested we name the streets Teddy Bear Lane, Baby Doll Avenue, and Miss Calico Street." She chuckled. "Miss Calico is Mom's cat."

"I see." He enjoyed the way she met his gaze and her eyes lit up with purple sparks. Considering the rumble of machinery around them, a romantic opportunity seemed unlikely. However, when he imagined taking Trista in his arms and kissing her, he thought they should step inside the outbuilding for a quiet discussion that had absolutely nothing to do with work.

Trista pulled out her cell phone and snapped shots of the land and the large machines. "What are we going to do with the shed?" Her mentioning the old building right after he had pictured them kissing in it was perfect timing.

"I don't know. Let's look inside." Should he wink? Rock his eyebrows? Anything to let her know he was thinking of them doing something other than discussing the shed's usefulness?

"Okay."

He followed her toward the tiny building with his heart pounding a furious beat. "It'll probably get torn down, right?"

"That would be a shame." She paused and pointed her cell phone at the dilapidated structure, taking a few shots. "It's where we first spent the night together. Where I first felt your heartbeat." She met his gaze like she was enjoying the same closeness he was experiencing with her.

"Are you saying you want to keep it as a memorial to our love?" he asked softly.

"I didn't say love." Her face turned pink. "It could be used for supplies."

"Oh, sure." He brushed her cheeks with the back of his cool knuckles. Heat emanated from her skin to his. "You're beautiful, Tris."

"Hud—"

"Even though we're working, I'm going to tell you how I feel. Is that so wrong?"

"No. But don't we have to keep a professional air between us?"

"Do we?"

"It's difficult to concentrate when I'm distracted with you."

"I'm distracted with you, too. In fact—" He clasped her hand and tugged her toward the outbuilding.

"Where are we going? What are you doing?"

"Let's peek inside the shed and see if it has potential." Of course he was thinking of its usefulness as something other than a supply shed.

"You need to hold my hand for that?"

"I sure do." As soon as they entered the building, memories of the night they spent here flooded his thoughts. Even the musty scent had a familiarity that invited him to hold Trista tenderly and kiss her.

But before he made a move toward embracing her, she said, "We could have died that night." She gazed under the counter like she was picturing them cuddled up there.

"But we didn't. We clung to each other." He clasped her other hand, hoping all the feelings in his heart shined from his gaze. "Now we're married, Tris, and close to diving into a loving relationship."

He was exposing his heart. But if not for his wife, who else would he share such deep, unexpected emotions with? He drew in a thready breath. "I never want to return to a platonic office association with you. I want to explore what we can have together romantically wherever we are, wherever the journey takes us. How do you feel about that?" He moved closer to her, wanting to hold and kiss her like he hadn't been able to do the night of the mudslide.

"I don't think I'm quite ready for all that."

"Oh. You're not?" He leaned back, trying to gauge her reaction. She was smiling at him, so he took a chance. "Is it all right with you if we—" He kissed her whisper-soft, using all the gentlemanly restraint he possessed. But when her arms slid around his shoulders and she initiated a passionate kiss, his heart rate skyrocketed. He held her snugly around the waist, loving the feeling of her being in his arms. *Ah, Tris.* If only she knew how much he cared for her already.

"Okay." She pushed back from him, breathing unsteadily. "Enough reminiscing about the night we spent here."

"If you insist." Smiling, he stroked her cheek and gazed into her indigo eyes.

"We should get back to the office, don't you think? We have lots of work to accomplish."

"Can we not act like platonic coworkers?"

"Hudson—"

"Yes, Mom?" he said teasingly.

"Hud."

"Yes, sweetheart?" Everything within him wanted to take her in his arms again, but the cautious look on her face kept him from embracing her a second time.

"I'll concede if you behave."

"I promise." However, he didn't promise not to kiss her. He wouldn't stop doing that unless she told him to cease. By the eager way she'd kissed him, he doubted she wanted them to stop being romantic together any more than he did.

"What about us repurposing this shed as an artist's supply closet?" Trista gazed at him intently. She'd gone into work mode faster than he had.

"If it's stable, that sounds like a good use for it."

"I'll call the foreman when we return to the office."

"All right." He held out his arm to her. "May I escort you back to the truck, Mrs. North?"

"You may, Mr. North." She blinked a few times, her gaze studying him. "Did you mean what you said about us being closer, even at work?"

"I meant it with all my heart." He brought her hand to his lips. "I can't wait until we're all the way married, Tris."

"I have some catching up to do with my feelings. But I like us being romantic more than platonic partners, too."

"Am I ever glad to hear you say that!"

Chapter Twenty-nine

A couple of days later, Hud was sitting across from Trista at the table in the office, studying some project drawings, when she held up her cell phone. "I got a text from Mom. She wants you to come over for a celebration dinner tonight."

"What's the occasion?"

"It's her way of saying thank you for bailing her out financially."

"That's not necessary."

"I know." She reached across the table and squeezed his hand. "But she wants to do something special for you. You might as well let her. You are, after all, her son-in-law."

"Yes, I am." He adjusted their hands until their fingers intertwined. "Are you going to let me act husbandly with you around her?"

"Husbandly? Goodness." She drew her hand back. "After the way Layla acted at the wedding when we kissed, I'm worried about us even holding hands around her."

"And if I try kissing you?" He was having a hard time holding back from doing that now.

"Unfortunately, she might yell or throw a tantrum. Layla's been very protective of me lately."

"When did I become the bad guy?"

Trista leaned toward him like a conspirator, her eyes sparkling with the purple hue he loved. "When you took some of her mama's undivided attention away from her."

"Did I do that?"

"You did," she whispered.

"Then we should hold hands around her more often and help her adjust to us being a couple."

"I don't know if that will work."

"Anything to speed up the process of you moving in with me would be nice."

"Until we find a bigger place—"

"Or until you have stronger feelings for me—"

"I like the idea of us." She touched the back of his hand, causing sparks to shoot along his nerve endings. "If that's any consolation."

Consolation would be hearing her say she'd stay at his apartment starting today. That she was eager to begin the romantic part of their marriage together. But he feared she might say that since Layla disapproved of him, she planned to stay at her mom's house until her daughter was ready to move out, even if that took until she turned eighteen! A sigh escaped his mouth.

"It'll take time, that's all," Trista said in a more serious tone. "Layla hasn't seen me around other men, so my being with you is unsettling for her." She patted the blueprints in front of them. "Now, we were going to talk about the interior designs of the first two units."

"Before we jump into more work, do you have any suggestions on how I can win her over?" That would probably be a huge step in them moving forward as a family.

"She likes presents. Maybe give her a small stuffed animal?"

"And you?" He stroked her hand as she'd done with his. "How can I win you over to my side?"

"I am on your side, Hud."

"Are you?" When she gave him a tense look, he folded his hands over the drawing and sighed. "Never mind." Just because he wanted things to move faster toward merging their lives, any cajoling on his part wouldn't make it happen and would probably annoy Trista.

Maybe now was a good time for him to try being more patient and continue praying for God to work everything out for good in their marriage and family. Granny Trish would surely approve of that plan!

Chapter Thirty

Hud's hand at the back of Trista's waist was reassuring as they hurried through the pouring rain to reach Mom's front porch. She was nearly soaked in the time it took to get from the truck to the house. "Can you believe this rain? Haven't we had enough?"

"I think so. But as you often tell me, it's Southeast Alaska! It rains a lot here!"

Mom opened the door before Trista had a chance to turn the knob. "Welcome! We've been waiting for you two."

"Mommy!" Layla lunged into her arms as soon as she crossed the threshold.

"Sweet pea, I've missed you." Trista kissed her daughter's warm cheek, trying not to get raindrops all over her.

Layla scrubbed her fists over her face. "Mommy, you are wet!"

"Sorry." She removed her dripping coat. "How are you?"

"Someone's here. Someone's here!" Layla jumped up and down.

"Is that right?" Trista hung her jacket over a hook on the coat tree. Who else had Mom invited to dinner?

"Come see who it is, honey bear." Mom waved them toward the living room. "Hud, I want to say thank you for all you've done to save my home." She hugged him and kissed his cheek despite his coat being wet.

"You're welcome, Mrs. Dunmore."

"It's Beth. Or Mom." She patted his arm affectionately.

"Okay. Thanks, Mom." Hud smiled and hung up his jacket. That's when Trista noticed a small package tucked under his arm. Was it a gift for Layla like she'd suggested? She smiled appreciatively at him, and he clasped her hand as they strode into the dining area.

"Surprise!" Arms spread wide, Lake stood in the center of the room, grinning like he'd pulled off the biggest surprise ever.

"Lake?" Hud went straight to his brother and shook his hand. "What are you doing here, man?"

"I came to check out the place for myself. Talk shop. Just a quick trip."

"Hey, Lake." Trista briefly embraced him. "It's nice to see you again."

"Is something wrong? Are the folks okay?" Hud asked.

"Everyone's fine. We'll talk later, huh?"

"Sure." Hud met Trista's gaze and shrugged, obviously surprised to find his brother here.

"Dinner's ready!" Mom called. "Everyone sit down, and I'll get the roast. It's already sliced and ready. The potatoes and gravy are near perfection, if I say so myself. Sit. Sit!"

"We better do as she says." Trista nodded toward the table laden with salad, a fruit bowl, and various condiments.

"I'm stunned that you came here without mentioning anything to me." Hud dropped into the chair next to Lake.

"You surprised me with a couple of unexpected visits, too. Call it payback."

"All right. I see how this goes." Hud chuckled.

Trista sat on the opposite side of the table beside Layla, leaving the head of the table for Mom and the other side for Hud and Lake.

Mom set down a delicious-smelling roast, then dropped into her seat and promptly said grace. "We thank You, Lord of heaven and earth, for blessing us with food, family, and good fellowship. Amen."

"Amen," everyone else said.

"Where's Irish?" Trista helped load up Layla's plate.

"Taking care of our dogs and working at the shelter. She's eager to bring Little Dipper home for good, but he still needs his mama a little longer." Lake forked some roast beef into his mouth. "Mmm. It's delicious, Mrs. Dunmore."

"Thank you. And it's Beth."

"I want a puppy!" Layla rocked in her chair, her eyes wide.

"Easy there," Trista warned.

"Can I have a puppy, Mommy? Can I?"

"Maybe someday."

Hud made a coughing sound. Didn't he ever want to have a pet?

"How did you meet Trista's mom?" Hud waved his fork toward Lake. "How did you know to come here?"

"Well, she—"

"Never mind about that." Mom passed the dinner rolls toward Hud. "Eat up. Have another roll."

"Mom, what's going on?" Trista asked.

"Nothing sinister. I just want you all to enjoy your meal."

Trista wanted to press her for answers but didn't. Hopefully Lake wasn't here for any unpleasant reason. What had brought him to Alaska today?

Chapter Thirty-one

Lake's presence at Hud's mother-in-law's table seemed suspicious. Was there a problem at home? He said they'd talk about it later, so Hud would have to wait, but he was curious. "So, Lake, how are your plans for the spring build coming along?"

"Great! It will be a smaller house than I originally planned. But Irish and I compromised, and we're moving forward with our plans."

"Good for you!" Trista said as if they'd won a personal victory.

Hud set his fork down with a clink. "How did you compromise on such diverse ideas?"

"I agreed to a more modest house. She accepted it wouldn't be as minimalistic as she preferred."

Something about that arrangement bugged Hud. "Why shouldn't you have a bigger house? Why do you have to give up what you want?"

Trista squinted hard at him. *What?*

Lake chuckled nervously. "Compromising is what marriage is about, bro. Sometimes it's about getting along for the day."

"Isn't that the truth?" Beth muttered.

A gnawing sensation in Hud's gut didn't subside. Why did Lake have to settle for less when it came to his dreams and wishes being fulfilled? Why did *he*? "Maybe it wouldn't have been so rough to work things out between you if you married for love in the first place."

"Hud!" Trista gaped at him.

"I meant if they—"

"If 'we.' Isn't that what you meant?"

"I wasn't talking about us."

"No?" She tossed her napkin onto her empty dessert plate. "Weren't you digging at what you're unhappy about in our relationship?"

"No." Heat rushed up his neck and face. He couldn't believe she mentioned that in front of her mom and his brother and Layla.

Lake cleared his throat like he felt uncomfortable.

His words, *"If you married for love,"* pounded through Hud's thoughts like a hammer hitting a nail head. No wonder Trista took offense! "Trista, I—"

"Come on, Layla, help Grammie clear the table." Beth stood and drew Layla away from her chair, casting Hud a scathing look before hurrying into the kitchen.

Trista stared at her hands in her lap.

What had he done? What had evoked such strong emotions in him that he offended his wife and made the others at the table feel awkward and angry toward him? Taking a deep breath, Hud turned to his brother. "I didn't mean anything disparaging about you and Irish. I already told you I'm glad things are working out well for you. When you spoke of your compromise, it seemed unfair to you—like you had to give up a lion's share of your dream for hers."

Trista's eyes lifted and met his gaze with misery etched in them. In his expression, he tried to convey his remorse and ineptitude as a husband to her but surely failed.

"That's okay." Lake shrugged. "It's tough to explain about building a smaller house without diving too deeply into personal details."

Hud turned toward Trista. "I'm so sorry." Apologizing was difficult for him, especially in front of Lake, but it was the right thing to do. "I wish we had a better solution for our housing situation. In time, we'll figure out how to make it work for us, too."

She nodded. "Why don't you go into the living room? I'll help Mom with the dishes." She stood and walked briskly into the kitchen.

Hud groaned, knowing he'd made a disaster of things.

"Let's help out." Lake scooped up some dirty dishes and empty serving bowls and strode into the kitchen. Hud filled his arms with dishes and followed his brother.

"You don't have to do that," Trista said when they carried their armloads into the room. "But go ahead and set them over there." She pointed to a vacant spot on the cluttered counter.

After they finished clearing the table, Hud grabbed the gift he'd brought for Layla and went into the living room with Lake. "So, tell me, what's this trip really about?" he asked as they sat in chairs opposite the couch. "I'd love to show you the land Trista and I have invested in."

"Actually, that's the main reason I'm here."

"Really?"

Lake leaned forward in his chair, elbows on his knees. "Irish and I would like to invest in your project. You need investors, right?"

"Absolutely!"

"She and I have been discussing how we might be a blessing with the inheritance, especially to our families. We thought of your plan to help A.W. and artists like him who'd like to pursue their gifting in art but can't afford it." Lake gazed at him questioningly. "What do you say? Can Irish and I donate to your cause?"

"Of course! With all the work Trista and I have done trying to get investors interested in our idea, I never thought about you becoming involved. Thanks, man." Hud placed his palm over his heart as a sign of gratitude. "What about the animal shelter? And your kennel business?"

"Both are covered, and we have extra funds in the bank." Lake settled back in his chair. "I've invested some money but want to do more. Would you mind showing me your property tomorrow?"

"I'd be thrilled. How did you happen to talk with Beth?"

"Trista gave Irish her mom's number in case of emergency." Lake nodded over his shoulder. "When I called, she suggested her house as a place to spring my surprise during a special dinner she was planning for you."

Hud groaned, feeling bad for bringing a pall over Beth's celebration meal. "I was definitely surprised. What you said about being a blessing with the funds … maybe we could do that together with our other brothers, too."

"Sure. As needs arise, we can rally funds and support them."

"That would be great." Hud drew in a calming breath. "Putting Granddad's money to good use feels like we're making some restitution for his bad decisions in the past."

"I agree."

"Does anyone want some coffee?" Trista stood in the doorway between the living room and the dining area as if reluctant to intrude.

"I'm good," Lake answered.

"I'm fine as well. Will you send Layla in so I can give her my present?" Hud picked up the paper bag with the stuffed animal he'd bought in a downtown souvenir shop.

"Of course." Trista disappeared around the corner.

"Are things okay with you guys?" Lake nodded toward the place where she had been standing.

"Other than me sticking my foot in my mouth?"

Lake grinned good-naturedly. "Been there, done that."

"Things are good considering we are two weeks into a marriage neither of us anticipated or planned." Hud drew in a deep breath and let it out slowly. If anyone could understand the complexities of a marriage like he and Trista were in, it would be Lake. Yet Hud didn't want to talk about his struggles, even with his closest brother.

His past experiences with women hadn't prepared him to be a husband or to put his wife first. Unfortunately, most of his other relationships had centered selfishly on him. As Trista's husband, he hoped to do better at putting her needs before his own. Unfortunately, he failed epically at that tonight!

"If there's anything I can do, let me know." Lake ran his hand over a pillow with some fancy stitching on it. "Mom mentioned she and Gran were praying for you guys."

"Tell her thanks."

Layla skipped into the room. "Mommy said I'm supposed to get my present."

"That's right." Hud handed her the bag, and she peered inside.

"It's a puppy!" Layla pulled out a small husky stuffed animal and hugged it. "Thanks, Hud."

"You're welcome."

"I have three huskies of my own," Lake said proudly.

"You do? Mommy says I'm too little to have a dog." Hud was relieved to hear that, considering his high-end condo and expensive furnishings.

"Maybe when you're older, she'll let you have a pet," Lake said. "I was eight years old when I got my first dog."

"Eight?" Layla scrunched up her nose like that was too long to wait.

Trista entered the room and dropped onto the couch with a sigh.

"Look, Mommy!" Layla sat beside her and petted the toy dog. "He has three dogs." She pointed at Lake.

"I know."

"I was telling her how old I was when I got Brownie. We were both eight."

"You guys are twins?" Layla gawked back and forth between Lake and Hud.

"Not twins, sweet pea. They are cousins raised in the same house as brothers."

"Oh." Layla nodded, then frowned as if she was confused.

"Lake's dad and mom adopted my brother and me after our parents passed away," Hud explained. "Now there are nine brothers."

"Nine is too many boys!"

"Sometimes."

Lake chuckled and stood. "It's getting late. I should probably head over to the motel. It was great to catch up."

"Why don't you stay at my place?" Hud stood also. "I have a spare room."

"Are you sure it won't be an inconvenience?"

"Not at all. It's just me." As soon as he said the words, he cringed, hoping he hadn't offended Trista again.

"I'm staying here with Layla for now." She smoothed her hand over the girl's hair.

"I understand," Lake said.

"Let's head out." Suddenly eager to head home, Hud said goodbye and moved toward the kitchen.

At the sink, Beth set a large pan on a dish rack. "You boys leaving now?"

"Yes, we are," Hud answered. "Thanks for the fabulous dinner. I'm sorry for making things uncomfortable during dinner."

"Eh, things happen." She stared intently at him. "Are you going to work things out with my daughter?"

"Yes, ma'am."

"Then we'll see you next time."

He retrieved his wet coat off the rack and had his hand on the doorknob when guilt hit him like a bad stomach ache. How could he step out the door without attempting to fix things between him and

Trista? Even though they weren't intimately involved yet, they were emotionally involved. She was his wife and someone he cared about. Hadn't he already determined her needs were going to come first? He nearly ran back into the living room.

"Did you forget something?" Trista met his gaze.

"I want to say again how sorry I am for what I said earlier."

"Thanks. I appreciate that."

He leaned over and kissed her cheek. "See you tomorrow?" He gazed into her dark blue eyes, hoping to communicate his feelings for her.

But then, taking him by surprise, Layla kicked him hard in the shin. He jerked back, pain shooting through his leg.

"Layla Louise Dunmore!" Trista exclaimed. "I can't believe you did that."

Hud couldn't believe it either.

Layla backed up against her mother, holding the husky tightly as if she thought he might take it back, but glaring at him, nonetheless.

"You apologize to Hud right now."

Layla pressed her lips together and shook her head.

"Layla!"

Trista had warned him about her daughter possibly retaliating against him if he tried kissing her. Now he knew what she meant, and he was fuming about it. Not trusting himself to keep his thoughts to himself, he strode to the door and forced himself not to limp— and not to punch Lake in the arm for snickering at him.

Chapter Thirty-two

Hud wrapped his hands around a cup of hot tea, facing the ocean view he loved from his third-floor condo. His leg ached, and he still couldn't believe Layla had kicked him like that. How was he ever going to get Trista's daughter to accept him?

Lake dropped into another chair and picked up the teacup Hud had left for him. "Nice place."

"Thanks. It would be hard to let it go."

"Why would you? It has two roomy bedrooms."

"I know. But since things are—" He shook his head, then sipped his drink.

"You don't have to explain. I'm acquainted with the awkwardness of living with a stranger who you're hoping and praying you'll fall for … and that she'll fall for you." Lake drank from his cup. "You are praying for that, right?"

"Sure. But Trista isn't a stranger. She's been my business partner for six months."

"Right. You have a different situation than Irish and I did. Any warming up toward you on her part?"

Their kisses flitted through his thoughts. "Just when I think so, something happens. Like what transpired at Beth's tonight." He was usually better at thinking before he spoke, but earlier, the self-control he thought he possessed had failed him.

"Two feet forward. Three feet back."

"So it seems."

Both men sat quietly for a few minutes, gazing at the harbor. Hud couldn't help feeling embarrassed and regretful over his mistakes this evening.

"How did you get Irish to feel differently toward you? If it's too weird of a question, forget I asked."

Lake was quiet for so long Hud thought he might not say anything personal about his marriage. He wouldn't push, although they had discussed dating when they were younger and lived in the same house, which seemed like a century ago.

"Remember how you told me Irish was a fire?" Lake finally said. "That she might be too much for me?"

"Yeah. Forget I said that. I'm sorry for mouthing off. I had no right." Shame and remorse flooded him over what he'd said to Lake about his choice of a marriage partner and how he'd accepted the terms of the inheritance. Now he had done the same thing! Talk about hypocrisy!

"It's okay. The truth is, Irish is perfect for me. Don't get me wrong—we are opposites. We disagree about some of the smallest things." Lake chuckled like he was thinking of something in particular. "You were partially correct. She is a fire. But it's an impressive fire! When God sent her my way, He knew who could pull me out of my discouragement over Laurie. He brought me someone who shoots gazes in my direction that smoke in the air like a flame about to combust. We've been married for seven weeks, and I can't wait to get back to her!"

"Lake, bro. You are one love-struck husband!"

"I am!" Lake set his teacup down. "I hope our passion lasts. That it doesn't burn out of control, using up all the energy and power it has, then fizzles."

"You think that might happen?"

"Not really." Lake gazed intently into the night sky that bore a slightly green hue around the mountains. "I think love energizes and multiplies more love between us. I pray it happens like that for you and Trista. And soon, you'll be experiencing an endless supply of love and passion with your wife."

"I hope for that also." A clog of emotion stuck in Hud's throat.

Lake pointed at the sky. "That's an amazing view. Even some Northern Lights." After a pause, he said, "Trista seems like a nice woman. She took a risk in marrying a guy like you."

"Hey, now."

"She has a daughter, and that's a game changer." A serious expression crossed Lake's face. "Thinking of Jazzy being a single mom and how she puts Jasmine first, I can imagine Trista doing the same thing."

"You're right. It's something I didn't ponder well enough before our marriage." Hud rubbed the back of his neck. "How is Jazzy?" He hadn't thought about the tomboy-turned-woman who'd tromped around with him and Lake when they were kids in a long time. They had even dated a few times, although nothing came of it.

"She's good. She's working with Irish at the animal shelter."

Hud contemplated that briefly, then returned to their previous topic. "I didn't realize how much Trista being a mom might affect our relationship before I asked her to marry me. Not that I would change anything. Other than—" He shrugged.

"You guys will work it out. Give it time. Giving it your all goes without saying."

"What's that supposed to mean?" Was Lake saying he wasn't giving his and Trista's marriage his all? Like he wasn't committed enough? "We're busy with work. She has a daughter who hasn't accepted me. Things are complicated. It's not my fault—"

"Whoa. Chill, bro. I didn't mean anything derogatory. Marriage and a relationship take prioritizing, that's all."

Hud released a tense breath. He was being overly sensitive. "Everything is confusing right now. It seems she likes me and enjoys kissing me. Then, wham. There's a wall."

"It'll get better. I promise."

"I hope so." Hud met his brother's gaze. "Any advice for a brother who went against all his plans and married a woman who doesn't love him to access his grandfather's funds?"

"That still bugs you, doesn't it?"

"I'd say you have no idea. But you do."

"Our brothers being up in arms about it hasn't helped." Lake squinted at him.

"Yeah. I admit I contributed to their outrage about you." Hud released a heavy sigh. "I'm sorry about that."

"It's okay. So you decided to marry and get the money for your art community. What now?"

"We work hard at getting it built and running. Everything is set in motion for the first phase to be established in six months."

"That's great! Have you told A.W. yet?"

"I did."

"Where's he at financially?"

"Not good." Hud yawned and stood. "Maybe we can talk about this some more tomorrow, huh?"

"Absolutely." Lake stood and shook his hand. "See you in the morning."

Just as Hud reached his bedroom, his phone vibrated. He checked the screen. Trista.

We need to talk.

Chapter Thirty-three

"Hey," Hud said when Trista answered his call. "What's up?"

"Sorry to bother you so late," she spoke in a subdued tone.

"No problem. It's never too late for us to talk." He sat down on the edge of his bed. "Is everything okay?"

"Not really. I'm worried about something."

"What's bothering you?" Was she still upset about what he said earlier? If so, he didn't blame her. He was still annoyed with himself, too.

"It concerns what you asked Lake about Irish getting what she wanted while he went without." She made a swallowing sound. "Were you referring to you and me?"

"No!" Less forcefully, he said, "Not really."

"Hud?"

He sighed, not wanting to hurt her feelings again. "I didn't think so at the time."

"And now?"

She was asking for honesty, right? "I can't help brooding over us still living in separate places after two weeks of marriage and being unable to sort through some of our difficulties."

"And you're worried you won't get what you want?"

"It's not that." He wasn't taking all the blame for their struggling relationship. "I'm trying to be patient and hoping for the best in our marriage." The following silence separated them more than the half mile between their homes did. "However, I'm truly sorry for what I said and for offending you. The words popped out, and I regret saying them."

"I'm more concerned about what you didn't say." Her voice grew more intense. "What you seemed to be implying was that I'm pushing for what I want—a three-bedroom house or us continuing with our arrangement of living separately—and you're going to dig in your heels because you deserve to have what you want!"

"Trista—"

"Am I wrong? Because if I'm way off base, I'll apologize. We can end this conversation now."

He blew out a long breath. "I really like my condo. I love the view of the channel. You should have seen the Northern Lights fanning across the edges of the sky tonight."

"And?"

"And it's big enough for a couple and one child." They were married. Why couldn't they share a bedroom? Layla could have the other room. It was a perfect apartment for the three of them.

"You mean for a married couple in a real, loving relationship."

"Which I hope for us to be in someday soon." He didn't want to let things go unsaid because physical intimacy was an uncomfortable topic. Love, too, for that matter. "I already care for you, Tris." He tried speaking in a gentle tone. "I'm hoping for a genuine crazy-about-you kind of marriage. I know it will take time. But we've kissed passionately. Why can't we—"

"No!"

"What about you and Layla staying in the guest room together?" He was grasping at straws. But Trista and Layla sharing the other room would work temporarily—not forever, he hoped.

"If Layla's attitude toward you improves, that would be a possible solution. I don't know what's gotten into her lately."

"What about her kicking me?" Some of his previous annoyance returned. "Should I expect more of that kind of behavior?" If so, he had no idea what he should do when it happened or how he was ever going to be a good father figure.

"I had a stern talk with her, and I hope it never happens again." Trista gulped. "I warned you about how she might react if you tried kissing me, although it was wrong of her to kick you. She still doesn't want to leave Mom's house or live in your apartment."

"Maybe you should try explaining to her about us."

"How can I tell Layla about our unusual marriage when I barely understand the intricacies of our relationship myself? When we aren't acting like a husband and wife?"

Hud bit back a tired groan. "Maybe you could explain why you married me so she doesn't resent me so much."

"Tell her I married you for your money? I don't want to explain that to my five-year-old daughter!"

He'd never heard Trista sound so bitter. "You regret it?"

"After tonight? Maybe."

"I'm so sorry."

"How do we flip the switch?" she asked in a softer tone. "How do we go from business acquaintances to lovers?"

Her use of "lovers" startled him … and made him smile. "We figure it out together. One day at a time. One hour at a time."

"Do you love me?" She wasn't pulling any punches. "I'm sorry if that's too forward of a question. I'm wondering where you are emotionally. I want us to be honest about our feelings, even if we must ask each other daily."

Hud closed his eyes. "I care for you. I'm falling for you. Not 'in love' yet. What about you?"

"More irritated than caring about you today."

Her honesty hurt his pride, but he tried not to dwell on it too much. "Thanks for telling me how you feel."

"I should let you get some sleep."

"Wait." Still shooting for honesty, he said, "I want you to know I have strong feelings for you already. If you and I were to share a room, it would be okay with me. We are married. Our feelings for each other will grow stronger over time."

"How can you be sure?" she asked so quietly he barely heard her.

"Trust me, I'm sure."

"Trust is a difficult commodity for me. But I'll think about it. Good night, Hud."

"See you tomorrow, sweetheart." He took a quick breath. "Is it still okay if I call you that?"

"It's okay if you mean it." She ended their call.

If he meant it? So she doubted his sincerity?

Before falling asleep, he spent a few minutes praying about their relationship. *Lord, help Trista and me to fall in love with each other. And somehow, please fix this thing with Layla hating me. I could really use some wisdom.*

Chapter Thirty-four

With thoughts of last night's phone conversation with Hud still swirling in her mind, Trista went along with him to show Lake the jobsite. Had he meant what he said about waiting for her as long as it took them to fall in love? After their talk and how he called her "sweetheart," warmer feelings were strumming through her heart toward him. That was also probably due to her prayer time and trying to release her negative thoughts to the Lord.

Hud was her husband—and she'd vowed faithfulness and love to him. She needed to try to work things out with him, even if they weren't living together yet, and even when it wasn't easy.

"What do you think of the place?" Hud asked as they walked along the perimeter of the property.

"It looks like a promising enterprise." Lake's gaze sparkled with interest as he peered out over the damp, dark earth rampaged by the mudslide, then flattened by dozers.

"They've done a lot of work to get it looking this good." Hud appeared animated as he spoke with his brother about their project. "I'm relieved they've accomplished it so quickly."

"Me too," Trista said.

Hud's and her gazes met, and they shared a smile. She was thankful they were closer to being on the same wavelength today. However, she was still embarrassed about Layla kicking him and didn't know how to deal with her actions. How was she going to get her daughter to warm up to Hud? He said he'd adopt her. But what did that mean to a five-year-old? Layla obviously saw him as a threat or competition for her mom's time and attention. How long would it take for her to feel like he was a genuine part of their lives?

"Isn't that right, Trista?"

"Oh. Sorry. What were you saying?"

"I said this place has changed a lot since the night of the mudslide." Hud pointed toward the leveled ground where the first house would be built. "I'm impressed with the progress so far."

"Me too. I had doubts that we'd ever see our dreams fulfilled."

"Sometimes things can turn around fast and be better than you ever imagined." Lake winked toward Hud like he was commenting on a previous conversation. Was he talking about the houses that would soon be peppering the landscape? Or was he implying Hud's and her relationship could be better than anything they'd imagined?

They skirted around the front of the property, with Hud pointing out the future layout of the land. He waved toward the empty area where a line of one-bedroom houses would go. He explained about the two communal art buildings where residents would be able to work together, seek advice and feedback, and share resources.

"Only artists will live here?" Lake asked.

"Mainly artists." Hud seemed to be walking taller, his shoulders back and head held high as he spoke about their development. "Project-based residents would be welcome also. Let's say someone came into town to do research for a book or an artist was giving lectures or seminars, they could stay in one of our bungalows."

Trista heard the pride in his voice as he explained their ideas, and she breathed easier, becoming more relaxed around him again.

This was what had drawn them together in the first place. Their shared desire to build an artist-based community had cemented their lives together before they ever spoke of marriage.

"Since you've seen an overview of the land, let's look over the plans." Hud led the way to the outbuilding where they'd spent that memorable night together.

"Wow. This place took a hit." Lake nodded toward the mud stain and large dent across the backside of the shed. "Are you going to tear it down?"

"No!" Hud and Trista spoke at the same time, then grinned at each other.

Lake's eyebrows rose. "I gather you have strong feelings about the building?"

"Something like that." Hud's cheeks hued ruddy. "It provided shelter for us during the mudslide."

"It's special to us." Trista wanted to clasp Hud's hand or kiss him in memory of their shared experience. But since Lake was here, she didn't.

Hud spread out the drawings on the wooden counter inside the shed. The three of them leaned over the plans while he pointed out the locations they'd been discussing. Then he explained about the art building they planned to have built during phase two of the project and the more profitable and much-needed apartment complex that would be constructed during phase three. Trista shared about the decorating themes she planned to use for the artists' houses and landscaping.

"Sounds like you guys have everything figured out." Lake glanced between them. "So how can Irish and I help with supporting your mission?"

"We had more investors before the mudslide." Trista took the lead. "Now we're looking toward the future and trying to get more financial supporters again. With more backing, we'll be able to finish this project and replicate the process in another area."

"Sounds great! Do you have a second location in mind?"

"We'd like to go where there's a strong artists' base." Hud rolled the plans into a long tube. "We're considering Kalispell, Montana, or Joseph, Oregon."

"Kalispell would be awesome! Irish and I do some skijor racing there."

"Oh, right."

Trista preceded the other two out the door, but she wanted to state her opinion, too. "My vote is for one of the other islands here in Southeast Alaska. It would be hard for Layla and me to leave my mom." Glancing back, she was relieved to see Hud nodding. "However, I'm committed to setting up specialty communities wherever God may lead us."

"Here's a thought." Lake grinned at Hud and then Trista. "Thunder Ridge might be the perfect location for an artists' community."

Hud chuckled. "Mom and Gran would love that."

"They sure would. So would I!"

But that would be a long way from Mom and all that was familiar to Layla. Trista released a long sigh.

"Whichever place you guys choose, I'm excited to be involved in your projects. Irish is too. She's the one who nudged me into coming up here." Lake rubbed his hands together. "We'll discuss the financial aspects and get back with you soon."

"Sounds good. Thanks." Hud shook his hand. "Tell Irish thanks for her interest too."

"I will." Lake hugged Trista, then clapped Hud on the back. "It was great seeing both of you, even for a whirlwind twenty-four hours." He checked his phone. "Looks like my flight is on time. I should head to the airport ferry."

"Let's go, then." Hud rested his palm on Trista's back as they returned to the truck, and she leaned slightly into him. "Heard anything from Coe lately?"

"Just that he's coming home soon. It'll be great to see him after his stint in India."

"We'll have to go back to Thunder Ridge to see him." Hud glanced at Trista, and she nodded. "Maybe we could bring Layla to meet her new grandparents if it works out."

"That would be nice. Your mom wants to meet her." She smiled, pleased that he was including her daughter in their plans. "I'd love to meet Coe, too."

At the dock where the airport ferry went back and forth between Ketchikan and Gravina Island, Lake grabbed his carry-on bag and hustled down the ramp. It was low tide, so the ramp was positioned at a steep angle, causing Lake to brace into the wind at an angle too. Hud and Trista sat in the truck, watching him until he disappeared into the enclosed area on the ship.

"Are you okay?" She'd noticed Hud's contemplative look as he watched Lake walking away.

"Yeah. It was great seeing Lake again. I miss my brothers more than I thought I would when I left everything and moved here." He ran his hands over the steering wheel, his gaze still on the airport ferry. "His wanting to contribute to our project was a nice surprise and a blessing."

"It sure was."

They sat there for a while, watching the ferry move across the choppy waters of the channel between the two islands. "I guess we should head back to the office," he finally said.

"If we must."

"Well, there are other things I'd rather do." He smoothed his fingers down her cheek, gazing into her eyes as if asking if she minded him touching her. She smiled at him, wishing for a meaningful connection between them. He leaned closer and brushed his lips against hers. An emotional tenderness toward him and a longing for their future as a married couple meshed inside her, opening her heart to accept and return his affection. "If I haven't said it lately, I am falling in love with you," he whispered near her ear.

His words and kisses made her want to forget all about their misunderstandings. She prayed that soon she'd know beyond any doubt that she was falling in love with him, too.

Chapter Thirty-five

On Sunday morning, Hud sat beside Trista on a church pew about halfway up the aisle from where they'd gotten married. Instead of sitting on Trista's other side like Hud had imagined her doing, Layla squeezed right between them and scowled up at him, showing her teeth in a grimace. Her animosity toward him didn't make sense. Hadn't he gotten her a stuffed toy? It had to be jealousy, plain and simple, but even that puzzled him.

Pastor Chad strode down the center aisle, greeting people. He stopped and held out his hand toward Hud. "Welcome to First City Fellowship."

"Thanks." He stood and shook the pastor's hand.

"How are things going in the Dunmore-North row?" The pastor shook Trista, Layla, and Beth's hands, too.

"Everything's good." Trista nodded, but Hud detected a hesitation in her voice. Was she thinking of something that wasn't going well between them?

"Couldn't be better, Pastor." Beth smiled widely.

Pastor Chad looked Hud in the eye. "I've been meaning to call. If you need anything, want to talk, or grab a coffee, text me, all right?"

"Uh, sure. Thanks." Now why did the pastor single him out? Was it because he was new to this church? Had he heard the hesitation in Trista's voice? Or was Hud wearing an expression that told the world he was floundering as a husband and stepfather?

Throughout the worship time, he sang along with the songs he knew, and he enjoyed hearing Trista's soft voice singing in harmony. Layla elbowed him in the ribs with her pointy elbow several times, but he tried to ignore her rude behavior. She was a kid. He was an adult. They weren't in a tug-of-war over Trista's affection. Yet that seemed to be exactly what was happening!

Layla hurried out of the aisle when the music ended and the children were dismissed to go to children's church. Glad for the reprieve from anticipating a problem with her, Hud scooted closer to Trista and slid his arm over her shoulder. She sagged against his side, and he was grateful for this time to be close to his wife. He tried focusing on the pastor's words and not letting his grumpy feelings toward Trista's daughter control his thoughts.

"My marriage and family are a testimony to the grace-filled journey God has brought April and me on. If it weren't for His touch on our lives, we wouldn't be married today. We wouldn't have our precious three sons." The pastor pressed his fist to his lips as if overcome with strong emotion. "As another anniversary passes of my pastoral time here at First City Fellowship, I want to thank my wife for putting up with my hectic lifestyle and loving our sons and me so well." Pastor Chad smiled fondly at someone toward the back of the room—his wife, no doubt.

The congregation clapped and cheered.

"They have a beautiful marriage reconciliation story," Trista whispered near his ear. He nodded to let her know he'd heard her.

After listening to the pastor sharing about God's restoration process and how the Lord had worked in his life, Hud wanted to walk forward with some of the others who accepted his invitation for prayer. Instead, he pressed his elbows against his knees, covered his face with his hands, and prayed silently in his pew.

Jesus, I'm so sorry for how I went my own way after leaving Thunder Ridge. Even before that, I made some decisions I'm ashamed of now. The pastor said I could drop my guilt and burdens at Your feet and take on restoration and grace as part of my journey. I want to do that. I want to live free and whole in You. Help me, Lord. I want to follow You and trust You.

Tears flooded his eyes, and he didn't fight them like he would have in the past. He let the healing power of prayer and God's love work through him. When he glanced up, Trista had tears in her eyes like she'd been praying, too. She clasped his hand and smiled as if she understood just what he was experiencing. Restoration and healing might be the best starting place for both of them in their marriage and life together.

Chapter Thirty-six

"What did you think of the pastor's sermon?" Beth asked when the four of them sat around her dining room table for lunch. The stew and biscuits she served smelled terrific.

"It gave me a lot to think about." Hud's thoughts had churned with unrest and a desperate need to pray during the sermon. But he'd felt comforted and encouraged by the prayer time afterward.

"Pastor Gray's sermons are like that."

"Have you attended his church for a long time?" He spooned some stew into his mouth and caught Layla staring at him with a begrudging look.

"I went to First City Fellowship even before Pastor Gray arrived."

"Did you know about the rough patch he spoke about today?"

"I did. It was a tough time for them and the congregation."

"How so?" He set his spoon down and gave Beth his full attention. Since he'd been raised in a parsonage, he knew some of the inner workings of a pastor's family.

"April left him for a while."

"Oh. That must have been difficult on both."

"It was. I prayed daily for their marital healing. I'd gone through a divorce myself, so I knew how challenging that could be." Beth lifted her spoon with chunks of potato on it. "As you heard in his testimony, God worked wonders in their marriage."

"That part was especially inspiring." Hud resumed eating his stew.

"Layla, how was children's church?" Trista asked, probably trying to include her in the conversation.

"It was okay." Rolling her eyes, the girl dropped her chin onto her hands resting on the table.

"Did something happen?"

"No." Layla gave Hud an intense glare that he tried to ignore.

"Would you like to tell me about it later?" Trista asked.

"No. Miss Conroy told us we have to love our enemies." Layla stuck her tongue out at Hud.

"Layla!" Trista said disapprovingly.

Hud winced. He'd never experienced a kid despising him before. Of course, he'd never married a child's mom before, either!

"Miss Conroy is right," Trista said. "Even if we don't get along with someone, we are still supposed to show them God's love and grace."

Layla grumbled something under her breath, then ate a few bites of food.

"What did you think of the pastor's sermon?" Hud tried to focus on Trista, remembering how she'd clasped his hand at the close of the service.

"I love how vulnerable he was about his and April's mistakes." Trista's soft, lilting tones reminded Hud of the notes of a beautiful song. "He could have been secretive and acted as if nothing bad had happened between them, even dismissing his own failures. But he didn't. His words about all of us needing restoration touched me."

"Me too."

They smiled at each other, sharing a moment of understanding. But then, Layla kicked his shin hard beneath the table! He jerked backward, his hand bumping his bowl. Stew sloshed over the edge and down his clothes. Quickly, he shoved his chair back and stood, biting his tongue to stop himself from saying something rude to the girl. How dare the little imp do these things to him!

"Layla Louise, how could you do that?" Trista ran into the kitchen.

Hud dabbed at the mess and tried stopping the stew from dripping onto the floor, but his napkin was useless. He marched into the kitchen, his hackles rising when he heard Layla snickering back in the dining area.

"I'm so sorry." Trista handed him a towel to sop up the broth trailing down his lavender button-up shirt and dark slacks. He nodded but didn't say anything. She returned to the table while he stayed in the kitchen, wiping his clothes free of small vegetable chunks and broth. "Why did you kick Hud?" Trista spoke sternly.

Hud leaned closer to the doorway, listening. He'd appreciate an answer, too.

"I don't like him making googly eyes at you."

Googly eyes?

"That's no reason for you to act so mean. I thought you were supposed to be loving toward everyone. You owe Hud an apology. And you will never kick him again! Do you hear me, young lady?"

"Yes," Layla said quietly.

However, when he returned to his seat, she still glared daggers at him. His clothes were damp, but it wasn't the worst thing that had ever happened to him at a dinner table, nor the most embarrassing. Thanks to having eight brothers, he'd had plenty of experience enduring unexpected mischief involving food!

"Dish up some more stew." Beth inched the tureen toward him. "We have plenty."

"Thank you." He filled his bowl to the top of the rim, almost daring Layla to try it again. He would be ready the next time she retaliated against him, although he sincerely hoped there wouldn't be a next time. They ate in silence for a few minutes.

Trista nudged Layla's arm a couple of times. "Sorry for kicking you," Layla finally mumbled. Since her mother had prodded her, the girl's apology didn't sound repentant.

"Thank you," he said with as much diplomacy as he could muster. His mom and dad had made him apologize for some of the stunts he'd pulled on his brothers when they were kids, too. Although a less-than-heartfelt apology usually got him into more trouble. "So, Layla, what are you looking forward to about spring?" he asked, searching for a topic they could discuss to get past the kicking episode.

"Nothing."

"Is there a special activity you do when nicer weather comes?"

"No."

"Why don't you tell Hud about us beachcombing after some storms?" Trista suggested.

"Who cares about that?"

"I do." He shrugged. "It sounds interesting."

"Tell him about the fishing float you found."

The girl sighed like a bored teenager. "After storms, we hunt for shells and stuff. One time, I found a glass ball."

"That's cool. What color is the fishing float?"

"Dark green."

"I've never found anything like that on a beach before." He decided to take a chance on getting Layla to warm up to him. "I'd like to see the float you found—if you don't mind."

"I suppose I can show you." She sighed like her offer was an inconvenience.

"Great!"

After they cleared the table, Layla asked, "Do you want to see my glass ball now?"

"Absolutely. Lead the way."

She clasped her mom's hand, and they went up the stairs with Hud following them. He was curious about the float, but his thoughts still reeled from Layla's resentment or jealousy, or whatever. Why did she dislike him so much? Had he said something that bugged her? Was she just causing trouble to create disharmony between him and Trista? At five years old?

In her bedroom decorated in light greens and pink, Layla picked up a dark green, hand-sized glass float from a wicker basket and handed it carefully to him.

"This is a real beauty." He held the globe up to the light and peered through it. "It's impressive that you found one in such good condition."

"I took it to school for show and tell. Miss Murphy made me let all the kids touch it." She frowned. "Zeke almost dropped it."

"You must have been worried about it."

"I wanted to sock him in the nose!"

"Layla!" Trista said sternly.

"It's true. He's mean to other kids' stuff too."

"I don't want you punching anyone in the nose." Trista lifted Layla's chin and looked her in the eye. "We don't hit or kick anyone. Remember what your children's church teacher said about loving everyone?"

"Yeah. But I don't love Zeke." Layla crossed her arms.

"Even Zeke needs Jesus's love."

Layla slanted a look at Hud.

He figured this was his opportunity to add something meaningful to the conversation. "I didn't get along with someone back in elementary school either." He passed the ball to Trista, and she placed it in the basket. "I wanted to fight with the kid daily for a month."

"That's how I feel about Zeke. I want to punch him in the face every day."

"Layla!"

The girl sagged against her bed. "My teacher says I can't hit anyone—same as Mommy."

"You should listen to her and your wise mom."

"Is that what you did when you wanted to fight the mean kid?" Layla removed her shoes and glanced away from Hud as if only half listening.

"Sure. My grandmother told me I should love everyone and be kind to the kid instead of fighting with him." He appreciated his grandmother's wisdom now more than he did back then. "She was right, so I brought him a frog."

"They let you have frogs at your school?" Layla faced him, her eyes wide.

"Nope. I brought it in a bucket and hid it behind a tree. Unfortunately, he didn't like frogs and kicked the bucket over."

"Did you become friends after that?"

"Not quite." Hud almost laughed but refrained. "Let's say we tolerated each other then."

"Thank you for showing Hud the glass ball." Trista patted Layla's arm. "Why don't you go downstairs and see if Grammie needs any help?" When Layla didn't move, Trista said, "Go on."

"All right." Layla shuffled out of the room, but at the doorway, she paused and squinted hard at Hud like she was dishing him a warning. So much for his showing interest in her glass float making a difference in her attitude toward him.

"Thanks for taking the time to share a bit of yourself with her." Trista clasped his hand after the sound of Layla's footsteps on the stairway faded.

"Of course. I want this to work between us. I want Layla to accept me as part of your family, too."

"This was a good start."

Was it? Man, he hoped so. But by the girl's departing glare, he doubted it.

However, Trista's shining gaze seemed to be inviting him closer. Was she hinting that she wanted to do more than hold hands with him? They were alone now. But considering Layla's recent behavior, he didn't know if he dared initiate a kiss in this house. Still, Trista's warm smile was too enticing to ignore. He brushed his lips lightly across hers. Planning to step back quickly in case her daughter returned, Trista's passionate response took him off-guard. She wrapped her arms around him and kissed him deeply, and he gladly returned her kisses. "Oh, Hud," she whispered against his mouth.

"Sweetheart, I—"

"Mommy!" Layla screeched from the doorway. Hud and Trista jerked apart. "Why are you kissing him like that? It's gross!"

"Layla, please go back downstairs. I'll be right there."

"Layla?" Beth called from the first floor. "Will you come down here, please?"

"Grammie is calling you." Trista tipped her head toward the door. "Go and find out what she wants."

"Why were you kissing him?" Layla jabbed her finger accusingly at Hud. He gulped.

Trista met his gaze tenderly, then crossed the room to her daughter. Squatting down, she smoothed her hands over Layla's shoulders. "Sweet pea, Mommy and Hud are married. We're going to kiss and hold one another sometimes. That's what married couples do."

Layla glared at him. "I want him to go home!"

"That isn't your decision." Trista peered into Layla's eyes. "And we don't tell people we want them to leave or go home. It isn't nice."

Hud tried relaxing his posture to avoid appearing frustrated or angry at the girl's conduct—except he was frustrated with the rude way their kissing had been interrupted. Everything about being with Trista felt so right a few minutes ago. Now, tension rifled through his emotions like a thief stealing all the finest things in the house. Should he leave and let Trista and Layla talk privately? Maybe that would be for the best. He took a step toward the door.

"We're going to be living with Hud soon. We're becoming a family." Trista's words made Hud pause. A measure of his frustration melted away.

"Not me. I'm staying here with Grammie!"

"No, you're not. Wherever I live, that's where you'll live too. But you may come and visit Grammie often."

"I don't want to leave!" Layla shouted. "You can't make me."

Hud clenched his jaw, waiting for Trista to refute that claim.

Instead, she sighed. "We'll talk about it later. Go see what Grammie wants, okay?" Layla threw Hud another glare of hostility before stomping out of the room. "I'm sorry." Trista moaned. "I didn't expect her to react so adversely to us being together."

"Should I give you time to work this out with her?" After their disrupted kisses, he wished they could spend more time alone, but he didn't want to push Trista. Layla's actions had obviously unsettled her, and she probably needed to have another conversation with her. "I was glad to hear you telling her we will be living together eventually."

"Except that didn't go so great." She thrust her hand over her hair. "I don't know what to do or say to convince her that our becoming a family is a good thing. I'll have to pray about it some more and try to be patient with her."

"Tris?" He clasped her hand that was raking over her hair and held it loosely between them. "I want us to be together. But I understand you need more time to work things out with Layla." He toyed with the wedding ring on her finger, longing to kiss her again. "I liked us kissing a few minutes ago."

"Me too—until all the fury of a five-year-old broke out!"

"Yeah." He let go of her hand. "I think I'll head back to my place. See you tomorrow, okay?" He kissed her cheek, then headed toward the door.

"Hud?"

"Hmm?" He pivoted back to her.

"Do you mind if I tag along with you?"

"You mean it?" Their gazes met and held. His heart rate accelerated.

"Yes. It would give us a chance to talk."

"Oh, sure. Talk." Did she mean just to talk? Or was "talk" code for something else entirely? Dare he hope?

Chapter Thirty-seven

Trista sat at the small dining table in front of the large window overlooking the harbor at Hud's apartment. He had such a fabulous view here. She understood why he didn't want to give up this place. And why should he? She'd love waking up and seeing the idyllic scene of the harbor with all the fishing boats, the channel flowing between them and the next island, and the lush mountains every day.

What if she just said yes to everything about a full marriage and life here with Hud? Was she ready for that? She fingered her coffee cup, mostly to give her hands something to do. Hud had fixed them coffee and set out cheese and crackers on a decorative wooden board, but she wasn't hungry.

How was she supposed to feel at ease, knowing the discussion she wanted to have with her business partner turned husband? They needed to learn to communicate on a deeper level other than as business associates, but how to do that was puzzling to her. Then there was Layla, with her strong dislike or jealousy toward Hud. Trista was still trying to figure out why that was happening and how to deal with her attitude. And she was trying to wrap her thoughts around her budding feelings toward her husband.

Was she falling for Hud? Truly falling for him? Earlier, when she was in his arms, kissing him with such abandonment, she felt ready to confess her feelings to him. Then Layla barged in! How embarrassing! And more confusing! Yet she had to consider her daughter's feelings. Was forcing Layla to move in with her and Hud the right thing to do? Trista sighed.

"Are you all right?" Hud reached across the narrow table and clasped her hand. Then he released it as if he was afraid she didn't want him touching her, which was far from the truth.

Warm feelings for him had been humming through her system ever since they kissed back at Mom's. But how could she move forward with a man her daughter didn't get along with? How could she not? They were already married! What if Layla's behavior was all an act to get Trista's attention? On the other hand, what if she emotionally scarred her by pushing her to accept Hud as a father figure too soon? She groaned.

"Tris?"

"I'm sorry. I'm just working through some things."

"I can imagine." He met her gaze tenderly, not looking away. She liked how he gave her his full attention and didn't keep checking his cell phone for texts or sports updates like some men she'd known in the past.

"I want us to talk." She wet her lips and smiled tentatively at him. "I mean, really talk."

"Okay. What about?"

"Us." She took a breath. "How would you feel about dating?"

He smiled in that masculine, flirtatious way that made shivers race through her and rocked his index finger between them. "As in us dating?"

"Mmhmm. Going out, having fun, being romantic." She'd veered away from the topic she planned to lead with. But they hadn't experienced many fun or romantic outings. "Spending time together away from the office would be nice. It might lead to more romance between us."

"I like the sound of that!" He reached across the table again, clasping both of her hands. "Is this what you wanted to talk with me about? Us dating?" He sounded so relieved she hated to break his bubble.

"Yes—and no."

Nodding, he released her hands. "I will go on as many dates with you as you want, whenever you want, Tris."

"You haven't even asked me out yet."

"I haven't?"

"We married without going out, remember?"

"Everything is topsy-turvy in our relationship, isn't it?"

"Uh-huh." Was she brave enough to expose her truest thoughts to him—to be completely honest and authentic? Wasn't that what marriage was all about—sharing their hearts and being real with one another? "I think it feels weird to be falling in love with someone, even contemplating sleeping together, without dating and getting to know one another first."

Hud's eyes pulsed wide. In one leap, he reached her side of the table, pulled her to a standing position and right into his arms. "Are you saying what I think you're saying?" He gazed at her, his eyes shining. His mouth was close to hers, hovering just above hers. She wanted to kiss him and allow herself to fall for him even more.

"What do you think I'm saying?" she whispered without closing the gap between them.

"That you're falling in love with me? That you want to take our relationship to the next step, which would be perfectly fine since we are married and falling for each other?"

Her heart pounded hard beneath her ribs, like it might jump out of her chest. "I might be suggesting something along those lines."

"Oh, Tris." His lips met hers with a sweet tenderness that morphed into a passionate exchange of hungry kissing between them. In his arms, she felt lost and complete, needy and giving, wanting more passion and tenderness, yet already so satisfied by Hud's embrace and loving affection that she wanted to melt into his arms and stay there forever. She wasn't fully in love with him yet. But she wanted to be as close to him as she could be, emotionally and physically.

"I still want us to date."

"Do you want to go out right now?" He stepped back but kept their hands clasped. "Shall we go to a movie? Dinner? How about a walk on the docks?"

"Yes. Yes. And yes." She took a breath. "But not right this minute."

"No? What do you want right now, Trista North?"

"I want my husband to say he's falling in love with me again."

He cupped her cheeks and gazed deeply into her eyes. "I am falling in love with you."

"I am falling in love with you, too." The words felt good and perfectly right to say.

"Ah, Tris. Really?"

"Really."

They gazed into each other's eyes as if they were having a whole loving conversation without saying a word. Then she met his mouth in a series of delicious kisses that left her bedazzled and hungering for more closeness with her husband.

"Is it enough that we're falling for one another?" He leaned back slightly, his eyes sparkling. "I mean 'falling in love' versus us being ready to say we love each other?"

"We are being honest. I only realized I was falling for you a while ago." She drew in a couple of breaths, steadying her pounding heart. "These stronger feelings for you have taken me by surprise. Your kisses sweep me away to a dreamy place I never want to leave. They make me want to be with you all the time—as your wife, Hud."

"I'm pleased, humbled, and so grateful to hear you say that." He kissed her longingly.

She wrapped her arms around his waist. "Are you planning to stay married to me?" Even with the romantic way she was feeling toward him lately, some of her trust issues had resurfaced. What if she and Hud moved toward intimacy, then he left her as Neil had done? What if she convinced Layla to trust him like a father, then he left them? How could Trista face both betrayals? She'd prayed about that very thing this morning at church.

"You mean, will I stay with you forever?"

"Yes," she whispered. "Until death do us part."

"Trista, I plan to love you and stay married to you, enjoying all the pleasures and challenges of married life, for the rest of my life." He tipped up her chin gently. "Are you worried about me not staying with you?"

Her gaze locked on his again. "Yes."

"Baby, I'm eager to experience a genuine, loving relationship with you. I care for you so much already. My feelings for you have surprised and amazed me, too. I think about you all the time. I want to be with you every waking hour, so I can confidently say I plan to be married to you until I die." He kissed her softly again and again. "What about you? Do you plan to stay married to me?" He gave her a roguish smile.

She chuckled over how the question sounded coming back to her. "Yes, my darling. I plan to stay married to you, loving you, and kissing only you, my adorable, sexy husband, for the rest of my life." She kissed him like a wife who wanted her husband to know beyond any doubt that she was serious about their marriage and a real relationship.

When he held out his hand toward her, she placed her hand in his, and they walked down the hallway. At his bedroom door, she leaned up and kissed him tenderly. This was the man she was falling in love with and the one she wanted to stay married to and love forever.

Chapter Thirty-eight

The next day, Trista and Hud had been busily working at their computer stations for a few hours, acting almost as if nothing personal had altered between them. But then, unexpectedly, he bent down and toyed with some of her hair around her ear. The ticklish sensation brought her entire focus to his silver-black eyes and his handsome face. "Will you go out on a date with me tonight, Tris? Dinner and a movie?"

She recalled how she'd told him she wanted them to go on dates together. How thoughtful of him to remember and act on it so quickly.

"I would love to go out with you." She leaned toward him to kiss him, but a promise she'd made to Layla flashed in her thoughts. Tonight she had to help her with a family-tree class project. Even though Layla was only in kindergarten, her teacher assigned a monthly project for them to work on together. Unfortunately, she'd saved this month's assignment for the last night.

"Good. Because I already made reservations for us. It'll be—"

"Hud, I'm so sorry, but Layla needs my help with a school project tonight. I promised her I'd be available."

"What?" He dropped down on the edge of his chair, his jaw dropping. "You said you wanted us to date."

"I did! I do! But Layla has to turn in her project tomorrow."

"Can't Beth do that with her?" He cringed. "Sorry. I know you must keep your word to her."

"I really must. I've passed off a lot of parenting responsibilities to Mom lately, what with our wedding and all." Had her lapse in attention contributed to Layla's angry reactions toward Hud? "This can't be helped. I'm sorry."

"I understand. I'll cancel the reservations."

"Thank you." She clasped his hand resting on his thigh. "I would love to go out with you tomorrow night. Will that work instead?"

"Of course. Does this mean you'll be staying at Beth's tonight?"

"Would you mind terribly?"

"I'll miss you terribly."

"I'll miss you too." The timing was awful for her to shirk their first post-wedding date. In her heart, Trista wanted to leave work right now and curl up with her husband for the rest of the day. But duty called. Motherhood called. She felt torn between the two worlds of being Hud's real wife and a good mom to Layla. How would she ever blend them successfully?

Trista heard Hud canceling the reservation. Then they worked for an hour before speaking again. She hoped doing the required monthly project with Layla wouldn't make things awkward between her and Hud, especially when their relationship had taken such a beautiful turn yesterday. She fixed two cups of coffee and brought one over to him. "Feel like taking a break yet?"

"Sure. Thanks." He took the cup and drank from it. "Mmm. Hits the spot."

She pulled her chair over to his and sat down. "I have a question about your condo."

"*Our* condo?"

"Yes. Would you mind if I decorated the guest room in colors Layla likes?"

"Oh. I guess not." He cleared his throat and looked away like the idea might bother him a little.

"I don't mean to push into your domain. But if we are going to convince her it's a kid-friendly place, we should probably make her room into a space she'll enjoy." She felt awkward even suggesting they redecorate his guest room like she was taking over. But he had called it "our condo." When he didn't meet her gaze, she asked, "Are you still upset about the canceled date?"

"Just disappointed. And it's not my domain. We're married, so it's yours too." He smiled kindly, but not with the wide compelling smile she loved.

"I'm disappointed about missing our date too."

"You are?" He expelled a breath as if he'd been holding it.

"Of course I am. I want to go out with you, Hud." How could she explain how she felt split between her desire to be the best mom she could be and wanting to spend time with her new husband? "Sometimes I'm going to be busy with Layla. She's a huge part of my life. You knew about my commitment to her when you asked me to marry you." She tried to say the words gently. "She's five. She'll need me for a long while still."

"I know. It's just—" He sighed. "Never mind. It's fine. Really. We should get back to work."

She tugged on his hand. "What were you going to say? I want to know what's on your heart—my husband's heart."

He gazed at her for several long seconds. "I enjoyed our time together yesterday. I was hoping for more time alone with you, that's all." Finally, he smiled at her in a way that looked more genuine.

Determined to let go of her coworker persona and embrace her newlywed role, if only for a few moments, she scooted onto Hud's lap. His eyes widened.

She took his cup and set it down, then stroked her fingers down his cheeks. He blinked slowly, an inviting smile crossing his mouth. She pressed her lips to his, kissing him like a chocolate connoisseur hunting for the richest chocolate in the land. Hud's gentle caress and how he molded her closer in his arms proved he was the perfect candy for her heart's desire. She broke the kiss first, leaving an inch of breathing space between them. "Did I mention I like kissing you?"

He chuckled lightly. "You may have mentioned that last night. Uh, Tris?"

"Hmmm?" She kissed him again.

"I thought you didn't want us doing this here."

"I changed my mind."

"I'm glad."

She scooted off his lap. "But now it's time to get back to work!"

"Yes, ma'am."

Their gazes held until she sat back down in front of her computer. She had to force herself to concentrate on the day's tasks instead of talking Hud into leaving work early and heading to his apartment. By the warm look on his face, it wouldn't take much convincing at all.

Chapter Thirty-nine

Hud finished his call, then glanced at his phone screen to make sure no one else had tried contacting him while he'd been conversing with a possible investor. Maybe he would run home and freshen up before the dinner meeting he'd scheduled. He checked off some items on his daily planning software, mentally shutting down business for the day. Suddenly, Trista stood beside him, frowning at him. "What? Is something wrong?" He stood quickly.

"Who were you talking to a minute ago?"

"Melissa Mills."

"And she is—?"

"A potential investor. What's with the look?"

"Were you making plans to meet her for dinner?" She dropped her fists to her hips.

"Yes. That's a problem because—?"

"We're married!"

"What does my meeting with an investor have to do with us being married?" Wasn't Trista going to be busy tonight?

"You know what a husband should do before inviting another woman out, right?"

"It's not 'out' like a date." His hackles rising at the implication, he picked up his jacket. "She's an investor. I have appointments like this all the time."

"You used to have appointments like this all the time." Trista thrust her hands in the air. "If you and I are married for keeps—and after last night, I thought we were—then you should talk to me about these things!"

"Of course, we are married for keeps."

"Then you shouldn't be meeting women alone for dinner!"

"But it's how I've always conducted business." He tugged the top button loose on his shirt.

"Yeah. Back when you casually dated some of those same women!"

"Trista." He groaned. He hadn't considered how doing business as usual might affect her adversely or how he should be making different choices now that they were married. He'd arranged the dinner meeting without giving it much thought. "Does this mean I shouldn't ever meet with a female investor for a meal?" He put his jacket on and contemplated how to gracefully back out of the invitation to Melissa. Then, what Trista seemed to be implying hit him. "Are you saying you don't trust me to be honorable?"

"No. That's not what I'm saying." Yet she grimaced like that was precisely what she meant.

Her previous assessment of him being a player came to mind and it irked him. After taking things further in their relationship and how she kissed him a while ago, she still didn't trust him to be exclusively devoted to her?

"Then what? Because I am one hundred percent committed to you and our marriage vows." He let out an exasperated breath. "Why don't you trust me, Trista?"

"I am trying to trust you, Hud."

"Are you?" She cast a glinting gaze at him, and he said the first thing that came to mind. "I don't understand the big deal about my meeting with someone as long as it's in a public place."

"Even if it is," she said tightly, "I don't think you should be meeting alone with a woman."

He raked his hand over his hair. "Why—"

"Never mind." In jerky movements, she put on her coat. "I have to pick up Layla."

"Hold up a sec." He rushed to get between her and the door. "Let's finish this."

"Why? You're stubbornly going to do whatever you want without taking my concerns into account, aren't you?"

"Where is all this mistrust coming from?"

"You really want to know?"

"Yes, I do!" He'd never known Trista to be controlling or manipulative before.

"Why didn't I want to get involved with you in the first place?"

"Because you didn't love me."

"It was because you were a player—Mr. Butterfly tasting all the flowers."

"Trista—"

"Then you convinced me you hadn't gone out in a long time. That you were trying to change and become a man of integrity. Did I misunderstand you?"

"No. I was changing! I am changing! I want to be with you for the rest of my life." He paced six steps, then turned back. "What must I do to build your trust in me?"

"Start by not meeting alone with female clients. It gives the wrong impression."

"To whom?"

"Are you really this dense?"

"Apparently, I am!" He thrust out his arms. "Do you want me to call Melissa and cancel the dinner I invited her to? Do you think she'll invest in our company after that?"

"Just go ahead and decide on your own. I need to leave. Layla is expecting me."

"Please." He clasped her hand. "Let's not fight, okay?"

"This was an honest discussion. There's a difference between talking and fighting." She didn't say goodbye, which added to his conclusion that it was a fight.

Chapter Forty

"Where's Hud tonight?" Mom asked for the second time.

Trista had avoided answering the first time by busying herself with drawing the shape of a tree on a piece of cardboard with a black marker. Then, while she cut out a half-dozen leaf shapes to represent family members, Layla colored the tree branches.

"Honey bear?" Mom sat in the living room, knitting a small blanket with blue yarn. "What is troubling you? You've sighed five times." Had she? "And you didn't answer my question."

"Sorry, Mom. Hud is out with a possible investor tonight."

"That's good for new people to be included in the project, right?"

"Uh-huh." Trista sighed again. What was Hud doing now? Was he sitting across from Melissa, smiling and being charming? She gnawed on the inside of her cheek to stop herself from sighing again.

As Layla finished coloring each leaf lime green, Trista printed a name on it. She didn't usually mind the once-a-month project. But tonight would have been a perfect opportunity for her and Hud to go on a date—and for him not to be at a restaurant with another woman.

"If you two fought, call him. You should settle matters quickly with your husband."

"Mom—" Trista nodded discreetly toward Layla. She didn't want her daughter to hear about her and Hud having disagreements already.

How had things taken such a sharp turn after their time together at Hud's condo? And following their kisses at the office? Had she overreacted to his meeting with Melissa? Was this more about her insecurities and trust issues—not because of Hud's past or his acting anything but sincere about their marriage? She started to sigh but stopped herself.

"If you need to say something to him, say it," Mom said firmly. "He's your husband. If I'd been more forthcoming with your father—"

"Mom." Trista gave her a sharp look.

"I was married before. I know things. That's all I'm saying."

"Can this wait until later?"

"Sure, sure." Mom resumed her knitting.

Layla glanced back and forth between them, frowning.

"Don't worry, sweet pea. Everything is fine. Finish your family tree." Trista smiled like nothing was bothering her. "You're going to have so much fun showing this to your friends tomorrow."

"Do I have to put Hud's name on it?" Layla asked in a grumpy tone.

Trista recalled her own contemplations about what might happen if she encouraged Layla to care for Hud as a father and then he left. But on the heels of that thought came the remembrance of his promise to stay with her forever, making her wish she hadn't stated her opinion about him meeting Melissa quite so forcefully. "You don't have to include him, but Hud is part of our family now. Putting his name on your tree would be nice of you."

"All right." Layla huffed out a noisy breath.

Finally, all the hearts had names—Layla, Mommy, Grammie, Great Aunt Fanny, Miss Calico, and Hud. Layla glued each one to her tree, putting Trista's at the top, Hud's at the bottom, and the rest in between. With another monthly project completed, Trista sent Layla upstairs to brush her teeth and get ready for bed.

In a few minutes, she'd head up to read her a bedtime story. But first, she wanted to check her cell phone in case Hud had called or texted. He hadn't. Earlier, he'd told her he would be faithful to her—and she had been trying to trust him. So why did she keep entertaining doubts about him and comparing him with her louse of an ex? That wasn't fair to Hud. And it wasn't honest to herself, either. Hud wasn't like Neil!

But when she first met Hud, he had dated several women in the same week, some of them potential investors. The fact he'd planned a dinner with another woman today still ate at Trista like a bear devouring honey! Even though Hud hadn't done anything to make her think he was flirting with other women recently, what was to stop him from allowing a flirtation to go too far? Was he gazing at Melissa with shining eyes over candlelight? Were they laughing about their common goals? Attracted to—

"Mommy!"

"Coming!" Hurrying up the stairs, she silenced her inner turmoil so her daughter wouldn't sense her misery and become more agitated with Hud. After reading the next chapter in the book she and Mom had been reading nightly, Trista kissed Layla's forehead. "Love you, sweet pea."

"Love you, Mommy."

She sat on the bed for a few minutes longer, silently praying for her daughter and her adjustment to their new family dynamics. Now to face Mom. However, when she reached the last step of the stairway, Mom wasn't the one waiting for her in the center of the living room. "Hud." She gulped.

"Hey, Tris." He dug his fists deep into his jacket pockets. His hair appeared wind-tossed, or else he'd been raking his fingers through the strands. "Your mom let me in, then said good night and went into her room."

"You want some coffee?"

"No thanks. I thought we should talk in person." He blew out a long breath. "Can we sit down for a few minutes? I'll go if you want me to."

"We can talk." She sat on a chair near the couch.

He dropped onto the edge of the couch cushion, his elbows on his knees, his hands clasped loosely. "I'm sorry about our disagreement this afternoon." He met her gaze without looking away. "I didn't mean to disregard your feelings. I didn't understand them, but I always want to know your thoughts. My wife's thoughts are important to me."

His soft tone and how he called her his wife sent shivers through her. They had given themselves to each other as husband and wife. They needed to learn to work things out, no matter how embarrassing or difficult. She appreciated him coming over and attempting to do so now. "Thank you. And your dinner with Melissa?" she asked with a tight feeling in her throat. "How did that go?"

"It didn't. I cancelled."

"You did?" He'd listened to her and altered his plans? Warmth oozed through the cold, aching places in her heart.

"I wouldn't disregard your feelings and go to a dinner I knew would cause trouble between us. I'm sorry for setting it up in the first place." His eyes moistened and a tender expression crossed his face. "I'm hoping you'll be free to meet with us tomorrow night."

"Really?" This wasn't what she expected to hear when he didn't text her and then showed up here unannounced. She assumed he was stopping by following his dinner engagement with Melissa. She needed to work on not making assumptions about Hud and their future together. Now she felt foolish—and relieved beyond measure.

"I want to be a good husband for you, Tris. I confess I don't know how to do that." Shuffling his shoulders, he glanced around the room. "But if something makes you feel uncomfortable, even if it's a trust issue with me, I want to know about it. I will back off as much as possible and give you room to explain, breathe, or whatever."

"Oh, Hud." She nearly ran around the coffee table and dropped beside him on the couch, clutching his hands. "I'm sorry for over-reacting." She dug her upper teeth into her lower lip, closing her eyes for a second. Then, forcing herself to be honest and open with him, she gazed into his dark eyes. "I wasn't being fair to you. I was judging you based on how my ex treated me. And, admittedly, on your dating history. I know you aren't that kind of man anymore. However, I still have some insecurities about it."

"I appreciate your telling me." He let go of one of her hands and stroked some hair away from her cheek. "My insides were churning. I thought I ruined everything."

"If we're going to make our marriage work, we must talk things through even when we don't understand each other." She stroked her palm down his arm, letting go of the remainder of her angst. "I want to feel like you're listening and taking my thoughts seriously. Your doing that tonight touches my heart."

He linked their fingers together. "After I took a walk and considered what you said, I called Melissa. She was gracious about my needing to postpone. I didn't want her to get the wrong impression, either. I want you, and only you, Trista."

"Thank you. I apologize for my emotional upheaval and my suspicions about you."

He kissed her softly. "I apologize for being so dense."

"Thank you for coming over. I'll sleep better knowing we talked and cleared the air."

"Me too." Leaning back against the cushions, he tugged her next to him, and his chin came to rest against her head. She relaxed beside him, feeling like she was right where she belonged, finally. She sighed and closed her eyes.

At two a.m., she awoke to darkness and Hud snoring softly beside her. His arms were around her, and her cheek rested against his chest. Had Mom found them this way and turned off the lights? "Hey, sleepyhead." She moved slightly, peering at him through the dim light emanating from a night-light near the stairway.

He squinted at her. "We fell asleep?"

"Uh-huh. Do you want to drive home?" She lifted her chin toward the second floor. "Or do you want to sleep here tonight?"

"Wherever you are, that's where I'd like to be," he said huskily.

"All right." She stood and held out her hand toward him. "Come with me, then." And he did.

Chapter Forty-one

The next evening, Hud was grateful that Trista sat at the restaurant table with him and Melissa. The blond had come to dinner dressed in a wine-colored dress that plunged deeply at the neckline, and from the get-go, her mannerisms toward him were flirtatious. Hud assumed she acted that way around all men—not just him—but she repeatedly batted her eyes, smiled coquettishly at him, and reached across the tablecloth and stroked his hand or wrist. Every time, he discreetly moved out of her reach, but it was getting annoying.

After one of those awkward moments, Trista patted his thigh beneath the table like she was sending him a message. *"See, this is exactly what I was talking about."*

Throughout the meal, Hud kept trying to bring the conversation back to their mission of providing residencies for artists. Melissa seemed equally intent on discussing a big party she was hosting where he might be able to share his ideas with her guests. The way she singled him out made him more aware of the validity of Trista's concerns about him dining alone with Melissa. And to top it off, near the end of the meal, the woman confessed she'd already maxed out her annual charity budget.

"No worries. Thanks for giving my wife and me your valuable time this evening." As soon as it was polite to do so, Hud signaled the server for their check.

On her way out to her Uber vehicle, Melissa kissed Hud's cheek and smiled faintly at Trista, who had her hand linked in the crook of his arm. "It was lovely meeting you both."

"Likewise." The car pulled away, and he heaved a sigh. "Are you going to say it?"

"Say what?" Trista's eyes sparkled with mirth.

"That you were right about her?"

"You mean that Melissa Mills came to dinner for one thing—you? That the wedding ring on your finger did nothing to stop her from touching you. 'Oh, Hud, darling, you are such a great listener,'" she said dramatically, imitating Melissa's voice.

"All right." He pulled Trista into his arms and kissed her softly. "This is what I wanted to do all evening."

"Oh, yeah?" She smiled at him.

"Definitely." Tucking her hand back into the crook of his arm, he led her toward the rental truck they were using until their new vehicle arrived. "What shall we do now that we have the rest of the evening to ourselves?"

"Do you think Melissa was being honest about her funding being exhausted?"

"I guess. At least, we might be invited to a party to share with potential investors."

"You mean *you'd* be invited to a party as her guest!"

"I'm wiser now." He kissed her cheek. "I'll only go to her event if my lovely wife and business partner accompanies me."

"That's a relief to hear."

"Are you returning to your mom's or coming over to my place? I mean, our place?" He cringed over the mistake.

"Do you have any ice cream?"

"We did miss dessert." He tried picturing what he had left in the freezer as he helped her into the truck. "Will a quart of vanilla suffice?" Trista frowned like vanilla ice cream wasn't enticing enough. "And some delicious chocolate syrup?"

"That's more like it! Vanilla ice cream and chocolate syrup will be a perfect remedy for any disappointment I might have about tonight's dinner."

"Wait. Are you disappointed in me? Or in us?" Concerned, he stood outside her door, waiting, his heart drumming a strong beat in his chest. Was something about tonight's dinner troubling her? Had he said something stupid?

Grabbing hold of his jacket, she tugged him toward her and pressed her lips against his in a hungry kiss. "Does that answer your question? If not, let me say I am not disappointed in you or our marriage. We're figuring things out as we go, aren't we? And this part?" She kissed him softly three more times. "I like this part with you a lot." She winked playfully. "However, I may have been a tad disappointed about sharing you with someone else."

"That, I understand." He gave her a quick hug. "I don't like sharing you with anyone, either."

Back at the condo, they dished up bowls of ice cream with warmed-up chocolate syrup drizzled over the top. Then they sat close together on the sofa, eating dessert and watching *Sleepless in Seattle*.

"This is a perfect date." Trista put a bite of chocolate and ice cream in her mouth. "And great ice cream!"

He could sit here all night, watching her eat dessert and never tire of it. A dab of dark syrup teased him from the corner of her mouth. Only one way to fix that! He kissed her cool lips, and Trista responded to his affection with a kiss and a soft smile.

This woman who used to be only his business partner was quickly becoming someone very special to him. How long would it be until they both fell completely, irrevocably in love with each other?

Chapter Forty-two

A few days later, Hud sat at his desk, sipping coffee and checking the most recent data from their contractor. He double-checked the list of materials for the first houses, including all the supplies they would need for the project's initial phase. He was trying to be as thorough as possible to circumvent any missing parts, especially considering Ketchikan was on an island and all the building materials would be arriving via barge.

Timing for this build was critical. Between the current rainy time of year and the rainy fall season, he hoped the crew had enough time to get the first row of single-bedroom houses finished. Then Trista would oversee all the interior decorating operations. Before long, they'd get to see their dream come to life.

Today, the retaining wall was being built. Hopefully it would keep any mudslides from hitting the houses in the future. Since a good portion of the hill behind the property had come down, the inspectors assured him the wall would be the final line of protection in the future.

Deep in thought, Hud barely heard his phone buzzing. He glanced at the screen. Aiden? "What's up, bro?"

"Not much."

"I haven't heard from you in ages. Did you get my text about me getting married?"

"Yeah, man. I can't believe you married your business partner," Aiden spoke methodically as if mulling over each word. "You and Lake both getting married for money? Dude. That's not cool."

Hud clenched his teeth to stop himself from saying something rude to his only biological brother. "But you understand why I did it, right?" He made a conscious decision not to say, "why I *had* to do it." Marrying Trista had been his choice—one he was becoming more thankful and pleased about every day.

"Because you needed the money? Who doesn't? I wouldn't marry someone for the evil mammon!"

Hud bit back a groan. It wasn't like he'd planned to take the money or marry as he did. In the past, he would have verbally contended with anyone who even hinted that he'd go along with a less-than-ideal marriage to get the inheritance. So why was he frustrated with his brother's negative opinion about it now? "I meant about us building the artists' community."

"Yeah. But you promised not to take the money, even to stop a national disaster or to avoid bodily harm." Aiden moaned. "Sounds like you got Spur and Wilks awfully riled up."

"Lake and I took care of them in our way." Hud was ready to move this conversation to another topic.

"Does Mom know about you guys fighting?"

So he'd heard about that. "Is that what you called to harass me about?"

"Not just that. Were you serious about me having a place to stay rent-free?"

Hud breathed a sigh of relief that Aiden hadn't called just to argue about his and Trista's marriage. "Absolutely. We plan to have ten houses ready by September."

"What's the catch?"

"No catch. Each resident must give back something artistically to the community."

"Like a sculpture?"

"Right. Or speaking at seminars or giving art demonstrations, that sort of thing." Hud cleared his throat. "Are you ready to take a break from Denver and see some Alaskan scenery?"

"I'd like to scrounge around for metal there."

"Great! Does this mean you're interested in the first house we have finished?"

"Totally interested. Money is scarce." Aiden coughed. "But I'll figure out a way to swing a plane ticket."

"The flight is on me."

"No way. I can't take your charity."

"Aiden. The funds for your flight will not be a problem." Hud rarely pondered his enormous bank balance—even after the hefty payouts for their project, paying off Beth's house, reimbursing Trista's savings, and buying a new truck. But he'd gladly provide a ticket and whatever else his brother needed to transition to Southeast Alaska. He was the main reason Hud had wanted to build the art community in the first place. "I mean it. I will buy your ticket up here."

"If you're sure. Thanks, bro." After a pause, Aiden asked, "So, how is the marriage to a stranger going?"

"It's none of your business!" Hud wanted to say. But since his kid brother sounded more curious than rude, he answered honestly. "Trista isn't a stranger. I already care for her a lot."

"As in how you cared for all your other dates?"

"Aiden. It's private, okay?"

"Yeah, yeah. So is she nice?"

"Very nice. Beautiful and sweet. However, she has a five-year-old daughter who hates me."

"Hud, the kid repellant!" Aiden chortled. "You know what works great with kids?"

"No, what? I could use some pointers."

"Paint."

"Huh?" Hud scratched his scalp.

"Paint with the kid." Aiden's voice rose passionately. "Let her splatter colors all over a wall like confetti. She'll love you forever." Art was Aiden's love language. Hopefully, one day, he'd meet a woman who appreciated his artistic side. "Make sure you get lots of pink paint."

"Pink, huh? I'll think about your suggestion."

"You'd better."

They chatted for a few more minutes, then Hud ended the call. He didn't know if painting a room pink would help Layla like him better. Trista had mentioned redecorating the guest room for her. Would an activity like painting together be a chance for him to get Layla to warm up to him as a potential dad? It might be worth a shot.

Chapter Forty-three

The decorating crew Trista had hired for their project agreed to secretly create a pink bedroom for Layla at Hud's condo. Over the next few days, they painted the walls of the guest room a rosy color and brightened up the bed with a matching bedspread and pillows with princess designs. They piled one corner of the bedroom with stuffed animals, and another nook looked like a cozy reading area with a small rocking chair and a bookshelf filled with books.

Hud was delighted with the team's work. But would the decorated room be enough to entice Layla to leave her grandmother's house and move in with Trista and him? One wall remained untouched. Taking Aiden's advice, Hud planned to ask Layla to paint the feature wall with him.

Eager to show Trista and Layla his surprise, he invited them over for a homemade spaghetti dinner on Friday night. The simmering sauce filled the room with delicious scents of garlic and onions. He was just finishing up lighting the three candles he'd put on the table, when he heard Trista using her key to open the door.

"Hud? We're here. It smells fantastic!"

"I'll be right there!"

"Do we have to eat here?" Layla asked in a grumpy tone.

"Yes, we get to eat here. Please, be nice."

Hud hustled into the entryway. "Sorry about that. I had some last minute details. Welcome!"

"That's okay." Trista kissed him lightly on the lips.

He stepped back abruptly so Layla wouldn't get upset about them kissing. "How are you doing, Layla?" He took her coat and hung it up on the rack.

"Not good. I didn't want to come over here."

"Layla!" Trista said.

Hud slapped his forehead dramatically. "Don't tell me you hate spaghetti?"

"No. I love spaghetti!" Layla made a face like she thought he was ridiculous.

"You hate chocolate cake, then?"

"Huh-uh. I love chocolate cake!"

"That's good because we're having both for dinner." He winked at Trista and led them to the table that was already set.

"Everything looks great!" Trista said, then let out a soft gasp. "When did you have the photo done?" She was staring up at a photo of them that he'd had enlarged and placed above the mantle. It was a snapshot of him with his arm over her shoulder in front of Mom and Dad's house the day they left Thunder Ridge.

"Mom sent it to me, and I got it enlarged locally."

"I love it!" Trista put her hands over her heart and sighed.

"Where's my picture?" Layla asked.

"We can have one of you made, too, if you'd like," he said.

"Wouldn't that be nice?" Trista smiled. "Maybe a family photo of the three of us?"

"And Grammie!" Layla lifted her chin and shuffled over to the table. "Why are these candles going?"

"To make the table look pretty." Trista met Hud's gaze and shrugged as if her daughter's attitude stymied her, too.

"Everything's ready. Let's sit down." He helped Trista with her chair. By the time he got to Layla, she was sitting in the chair he'd planned to use for himself, so he dropped into another seat.

"It looks and smells delicious," Trista said.

"Shall we say grace?" Hud led them in a prayer. Then he served noodles and meat sauce and made sure they each had enough cheese, garlic bread, and napkins. Before he'd even taken a bite of his food, Layla spilled her water. He hopped up, grabbed a towel, and mopped up the liquid, trying not to let anything dampen his mood. This was their first family dinner at his place, and he couldn't wait to share the guest room surprise. Much of their future happiness rode on Layla adjusting to living here, so he would do whatever he could to make that happen.

"That was so good, Hud. You are an amazing cook!" Trista said after they'd eaten the spaghetti and chocolate cake without any other spills or catastrophes.

"Thanks. I'm glad you liked it."

"What do you say?" She prompted Layla.

"Thanks, Hud. Can we go home now?"

Hud stood quickly. "I have something I'd like you to see first." Waving for them to follow, he hurried to the guest room door and flipped on the light. "Surprise!"

"Oh, Hud!" Trista stepped into the room, tugging Layla along with her.

"Whose room is this?" Layla sniffed. "It smells funny."

"It's the scent of fresh paint. This room is for you."

"I have a room at Grammie's house."

"I know. But this is your room, too."

"I don't need another room."

"Layla. Let's see what Hud did for you, all right?" Trista drew her toward the reading corner. "Look at all these books. And the cute chair, a lamp, and everything!" Trista glanced back at him. "When did you do all of this? It looks fabulous!"

"Thanks. I had some help from the design group." He obviously hadn't won Layla's heart with his actions, but Trista seemed pleased.

"Now can we leave?"

"Layla," Trista said firmly. "What do you say to Hud after he's gone to all this effort to make a nice space for you?"

"Thank you." She didn't sound the least bit appreciative.

"No problem." He pointed at the blank wall. "Did you notice this wall isn't painted? It's a feature wall."

"So?"

"Would you like to come over tomorrow and paint it with me?"

"Why would I do that?"

"I thought we could do some splatter painting together."

"Doesn't that sound like fun?" Trista nodded.

Layla nibbled on a fingernail and didn't answer.

"My brother, Aiden, is an artist. He says painting is great fun."

"I like painting." Layla's half-hearted admission was the only sliver of hope that Hud's efforts hadn't been in vain.

"So, how about you and me having a painting party?"

She shrugged and scrunched up her nose like she wasn't that interested.

Trista met Hud's gaze over Layla's head. "Thank you," she said quietly. "It's a genius idea to paint with her. She's going to love you."

"That's the idea." He kissed her cheek quickly. "Maybe her mama will love me too."

Chapter Forty-four

Layla cried for fifteen minutes straight after Trista dropped her off on Saturday morning. Hud didn't have a clue what to do with a weeping child! Even though he'd set a plate of donuts and a glass of chocolate milk on the table for her, she turned up her nose at them and continued crying.

"You're still going to paint with me, right?" He leaned against the wall near the hallway, waiting for her to snap out of her funk.

"I want to go home." She turned the easy chair toward the living room window, the back of it facing him. After a while, her loud cries subsided to low moans and sniffling.

His phone vibrated, and he glanced at the screen. *Any luck with Layla?*

Nope. He inserted a crying emoji.

Sorry. She's been upset ever since she woke up this morning.

Should we cancel? He hated putting off painting for another week. Trista wouldn't move in with him for months at this snail rate.

Is that what you want to do?

No. But I don't want her to hate me, either.

Let me know if you want me to come and get her.

He tucked his cell phone back into his pocket. "Would you like to splatter paint with me now?" Layla didn't answer. "Painting sounds like a lot of fun to me."

Slowly, she turned the chair in a counter-clockwise circle. She wiped her sweatshirt sleeve over her red face. "What is splatter painting?"

"We'll flick paint all over the wall like this." He acted out speckling paint onto the living room wall with an imaginary brush. "It'll be like an explosion of color!"

Her eyebrows dipped in concentration. "I've never done that before."

"Me either. I have turquoise, purple, orange, and pink paint."

"No lime?"

Great. The one color she wanted, he didn't have. "No lime. Sorry."

Layla huffed. Then, as if she were about to face a horrible ordeal, she stood slowly and straightened her shoulders. "I guess I can paint for a little while."

"Good."

"Then I want to go home."

"Okay." He led the way into the guest room that he hoped would soon be her room, even though this painting session wasn't off to a very good start.

Since they wore old clothes, they wouldn't have to worry about getting paint on themselves. Hud was mostly concerned about paint droplets landing on the carpet or the new bedspread, but he wouldn't stress out about it. He pointed to the small plastic containers he'd arranged in a line. "Let's each choose a color, then start splattering."

"Wait until I tell my friends at school that my *maybe* dad let me throw paint at my new bedroom wall."

Maybe dad, huh? Her assessment of him hurt his pride, even though she had claimed the room as hers. "What color do you want to start with?" he asked with less enthusiasm than before.

"Blue—since you don't have lime green."

"Okay." He handed her the small container of turquoise. "Stay on the plastic sheeting if possible. I'll do the pink." She gawked at him. "What?"

"You look more like a brown-paint guy."

"Why is that?"

"Your apartment looks like mud."

Mud? He sighed. Yeah, to a kid, his condo probably did look drab and boring. Most of his furniture and decorations were gray or black. "This room will be the most colorful room in the place."

"That's because I'm the most colorful!" She lifted her chin disdainfully, and he nearly burst into laughter.

Layla flicked turquoise paint onto the white wall, and Hud caught a brief smile crossing her mouth. Maybe she'd enjoy herself, after all. They worked for a half hour, splattering the four colors. When they came to a good stopping place, he convinced her to take a break and have some snacks while the paint they'd used so far dried.

They cleaned up and were gobbling down donuts and fresh chocolate milk when Layla tapped his arm. "Why did you marry my mom?"

"Uh. Well. It's complicated."

"When I asked her if she loved you, she didn't answer me, either."

What was he supposed to say to that? Hud swallowed hard. *Lord, some help here would be appreciated.*

"Do you love Mommy?"

"I'm falling in love with her." He wanted to be as honest as possible without divulging information better left unsaid. Trista wouldn't appreciate him telling Layla too much about their arrangement.

"Why isn't she falling in love with you back?"

"Good question." Hud decided to change the topic. "Do you like flying in a jet?"

"I don't know."

"I'd like you to meet my family—my mom, dad, grandmother, and some of my eight brothers."

"Eight boys are a lot of boys." Layla coughed on the large bite of donut she stuffed in her mouth, then drank some noisy swallows of milk. "I'm the only kid in my family."

That might not always be the case, but Hud figured this wasn't the time to mention it. Instead, he said, "I'd like to adopt you."

"Why?" She held the glass midair, halfway between her mouth and the table.

"Because I want your mom, you, and me to be a family." A thought came to mind. "You'll get eight uncles in the deal, too."

She set her glass down hard. "What about Grammie?"

"She will always be your grandmother."

"Do I have to stay in that pink bedroom?"

"I thought you liked pink. And I hope you will want to stay here."

"Not without Grammie!"

This subject might be more problematic than a single painting session would smooth over. If he said the wrong thing, he'd only make things worse.

"I want to go home!"

"Aren't you going to paint with me some more?"

"No!" She stomped into the bathroom and slammed the door.

Great. Hud sighed and pinched the bridge of his nose. *Heading your way,* he texted Trista. "Get your coat on," he said when Layla came out of the bathroom. "I'm taking you home."

"Good!" She didn't speak to him for the whole drive back.

So much for his grand idea about painting a wall together fixing the disparity between them. He'd give Aiden an earful when he spoke with him again!

Chapter Forty-five

"I'm sorry things didn't work out better with Layla." Trista was looking over some wallpaper swatches while Hud drove them to the jobsite on Monday morning.

"Yeah, me too. I had everything riding on that one plan."

"Give her another chance, will you?"

"You mean paint with her again?" He met her gaze with a scowl before returning his attention to the road. "Honestly, it was a disaster!"

"Please? She's a kid who doesn't know that doing fun things with a dad would be great."

"She called me a *maybe* dad."

"Oh, Hud. Where does she get these things?"

"I have no idea. But she wants your mom to move in with us."

"What would you think of that?" Trista bit her lip to stop herself from laughing at his horrified expression. "Relax. I'm teasing. However, I told you Layla is very attached to her."

"Where does that leave us?" He clasped her hand while steering with his other hand. "I want us to be together."

"I want that, too, but I have to work this thing out with Layla." They'd entered marriage so quickly. Perhaps she hadn't broached the topic of the three of them becoming a family with Layla well enough—especially about them moving into Hud's apartment. She had to tread carefully since she didn't want her daughter to have emotional problems at school or throw more temper tantrums. She was already resorting to tears too often. "Would you consider having another painting session with her?"

Hud returned both his hands to the steering wheel. "If I did, do you think she'll warm up to the idea of us living together?"

"I hope so. At least for her to get beyond calling you a *maybe* dad. We'll work out the rest, somehow." Did he hear the hesitancy in her voice? How long would the process take to get Layla to warm up to him?

At the jobsite, they went in separate directions with plans to meet up and compare notes later. However, the rain came down intensely while Trista was talking with the contractor, and she made a mad dash for the shed. Relieved to escape the pelting raindrops, she was pleasantly surprised to find Hud already there.

"Hey, Tris." He had blueprints spread out over the wooden countertop. "I thought I'd check a few things during the downpour."

"Good idea." She brushed raindrops off her shoulders before standing next to him and looking at the prints, too. Being in this cozy shed with him brought back a flood of memories. "Does being here remind you of anything?"

"I recall a cute woman resting in my arms all night here," he said in a husky tone.

"Is that right?" She smiled, enjoying meeting his warm gaze and hearing his flirty tone.

"When we're alone in this shed, I can't help but want to do something like …" He drew her to him, and they kissed tenderly. His gentle touch and the way he held her close ignited a string of heated reactions in her. Her heart pounded hard. Her thoughts whirred with memories of other times when they kissed like this. "Tris?" His cool lips brushed her jawline. "I love you."

She went completely still. He'd gone from *falling* in love with her to *being* in love with her already? Panic ignited in her brain. She leaned back and hesitantly met his gaze. How could he be in love with her when it had only been four weeks since their wedding? How would she ever catch up with him emotionally if it were true?

"I'm sorry if that was too soon for me to say the words."

"It isn't that." Yes, it was!

"Then what is it?" Hud brought her hand to his lips and kissed her knuckles, causing ticklish sensations to dance up her arm. "You went from kissing me hungrily to looking like you lost your best friend." He'd read all that in one look? "Is this about the problem with Layla not liking me?"

"No." She gulped. She didn't want to hurt his feelings or ruin the tenderness they'd shared over the last weeks, but she had to be honest with him. "I'm just not ready to tell you those words yet. I'm so sorry." Hud had caringly expressed his love for her, but she couldn't assure him of her feelings when she still felt uncertain about too many things.

"Don't worry about it." He stroked his fingers down her cheek softly. "They will be more meaningful when you're ready to say them."

"What if I never—" His lips pressed against hers again, stealing the words from her lips and heating her core.

"You will. When you kiss me back like that, I know." He grinned so confidently it unnerved her.

"Maybe I'm faking how I feel," she said jestingly. But when Hud tensed and backed away, she wished she hadn't been so flippant.

"Are you faking you enjoy my kisses, Trista?"

"Hud, no. I shouldn't have said that." She groaned. "When we kiss, I'm transported to a delightful paradise. It's when we stop kissing that I thud to the ground. That's when I must figure out how kissing you and being in your arms fit with me being a mom and your business partner."

He sighed and hugged her gently. Leaning her cheek against his damp coat, she closed her eyes and enjoyed the rhythm of his heart beating beneath her ear. But thinking of the responsibilities they needed to take care of while they were here at the property, and that any of the workers could enter this shed at any moment, she stepped out of his embrace. "We should get back to work." And she had a lot to think about.

"If we must. Any chance you'd like to have dinner at my place? Maybe stay over?"

"Why don't you come to Mom's and have dinner with us?" She combed her fingers through her damp hair. "That way you can talk to Layla again."

"Oh, right. I guess that would be okay."

"We can make plans for the weekend for just us."

"Sure. That sounds good." He closed his eyes, took a deep breath, and then faced her again. "I don't mean to keep pushing you about moving in with me, but we are married."

"In a highly irregular marriage." She didn't want to offend him, but she needed him to understand. "My daughter's adjustment period is taking longer than we expected, but we're going to have to be patient about it. I can't move in with you until she's emotionally ready to do so also."

"I know. But I enjoyed it when you stayed with me. I'm eager to be with you as your husband." His humble tone and honesty eased some of the tension that had risen within her.

"I liked being with you, too. However, I have this other life I must try to merge with ours."

"I get it. I'm sorry for pressuring you." He leaned over his blueprints again.

"About dinner?"

"Whatever works for you is fine with me." He peered down at the drawing without meeting her gaze like he had before.

"See you later?"

"Mmhmm."

Since the rain had stopped, she walked outside in search of the contractor, but she already missed the warmth of Hud's arms and his smile.

Chapter Forty-six

Hud was glad he'd stopped at the hardware store on his way home from the office and purchased a can of lime green paint, since Layla's eyes glistened like shooting stars when he handed her a cup of the bright paint. "I like this color a lot!"

"Good. Flick as much on the wall as you want."

"Thanks, Hud!" She smiled like she was genuinely happy with the activity this time. "Aren't you going to paint, too?"

"I thought you might like to do this part alone."

"I thought we were going to paint together."

"We can. I mean, if you'd like me to, I will paint with you." What was with the change in Layla's attitude? Why was she acting friendlier toward him? Nothing had changed in their circumstances other than his buying the lime-colored paint.

She pointed toward the row of cups with various paint colors. "You could paint with blue, and I'll do green."

"Sounds good." He slipped out of his shoes, then rolled up his sleeves. He would have put on grungier clothes if he'd known he was going to paint. But even if his blue button-up shirt got ruined, if today's session brought Layla closer to agreeing to live here, it was well worth it.

She splattered some bright green paint onto the wall and laughed. "This is fun!" Maybe she was in a better mood today. Or else God was answering his and Trista's prayers already. "Hurry up, Hud!"

"I'm trying." He picked up the cup with turquoise paint. Following Layla, he flicked the blue color higher, then lower on the wall.

After a few minutes of splattering paint, Layla said, "I'm going to switch to pink." Ah, the pink. It was a good thing he'd filled the cup with rosy tint nearly to the brim. "Are you going to switch to another color also?"

"What would you suggest?"

"Orange."

"Orange it is." They painted for half an hour, alternating colors every so often.

The topic of dogs came up, and he told her about Lake's fascination with huskies. "Someday, we could go to one of his skijoring races." He held his breath, waiting for Layla to shout that she didn't want to do anything with him. Instead, she smiled and nodded. Had the sky turned purple? Or the moon blue?

"I hope Mommy lets me have a dog."

"Er, um, well." He'd rather avoid that topic. "Did you ever have a dog?"

"No. Mommy says when I'm old enough to care for one, she might let me get a small dog." Layla sighed like she was exasperated with the world. "Come on! I'm five!"

"Do you help take care of your grandmother's cat?"

"Miss Calico is old and boring. Did you have your own dog when you were a kid like me?" She gazed at him intently with her big green eyes.

"Just family pets. Lake was the one who pestered our parents about having his own dog."

"Pestered?" Her face lit up.

He probably shouldn't have mentioned "pestered" around an unpredictable five-year-old.

A few minutes later, she spread her arms wide toward the multi-colored bespeckled wall. "It's *beeeaaauuutiiiful!*"

"You're right." The wall's overall effect was surprisingly lovely. Maybe he'd suggest to Trista that they do a similar feature wall in the artists' houses. Layla could even assist with the painting.

After they washed their hands, Hud set out milk and some chocolate chip cookies he'd made. Layla plopped onto a chair at the table and grabbed a cookie. "How about if you tell Mommy I can have a puppy here?" She nodded eagerly and nibbled her snack.

He stifled a groan. How was he going to tiptoe around this subject? "I'm sorry, but I don't want a dog in the condo."

"Are you kidding me?" She wiped cookie crumbs off her face with the back of her hand. "If I can't have a dog, I won't move here! I only came over here to get you to talk to Mommy about getting me a dog!"

"That was the only reason?" Hud had hoped Layla was experiencing a change of heart and might be warming up to him due to their painting project. He'd obviously assumed wrong.

"Yes! Since your brother has lots of dogs, I thought you liked them too."

"I do. But I'm not a dog person like Lake."

"I only want one little doggie." She stuck out her lower lip, tears flooding her eyes. "Please?"

"It won't work here. I'm sorry."

"Why not?" Her face turned lobster red. "I want a puppy!"

"Are you ready to head back to your grandmother's house?" He was ready to take her back.

"You're rich, aren't you?"

His shoulders stiffened. "What does that have to do with any-thing?"

"Grammie says you have oodles of money." She lifted her chin, and her stance looked just like Trista's when she was annoyed with him. "How much is oodles?"

"A lot, I suppose." Talking about his finances with a five-year-old felt absurd.

Layla slurped her milk, spilling some in the process. "If you have oodles of money, and Grammie says dogs cost an arm and a leg, you must have enough to get me a puppy." Her mouth spread in a precocious grin with a milk mustache.

"I think you should get your coat on. It's time for me to drive you home." He'd had enough of Layla trying to manipulate him. She didn't move. "Let's go." He grabbed his keys off the counter.

"Mommy says you're going to be my dad." She scrunched up her face at him. "But a man who is too mean to buy a puppy for his daughter isn't a good daddy at all."

"I'm sorry you feel that way." Hud felt miserable over how bad of a turn this conversation had taken. So much for painting together helping anything improve between him and Layla. Strike two! "Let's get you back to your mom."

"I'm never coming back here again!" Layla stomped down the hall in jerky movements. She yanked her coat off the rack, throwing glaring darts at him over her shoulder.

The drive to Beth's was silent.

As Hud walked Layla to the front door, she mumbled, "Mommy wants to be married to you. But I'm going to tell her the truth about you."

"What truth might that be?"

"That you're a stingy, empty-hearted *nothing* dad!" She stomped inside and slammed the door. The lock clunked loudly into place.

Hud blew out a long breath. His lofty plans for the three of them to move into his condo as one happy family had just been obliterated.

Chapter Forty-seven

On her way to Hud's apartment, Trista picked up takeout burgers and fries, hoping it would suffice as a peace offering. Since Layla returned from her painting session with Hud, she'd been mopey and short-tempered. Trista asked how the visit went a few times, but Layla just repeated that she never wanted to paint with Hud again.

When Trista texted him to ask if something had happened between him and Layla, his response was brief and lacked the explanation she sought. Something negative must have transpired. But what? Layla could be strong-willed about wanting things her way. Trista had gone around and around with her enough times to know that. If Layla was rude to Hud, she'd try to smooth things over—starting with the dinner she was bringing over to his place. But she was worried about Layla also. If her miffed attitude continued, how long would they have to continue staying at Mom's? It had already been a month since Hud's and her wedding.

Hud answered the door and welcomed her in but didn't embrace her or kiss her, which was odd considering how affectionate he'd been with her lately. It seemed like another sign that things had gone sour between him and Layla.

Trista took off her coat and went straight into the guest room. The colorful paint speckles on the wall were fun and lively and brought some extra pizzazz to the room that was already wonderfully decorated. Hud and Layla had obviously painted together. There weren't any paint splotches on the floor—no accidents for Hud to be upset about. "It's beautiful! You and Layla are quite the artistic team!"

"Thanks." He shrugged.

"I got sweet potato fries to go with your burger," she said, hoping to elicit a smile.

"Sounds great." Yet he sounded defeated.

She carried the food bag into the living room. Then they sat on the couch, eating their burgers and fries quietly.

"Thanks for bringing these over." Hud nudged his fries away from the ketchup on his plate.

"Sure. Is everything okay?"

"Uh-huh."

"Was Layla rude to you?" She jumped into the topic that needed to be addressed.

"We don't have to talk about that."

"But I want to. Was she disrespectful to you?" He stuffed a fry in his mouth. "Hud? What is it?" Trista turned on the cushion to see him better. His eyelids were barely open. His lips arced downward. He kneaded his chest with his fist as if he were in pain. Remorse swept through her, causing an ache in her own chest. She was the one who encouraged him to ask Layla to paint with him again. She felt responsible for whatever had occurred. "Please, tell me."

Finally, he said, "She has some extreme opinions."

"Yes, she does. What was it about this time?"

"She wants a puppy."

That's what this was about? "Listen, I've had that discussion with her." She leaned closer to him. "Did she cry big fake tears?"

A half-hearted smile crossed his mouth. "Yes. And called me stingy."

"Oh, Hud." She chuckled until he turned a mournful gaze on her. "She's a kid who wants her way about having a dog. But you are not one bit stingy."

"She almost convinced me."

"That's because you have a tender heart under your tough-guy business persona." Trista kissed him, tasting his ketchup and spicy fries. "Are you okay?"

"Better with you here." He set their plates down, took her in his arms, and kissed her softly. She responded to his kisses, loving the warm feeling of being close to this man she cared about so much. Hud sighed and kept holding her. She leaned her cheek against his chest, hearing his strong heart beating. It felt like they were already a devoted husband and wife, sharing their lives with all the ups and downs and sweet times in between. He let out another long sigh.

"She really got to you, didn't she?"

"Yeah."

"It's sweet of you to worry and be troubled about her." She stroked his back. "But you can't fall for a five-year-old's tricks."

"Is that all it was?" He leaned back and rubbed his brow as if to ward off a headache. "An act to get her way?"

"I think so."

"I thought boys were the masters of pranks and the power of persuasion."

"Huh-uh. You have been Layla-ized!" Trista smoothed her hand over his scruffy jawline, liking the feel of his stubby bristles against her skin. "Despite not wanting a dog, you may have to come up with a way to convince her of your kindness and sincerity."

Hud flopped back against the cushion. "Don't tell me I have to paint with her again!"

"Not painting. But something at which she won't win."

"You think she won?" He let out a low growl.

"I'd say she thinks that. She may be small, but she is savvy." Trista picked up her plate and continued eating her burger.

"Do you have any suggestions?" He grabbed his plate too. "I was worried about you taking her side and wanting out."

"Out of our marriage? Are you serious?"

"I'm not father material—Layla made that clear!" He snorted. "You told me you have to blend the two sides. If it isn't going to work—"

"Hey now. I didn't say I was giving up. I'm here, aren't I?" She bumped her arm against his. "I could have joined Mom and Layla at the movie tonight. Instead, I'm sitting next to my kind, handsome, kissable husband." He gazed at her intently, his eyes moist and shiny. "What?"

"You're beautiful. I've been feeling self-absorbed, grumpy, disheartened, and inadequate. But you came here and cheered me up by talking with me and kissing me."

"That's how spouses should feel when they're together—like they are facing the world as one. And I like kissing you." She kissed him once to prove it. "However, I am sorry Layla is being such a pill." She picked up a fry off her plate. "You went to all that effort to have an activity with her, and it didn't turn out as well as we hoped. But the wall looks amazing!"

"Thanks." He set his arm over her shoulder. "I thought a similar feature wall might be nice in some of our artists' houses. It was easy to do."

"That's a great idea! I'd enjoy throwing some paint."

"Yeah? If we threw paint all over the wall right now, it might relieve some of my angst."

"You want to? I'm game."

"On second thought, I prefer this." He tugged her closer to him again. "Sitting together. Talking. Chilling like a romantic couple."

His lips met hers, causing a streak of heat to course through her internal system. Yes, this was much better.

After a while, Hud let her pick a movie. They dimmed the lights and watched *Leap Year* on his big screen TV. Sometime before the end, Trista dozed off.

Around midnight, she awoke, hearing Hud snoring softly in her ear. Unsure whether she should wake him up, she leaned her cheek against his chest again and fell back asleep, cozy and warm in her husband's arms.

Chapter Forty-eight

For breakfast the following day, Hud prepared his favorite homemade pancakes with huckleberry syrup. "You've never had pancakes until you try them like this!"

"Mmm," Trista said after the first bite. "These are fluffy and moist and amazing!"

"Thanks." Grinning, he lifted a whipped cream can. "It's even better with this."

"I'm already having a sugar buzz, but okay." She held out her plate to him. He swirled a glob of whipped cream in the center of her large pancake. She took a bite of pancake topped with whipped cream and sighed. "This is heavenly. Did you use a packaged mix?"

"Not on your life! A North man knows how to make pancakes from scratch. It was a staple in our household."

"You are officially in charge of making pancakes for the rest of my life!"

"Deal." He kissed her slightly syrupy lips. "And sealed with a kiss just like during our mock wedding ceremony."

"Only then I didn't do this." Grabbing hold of his shirt fabric, she kissed him. "Us having the place to ourselves is quite nice. It's like we're on our honeymoon."

"My thoughts exactly. We need more times like this." He was hoping they could spend the day kissing and being together.

"Enough distractions!" Giggling, Trista picked up her fork. "I have to focus on devouring all the pancakes in the land."

"Then what?"

"Then we should make plans and figure out what we're going to do about Layla being obstinate about living here."

"Oh, right." He felt some tension tightening up his neck and shoulder muscles. "What can we do about it? She seems determined to hate me."

"I'm sorry for how she's been acting." Trista moved her food back and forth on her plate. "I'm not excusing her behavior, but Layla is still adjusting to the idea of you and me being a couple, let alone having to move away from her grandmother." She linked her fingers with his and rubbed her thumb over his palm in a caress. "You and I are still working out our arrangement, too, right?"

"Yeah. I just thought—" How could he put his feelings into words? This closeness he was experiencing with Trista was the first time he'd desperately wanted to know everything about a woman and for her to honestly know his heart. It was tearing him up inside to be living separately from her. Yeah, he was probably being too impatient. But he hoped she felt the same way and wanted to know everything about him, too.

"What did you think was going to happen?" She tipped her head, smiling at him flirtatiously. A bit of whipped cream lining her upper lip tempted him to forget about eating pancakes and kiss her.

"I guess I thought after being together intimately that things would be different between us."

"You hoped I'd want to spend all my time here in your arms?" She grinned, and he couldn't resist kissing her.

"Something along those lines," he whispered. "I miss you when you aren't here with me. I'd like us to act more husbandly and wifely."

"Wifely, huh?" She winked and lifted her chin toward the sink, partially filled with bowls and mixing spoons. "Like me doing my share of kitchen duty?"

"I'm fine with loading the dishwasher and washing pans." He smoothed his fingers down her cheeks. "Doing it together would be even more enjoyable."

"Good to know." She ate a few bites of her pancakes, her gaze still latched on his. "Let's do something fun today."

"Yeah?" He felt a catch in his throat. Having fun sounded inviting. "Like what?"

"Let's do some things a married couple might do together."

"Hang out here? Go to a movie? How about dinner at a nice restaurant?"

"What do you think about us going to church?" Her eyes lit up. "Then we could grab a picnic lunch and go for a nice drive."

"Oh, right. It is Sunday." He ran his palm over his scruffy chin. "I suppose I'd rather hang out here with you, but I'll do anything so long as we can be together." Taking a breath, he returned to the food on his plate. "We should finish breakfast and get ready if we're going to make it to church on time."

"I usually go to church on Sundays, Hud."

"I know. I'm trying to do better about attending services, too." Despite his previous thoughts about staying here with his wife, going to church and talking to God about their situation was probably the best thing for them to do. No doubt his grandmother would heartily agree.

They slipped into a pew next to Beth and Layla an hour later. The girl dove into Trista's arms, and Hud scooted slightly away, knowing what kind of mischief she was capable of doing. But he wouldn't back away altogether. He and Trista needed to face this situation with Layla together.

Pastor Chad came by and shook their hands. He invited them to call or stop by his office if they needed anything or wanted to talk. Had Trista mentioned their situation to him? Or did Pastor Chad assume they might need counseling since they were newlyweds in a unique marriage?

Did they need to talk to someone? They got along well in business matters. Yet taking their relationship deeper into emotional closeness was more complicated than he'd imagined—especially with Trista's daughter acting so bad-tempered toward him. How were they going to get beyond that? *Lord?*

"Are you okay?" Trista whispered after Layla left for children's church without incident. He nodded but didn't want to explain his concerns here.

Holding hands with his wife through the sermon, Hud relaxed and listened to Pastor Chad discussing church history and people whose faith had made a difference for Christ. His interest was piqued when the pastor mentioned several names he'd heard about growing up. Pastor Chad spoke of John G. Lake's belief in the healing power of God, Jack Coe's radical faith, and the way God had used Smith Wigglesworth in his later years.

Then he told of a man who'd turned to God at an early age and had a burning desire to go to China as a missionary. His voice warming with the story, Pastor Chad shared how James Hudson Taylor pursued following God's will at any cost, then he encouraged the congregation to have a similar faith and purpose.

Hearing about Hudson Taylor, someone Smith had talked to Hud about many times during his formative years, warmed his heart and caused him to ponder some personal things. Was he willing to follow God's will at any cost? Even if that meant doing whatever was necessary for his new family? Was he willing to do anything he could for Trista and Layla?

Chapter Forty-nine

After church, Trista and Hud ate their deli sandwiches in the truck due to the windy, rainy weather, but the pullout overlooking the Tongass Narrows was a lovely viewpoint for a picnic. Hud had been quiet or introspective ever since they left the church, leaving Trista to wonder if something in the sermon had hit a nerve or if he was troubled about their marriage, the business, or something else entirely.

"This is a great sandwich." She lifted her ham and cheese on sourdough bread.

"I could have made it better," Hud said with a shrug.

"After the pancakes you fixed this morning, I don't doubt it!"

"When you move in with me, I'll make you as many delicious foods as you'd like."

"I'm looking forward to that part of our marriage."

"Just that part?" There was a catch in his voice.

"I'm sure there are plenty of fine things to look forward to about our marriage. Like the way you keep your bathroom clean and how you don't mind loading the dishwasher"—she attempted a teasing tone. "A girl appreciates such fine traits in a man." A more serious thought came to mind. "You do have large oceanside windows without any fingerprints on them."

"And?"

"Have you considered what a five-year-old living in your apartment might do to your attempts at tidiness?"

"I guess not." Frown lines creased his forehead. "Won't she clean up after herself?"

"Oh, Hud." Trista laughed.

"Does that mean no?"

"Did you and your brothers always clean up after yourselves when you were growing up?"

"No. But our parents and grandmother kept after us about it."

"And Layla has a mom and a grandmother who do the same." She felt riled over his implication otherwise. "However, I won't fight with her about it every minute. I'm saying you need to consider what Layla staying at your place will mean. Having a child underfoot may be difficult for you since you've lived the bachelor lifestyle for so long."

"You're probably right." He exhaled a weary-sounding breath. "I wanted you to move in with me quickly. I didn't consider all the other stuff. Still, we'll adjust. I'll adapt. I want to do whatever I can to make the transition easier for both of you."

"Thank you for that." Taking a few bites of her food, she let her reactions mellow before mentioning another topic that might be touchy. "What about us having other children? When we talked with Pastor Chad, you said we'd discuss it."

"You want to talk about that now?"

"Sort of. My biological time clock is ticking." He looked aghast like she might be suggesting they have a baby today. She patted his knee. "I'm not trying to pressure you into fatherhood, but I want another child. I'd like a sibling for Layla. Also, when we have stronger feelings for each other, it might be nice to have a child born of our love."

"I have strong feelings for you already, Tris." He clasped her hand gently. "About having a child, I want that too. Just—"

"Not right now?"

"Exactly. I hope we'll get closer and figure out about being married and being a family with Layla."

"I agree. And thank you." They had a lot of stuff to work out together, but every time he included Layla in their plans, it endeared him to her even more. "Eventually you'll be okay with us having more kids?"

"Yes."

"Good. That's all I'm asking."

They finished their meals in silence, watching the stormy winds churning the sea in the channel.

"What did you think about the pastor's sermon?" Hud's question brought her attention back to him. "It made me consider some things I heard growing up and stuff about my name."

"Tell me about it." She enjoyed hearing his stories about being raised in a household of nine boys.

"My birth parents named me after my maternal grandfather, but Dad—Smith—wanted me to be named after Hudson Taylor, the missionary, too."

"Did that bother you?" She inched closer to him, gazing into his eyes.

"Not when I was little. The stuff about names made me feel more like Lake and Coe's brother. Dad often told us stories about John G. Lake, Jack Coe, and Hudson Taylor." He sighed and leaned back against the seat.

"Just like in today's sermon?"

"Yeah. Strange, huh?"

"God works in wonderful ways to speak to our hearts, sometimes even in meaningful sermons." She stroked his arm. "What changed for you?"

"Teenage angst, I suppose. Dad didn't approve of some of my high school girlfriends. In college, it got worse."

"Those girls got you into trouble, huh?"

"You might say that."

"I had a troublesome relationship too." She winced, feeling a pang of remorse over some of the choices she'd made.

"Dad wanted the girl I married to be—" He exhaled. "Never mind. That's all in the past, anyway."

"We both have pasts. I know you've been with other women, Hud."

His eyes moistened. "Dad was right about one thing. I do wish I'd waited my whole life for you."

"That's sweet of you. And I would say the same thing, but I don't regret having Layla. She is a blessing to me beyond anything I've experienced." Hopefully he wasn't offended by the comment, but it was the truth.

"You're lucky to have her. And I'm lucky to have you in my life." He kissed her cheek. "I care for you so much, Tris."

"I care for you, too, Hud."

He stared at her intensely, his mouth opening slightly as if he wanted to say something else. Was he about to tell her that he loved her again? She wanted to hear it—boy, did she want to hear it—even if she wasn't quite ready to return the sentiment yet. "Shall we head home?" he asked instead of declaring any deeper feelings.

"Sure." She felt silly for being disappointed. Why should she expect him to say he loved her when she wasn't ready to say the words to him? She was falling for him, and she truly cherished their time together as a married couple. Was it possible she was already "in love" with him and didn't know it? But if that were true, would she still have doubts?

Hud put the truck in gear and headed back toward town. "I've been mulling over what Pastor Chad mentioned about us talking to him. Do you think it would help?"

"Talk to him about what exactly?"

"Our situation. Maybe he could help us overcome the uncertainties of melding our lives together." He slowed down the truck to accommodate a car braking in front of them.

"It might. Or if you wanted to talk with Pastor Chad, I could talk with April." Hud met her gaze and frowned. "You don't like that idea?"

"If we go to counseling, I'd rather we spoke to someone together." He cleared his throat and grimaced as if troubled by the idea of getting counseling at all. "What if we talked with my dad? Maybe in a Zoom call?"

"Hud—" She did not want to discuss marital intricacies with his father!

"Does that sound terrible?"

"On so many levels."

"All right. Shall I set up a meeting with your pastor?"

"I'm willing if you are." She glimpsed the channel between a couple of houses, noticing the whitecaps whipping around turbulently. "What do you hope to achieve with such a discussion?"

"Us getting closer to being a real married couple, I suppose."

"And love?" Was he trying to force that to happen too? Maybe to push her into saying the words before she was ready to express them? "Do you imagine we'll love each other more if we go to counseling?"

"No."

"Then what?"

"I'd hope for a better understanding of each other. A nudge toward better communication and us interacting like marriage partners." He shrugged a couple of times. "I'm sorry for being impatient about your moving in with me. It'll take more time, and that's okay. Maybe I am jumping the gun." He sighed heavily. "We probably don't need counseling at all."

"Maybe not." But she couldn't snub his efforts to understand her better and win her heart—and for them to work things out about Layla together. "I liked being with you last night. Eating your homemade pancakes this morning was incredible." She smiled at the memory. But she knew Hud wanted more from her. If the roles were reversed, wouldn't she want more from him?

What held her back from saying she loved him?

Chapter Fifty

Despite the busyness of getting everything arranged and ordered for their project and all the business calls he'd been making recently, Hud had scheduled a counseling session with Pastor Chad for the middle of the week. Admitting they needed help and coming in for counseling were difficult steps for him to take, but he wanted to do whatever would help Trista and him move toward a stable, loving relationship. Hadn't he challenged himself to be willing to do anything for his new family?

They had been sitting in the pastor's office for several minutes, waiting while Pastor Chad stepped out to take a call. Trista looked pale and was twisting her hands together. Did she feel as nervous about being here as he did? The emotional bond he'd felt with her on the weekend when she stayed at the condo had seemingly evaporated over the last three days, probably due to their workloads and her still living at her mom's house. "How are you doing?"

"I'm okay." Trista met his gaze briefly. "And you?"

"Okay." Although he was frustrated that they'd reverted to acting more like coworkers than spouses. Would this counseling session help with their transition to living under one roof? Would it do anything to bring them closer as husband and wife? As a real family? "Sitting in a pastor's office brings back bad memories of me being called into my dad's office."

The door opened, and the pastor rushed in. "Sorry. A parishioner needed prayer. Duty calls when it calls!"

"No worries." Hud faced him like he might face a judge—or his dad! How much gut honesty would be expected of him in today's session?

"I see apprehension written all over your face, Hudson." Pastor Chad settled into his chair.

"It's Hud. And that would be correct."

"Let me assure you, I am only here to listen and offer advice if needed." The pastor smiled and folded his hands on the desk. "Zero condemnation or judgment."

"That sounds good to me." Hud's uneasiness lessened. He glanced at Trista to see how she was fairing. Her hands had stilled. Her expression seemed less tense.

"So, Hud and Trista, what brings you here today? How is your newlywed adventure going?"

Hud figured he should take the lead since he was the one who'd suggested this intervention. "We're doing as good as can be expected considering the irregular beginning of our marriage."

"Are you here to discuss some of the problems you've encountered so far?" Pastor Chad glanced back and forth between them.

"Yes. As we navigate marriage without—" Hud cleared his throat. "We've had a few bumps in the road without both of us already being in love."

Trista's face reddened. Had he expressed the sentiment poorly? Pastor Chad had been her pastor for a long time. Perhaps she didn't want him to know certain aspects of their private lives. If so, they should have set some ground rules before coming here.

"Are you taking steps to improve that part of your lives?" Pastor Chad asked. "You're married, but are you spending quality time together? Going out? Doing romantic things?"

"Yes. But not as much as I'd like," Hud said. "Our work schedule has been frantic since we're in crunch time with a project. Always things to do."

"Sure. That's how it usually is with work, marriage, and life."

"I'm still staying at my mom's house," Trista said as if her place of residency was the cause of all their woes. That wasn't their only problem, but Hud appreciated her recognizing their staying in two separate places was part of the dilemma. As business partners, they'd worked through plenty of difficulties and complications. Why was working through personal and family obstacles so complicated?

"That's understandable, given the situation," Pastor Chad said. "Is there anything keeping you from moving in together?"

"My daughter is upset about leaving my mom. And about us moving in with Hud."

"So, you two still haven't—"

"We have." She lifted her chin, but her face flushed like she was embarrassed by the admission. "However, it's difficult to adapt to a married lifestyle while living in separate places. And working together while trying to figure out our feelings is challenging." She met Hud's gaze, and her shoulders sagged. He clasped her hand gently.

"Sounds like a rough beginning." The pastor nodded understandingly.

"It's been unusual," Trista said. "I've never been married before, and my parents divorced when I was young, so I have nothing to compare it to."

"Neither of us has been married," Hud added. "Any words of advice?"

"Falling in love takes time spent together. Building a marriage and family takes longer." Pastor Chad spread his hands toward them.

"You married before you had strong feelings for each other. Perhaps, you want to advance things faster than your circumstances dictate."

"I'd say that's right. I admit to being impatient about the process, even though I'm trying not to be." When Trista looked at him with a sympathetic expression, some of the internal weight he'd been carrying eased.

"Hud, as the man of the family, have you been praying with Trista?"

"About?" He turned his attention back to the pastor.

"About your marriage and trusting God to work everything out with your new family." That sounded like something Dad or Gran would say to him.

"Not really. We haven't been together that much—outside of work, that is."

"All right." Pastor Chad stared at a blank sheet of paper as if seeking an answer. "Trista, how would you feel about you and Hud praying together?"

"I don't have a problem with it." She let go of Hud's hand and combed her fingers through her hair like she needed something to do with them. "I've been praying about our relationship and Layla's attitude. But it would be nice if we prayed about those things as a couple, too."

"You could even pray over the phone if you weren't staying in the same house yet." Pastor Chad tipped his head, the gray streaks in his hair reflecting the overhead lighting. "I believe in couples praying together and trusting God for whatever situations they face in marriage or life."

Trista glanced at Hud. "Would you be okay with us praying together like that?"

"Sure." He took a deep breath. "If we stayed in the same place, it would be easier. Maybe you should explain about Layla." He'd appreciate some clarity about her, too.

"Okay. Layla has been my priority for five years." Trista picked at a cuticle on her thumb. "I've been a single mom for her whole life. I think that explains a lot."

"It does. With us having three boys, April's world revolves around our sons." Pastor Chad stroked his chin. "However, there was a time I feared her devotion to children and my commitment to the church wouldn't mesh."

Hud sat up straighter, listening closely.

"Fortunately, God shined a light on my heart. I desired a close relationship with my wife but didn't know how to achieve that." He tapped his Bible. "By basing our marriage on God's love and praying together, I became more vulnerable and honest with April. More tender toward the Lord, too."

Was the pastor implying that Hud had to be more vulnerable and honest with Trista? Like their inability to get past this thing with Layla was his fault? Like he wasn't doing enough to help them work things out? Feelings of pridefulness and being unjustly blamed rushed through him like a runaway train, combatting his peace of mind and newfound hope for their marriage.

Sure, he was the one who had asked Trista to join him on this unusual journey. He should be more patient. But wasn't he also the one who'd confessed his love for her? Hadn't he put up with the elbow jabs and kicks from Layla? Hadn't he gone the extra mile by having two painting sessions with her? Look how those efforts turned out! He sighed and stared up at the ceiling, questioning his decision to ask for this counseling session.

"Is there anything, in particular, troubling you, Trista?" Pastor Chad asked in a calming tone. "Is there a problem with Layla you'd like to discuss?"

"She isn't adapting to our new family as I'd hoped she would." Trista made a gulping sound. "Layla has become so attached to my mom that she doesn't want to leave her even for a night. Yet I feel a strong pull to live with Hud as his wife."

She did? Really? Hud's internal fuming sieved from him like sand trickling out of a funnel. He met his wife's teary gaze and felt compassion for her situation with her daughter. She'd agreed to marry him to help them both out of a financial bind, but she was facing a lot of personal adjustments—much more than he was. Man, he really needed to be more patient. And they needed more time to work things out together.

"I agreed to this marriage. I owe Hud my devotion and love, but I'm not there yet. I'm sorry, but I don't want to drag Layla to his apartment with her throwing a huge tantrum about it. I confess my mixed-up feelings about our relationship have been confusing." She gulped like she was near tears. "They are probably the cause of the problems between Hud and me." She shrugged and made an uneasy facial expression toward him like she was apologizing.

"It's okay. We're going to work this out together." He stroked a strand of hair back from her face. Even that slight touch between his fingers and her cheek sent warmth barreling through his internal sensors. "I want to know your heart, Tris, and for you to know mine. That's why we came here today—to figure things out together, right?" She nodded and sniffed. Seeing her even a little emotional made him want to pull her into his arms and comfort her. "Are you okay?"

"I will be." She took a tissue out of her coat pocket and wiped her nose. "Sorry. This is silly. I didn't think I'd cry."

"It's all right." Pastor Chad nudged a tissue box to their side of the desk. "Hud, what steps are you taking to help in this transition to a family of three? What are you doing to help Layla adjust to you being her dad?"

What was he doing? Had he done anything that had helped? "I offered to adopt her. And I painted a wall with her in the room that will be hers."

"That sounds like a creative thing to do." Pastor Chad eyed him. "Did she enjoy the activity?"

"Not really. She called me a *maybe* dad." Hud rolled his tight shoulders.

"Why did she call you that?"

"I don't know. It baffles me." Hud glanced around the small office with its tall shelves packed with books, feeling restless. "It's not much of an excuse, but I haven't been around little girls much. I'm from a family of all boys."

"A household of boys is different from one with girls only." Pastor Chad chuckled. "Although some things are the same. All kids want to have fun. Snowball fights. Sledding. Watching funny movies. Why don't you try some of those things?"

So earning Layla's trust really was up to him? When he'd asked Trista to marry him, he knew Layla was a big part of her life. Maybe he hadn't done enough to convince her that he'd make a good father. But how could he when he didn't know how to be a decent dad? And when he was still trying to convince Trista that he'd make her a good husband?

Chapter Fifty-one

Later that evening, Trista took a call from Hud. Closing her bedroom door so Layla wouldn't overhear her conversation, she tuned into his low voice. "I thought I'd check in and see how you're doing." While his words were polite and he sounded caring, Trista detected some tension, too.

"I'm okay." She sat down on her bed. "What about you?"

They'd returned to the office after their counseling session, but neither had mentioned anything about their talk with Pastor Chad. Since Hud clammed up after their discussion about Layla, Trista was left mulling over his reaction and his silence. What made him so contemplative? Was he questioning what he'd gotten into by marrying a single mom?

"I'm tired. Ready to call it a night." He paused. "I was wondering if we should, uh, try praying together."

Ohhh. He'd called to pray with her? Warm feelings and a sprinkling of hope settled over her. "Sure. I'd like that a lot, Hud."

"Shall I go first?"

"Okay." She closed her eyes, relieved that he had called. Surely his praying with her was a positive step toward them becoming a couple and a family.

"Lord, praying aloud like this is hard for me. Praying in front of Trista feels weird, too."

With his humble admission and the way he sounded so sincere, her heart softened a little more toward him. Her thoughts drifted back to the one time they'd been intimate together. Their closeness had been beautiful and tender and everything she'd hoped for with her groom. But the emotional struggles in the three-and-a-half weeks since then had stolen some of the vulnerability and affection she'd experienced with him. How could they get that back? Would praying together help them feel closer and more like they were a part of each other's life?

"I want to be a good husband," Hud continued prayerfully. "A good father, someday." *Oh, Hud.* "I'm lightyears away from being either." He made a sniffing sound like he was fighting some emotion. "I want to do better at following Your ways. I ask You to bless Trista's and my marriage." A long breath. "And bless Layla."

After a silence, Trista prayed too. "Thank You for sending me someone so kind and understanding as Hud to share my life with. He's a good man, and I have strong feelings for him." Hud made a huffing sound. "I ask You to make us into a real family—one who honors and loves You. In Jesus's name." She took a deep breath, letting out some of her worries and stress about their counseling session and the future.

"Thanks for that," Hud said. "Any plans for tomorrow?"

"Just work."

After a quiet pause, a flirtatious idea came to mind. She didn't know if she should mention anything so lighthearted following their thoughtful prayer time. But Hud was her husband. She wanted them to make headway toward feeling closer and being more romantic, even though they weren't living together yet. She took a breath and playfully said, "There's one disconcerting thing about my job."

"Oh? What's that?"

"I have an adorable boss who makes my heart nearly pound out of my chest every time I see him." She fought a grin.

"Is that right?" Hud chuckled.

"Mmhmm. I can't keep my gaze off him. I keep wanting to ..." She bit her lip, unsure how far she should take her flirtation.

"What do you want, Tris?" His rumbly tones stirred her emotions. She imagined his soft kisses the last time they'd embraced—how he stroked her hair away from her cheek and gazed deeply into her eyes like he could see into her soul.

"I keep wanting to kiss him. At work, I mean."

"Ah. Kissing at the office is against the rules, huh?" She liked that he was playing along and the tension she'd detected in his voice when he first called was gone.

"That's right. Workplace fraternization is off-limits!"

He chuckled again. "I know what you should do the next time you run into this guy."

"Yeah? What's that?" She leaned back against the headboard.

"Kiss him like you can't take another breath without touching his lips with yours. And tell him all about the wild crush you have on him."

"What if he fires me?"

"Love is worth taking a risk, isn't it?" Was he still talking about their imaginary situation of boss and employee? Or had he switched to talking about them as husband and wife?

"I guess I'll find out in the morning."

"I guess you will. Call and tell me how it goes, okay? Good night, Tris."

"Good night, Hud." She closed her eyes, picturing a smooching session worthy of Fourth of July fireworks and shooting stars when she kissed Hud at the office in the morning. Maybe she'd dress up a little and enjoy playing the part of a flirty office girl pursuing her boss.

Chapter Fifty-two

As Hud prepared for work, he eagerly anticipated Trista's promised kisses. He'd gladly play along with her flirting on the job. However, when he arrived at the office, Trista wasn't the one standing by the front door waiting for him. Melissa Mills, dressed in an expensive-looking coat and matching hat, stood by the office door, her red lips spread in a pouty smile. "Hudson North, I've been waiting for you in the cold for five minutes."

"I'm sorry. Did we have an appointment?" Fighting disappointment and the urge to ask her to return later, he unlocked the door and strode inside. Despite the fact he moved swiftly, Melissa slipped her hand into the crook of his arm and walked into the office beside him.

"No appointment. But I must speak with you. It's urgent!"

"All right." He disengaged their arms and flipped on the light switch. "Trista should be here any minute."

"I need to speak with you only." He tensed and stepped back. "Don't look so shocked. I meant for us to talk—nothing else." Yet her flirty smile implied otherwise.

"Why don't you have a seat? I'll get the coffee going." He waved his hand toward the work table, hoping Trista would arrive quickly—and that Melissa meant what she said about only wanting to talk.

"It's a quaint office you have." She strolled around the perimeter, ending up next to Hud as he prepared the coffee.

Where was Trista? Not only had the flirtatious exchange he'd been anticipating with her been thwarted, but Melissa being here might cause a problem. The woman hovered too closely and grinned possessively at him, which made him feel even more uncomfortable. How could he convey to her that he wasn't interested in any flirtatious behavior without offending a potential investor?

"Sugar?"

"Yes, please!" She batted her eyelashes at him.

"Er, um, cream?"

"Just sugar," she whispered. "I like things sweet."

His fingers fumbled as he fixed her drink and added extra creamer to his cup. *Come on, Trista. Hurry up and get here!* Hud led the way back to the table, pulled out a chair for Melissa across from where he planned to sit, then sat down in his chair. He wouldn't assist her with sitting or taking off her coat. The quicker she told him why she was here and left, the better.

Melissa didn't sit in the chair he'd pulled out for her. Instead, she sank into the seat next to his and smoothed her fingertips over his hand. "I need your help, Hudson."

He jerked his hand away and picked up his coffee cup. "What kind of help?" She squeezed his bicep as if checking his muscles. "Stop—"

The glass door opened, and Trista sashayed into the room, smiling. She wore a short skirt, dark leggings, and high heels that made her appear taller—and so adorable! But within seconds, her gaze zigzagged between him and Melissa, and with a look of mortification replacing her smile, she scrambled out the door.

"Trista!" Hud shoved away from the table.

Melissa clutched his arm. "Can't that wait?"

"No, it can't!" He rushed to the door and yanked it open. "Trista!" But she was already fleeing down the sidewalk. He groaned. What should he do? Run after her? Leaving Melissa in the office alone was out of the question. He'd cut this meeting short and then find Trista. He sat down stiffly in his chair. "What can I do to help you?"

"We don't know each other well, but it's about my son."

"Your son?" He frowned.

"He's difficult." Melissa played with a flashy ring on her finger. "You know how teenagers can be."

"Sure. I was one. I have younger brothers." If Melissa needed parenting support, she should talk with Trista. She was a mom. He knew nothing about being a good parent. He wasn't even very understanding of his wife's situation with Layla. "What does any of this have to do with me?"

"Only that you're a part of the male species." Melissa spread her dark red lips in a provocative grin.

"And I'm a married man." He held up his left hand with the wedding ring on it. "If I can help you, I will. But that's all the further it will go. I love my wife. Do you understand?" He wasn't usually so forthright with someone he barely knew, but he was determined to prioritize Trista and their marriage. He was drawing a line in the sand about Melissa's seductive behavior toward him, too.

"I wasn't aware you felt so strongly about marriage."

"Well, I do!"

"Fine." Melissa sighed dramatically. "Greggory is causing trouble at school and getting into fights. Truancy. That sort of thing." Her list of offenses about her son reminded Hud of his brother, Stone. Melissa wiped a lone tear from her cheek. "I've tried to get him to see the error of his way. We fight a lot."

"I'm sorry to hear that." He glanced out the window, checking for Trista. "But why come to me?"

Melissa took a sip of her coffee and grimaced. "Of all the men I know who might influence his life, I thought of you." Hud snorted. He was the last person on the planet who should be asked to help a teenager. "You're shocked?"

"I am. I'm not a parent yet."

"Still, there's something honorable about you. You've shunned even my slight attempts at flirtation."

Slight? Trista wouldn't think so. "I'm one hundred percent committed to my wife." Had he spoken insistently enough for her to believe him this time? He wasn't the least bit flattered by her flirtations. All he wanted to do was escort her to the door, lock the office, and find his wife. "About your son—what were you hoping I'd do?"

"Greggory needs guidance."

Hud's phone vibrated, and he answered without checking the caller ID. "Trista?"

"Lake."

"Can I call you back?"

"Bad timing?" his brother asked.

"You could say that."

"Let's talk later."

Hud ended the call and glanced at the screen to check for any texts or calls from Trista. Nothing. Was she waiting for him to reach out first?

"Would you consider mentoring my son?" Melissa asked.

"Mentoring?" Hud barked out the word like he didn't know its meaning. "I haven't made a breath of headway with my stepdaughter. If I can't change a five-year-old's attitude, I doubt I can influence a teenager."

"Will you try? I don't know who else to turn to."

"What about talking with a pastor? I can give you the number of someone my wife and I are seeing. Pastor Chad Gray at First City Fellowship has been helpful."

Her penciled eyebrows arched. "I didn't know you were a church-going man."

"I'm surprised about that too. However, I'm a pastor's son who walked away from spiritual things for a while. But my wife, who I care a lot about," he reiterated, "goes to Pastor Chad's church. Now we're going together. The pastor might have suggestions for you and Greggory."

She eyed him like he was a strange curiosity. "I'll consider it." She tugged on her lips with her teeth. "Can you meet with my boy? As you said, you were a teenager. You have brothers. You might instill something beneficial in him."

"Like what?"

"Integrity. Doing what's right. Make him listen to his mother!"

Hud sighed. Should he run this by Trista first?

"Please, Hudson?"

"I guess I can try," he agreed, mostly to end the discussion.

"Thank you!" Melissa spread her arms as if to embrace him.

He backed away, palms out. "On one condition—no hugging or touching me again!" She froze, lips poised in an air kiss. "Do I make myself clear?" He gave her a stern glare.

She wilted against her chair. "Perfectly." She pulled white gloves out of her ritzy-looking coat pockets and slowly put them on. "I don't know why you're having trouble with being a parent. Your voice and how you acted was just like my father."

Her censure, or her honest appraisal, made him wonder if he did have what it would take to influence her son's life. Maybe even what it would take to be a good father to Layla.

Chapter Fifty-three

Trista peeled off the tight leggings and threw them into a heap with the black mini-skirt she'd already tossed on the bed in Hud's apartment. She came here because she didn't want to go to Mom's and have to explain why she was dolled up, weeping, and angry. Why had she dressed up like that? Anyone could have walked into their office. Melissa Mills did!

Now Trista would have to return to the office and face Hud, even though she was still embarrassed about what happened—and irritated with herself for not marching into the office and giving Hud and Melissa a piece of her mind! Was Melissa gone yet? Seeing her sitting beside Hud with her hand resting possessively on his arm had been shocking and hurtful. Wasn't the flirtatious scenario precisely what she'd feared? That Hud might return to his old way of behaving around beautiful women? And if he did, that she would be left feeling as wretched and destroyed as when Neil cheated on her. More unwanted tears flooded her eyes.

Just as she finished putting on jeans and a sweater, Hud's apartment door rattled. Was he home already? She groaned. "Tris?"

"I'm in here," she forced herself to answer. Too bad her idea of dressing up like a flirty office assistant and planting a whopping kiss on her boss's lips had backfired so horrifically. Otherwise, their being alone at Hud's apartment might have turned out differently. But she didn't want to think about that. She'd gather her things and leave quickly.

"Tris?" Hud nudged the bedroom door open. "Here you are."

"Here I am." She strode past him without meeting his gaze, hoping he didn't see her red-rimmed eyes.

He followed her into the kitchen. "I'm sorry about Melissa being at the office like that."

"You and me both." She ran water into a glass, then drank a few sips. "What did she want, other than to fawn all over you?"

He set a mixed floral bouquet on the counter in front of her. "I am sorry."

She eyed the flowers. "Are you going to tell me what happened?"

"Sure. When I arrived at the office, hoping to find you there, Melissa was waiting."

"Did she flirt with you?" She already knew the answer! Trista clutched the glass tightly, glaring at him. She didn't want to be a scowling, jealous wife, but that's what she felt like.

"A little." His cheeks reddened. "I explained that I'm committed to you, and there was to be no more—"

"Flirting? Touching you?"

"Yeah. But nothing happened." He huffed out a breath. "I didn't want her to be there any more than you did, so please don't blame me for her walking into our office. I'm sorry you weren't there to talk with her yourself. And I'm sorry your feelings got hurt."

So was she. Now she was ready to head to Mom's and stay there for the rest of the day—or the rest of the month! Oh, how she regretted working with Hud! And marrying him for his money? What in the world had she been thinking? But even as the tempestuous words crossed her mind, she despised them.

Wasn't she trying to trust God to work things out in their marriage and in their family? How quickly she forgot those things! How quickly she let herself get all riled up, imagining romantic things going on between Hud and Melissa. Even during their dinner at the restaurant, Trista had observed how forward and one-sided Melissa's flirtations were with Hud—while he'd been cordial and polite, nothing more. So when was she going to start trusting her husband and believing that he was committed to their marriage? When was she going to start having more faith in God and believing that He was working in their lives together?

"How did you find me?"

"I went by your mom's. She was surprised you weren't at work."

"Great. Now she'll know we're fighting." She set the glass down firmly in the sink.

"Are we fighting?" She glanced sharply at him. "I mean"—he strolled around the counter, coming closer but not touching her—"do we have to fight? What happened with Melissa wasn't either of our faults. You're here looking sweet and beautiful. I'm here bringing you flowers and wanting to kiss you."

She clenched her jaw. She doubted she looked sweet or beautiful. And kissing? *Not likely.* "I'm angry and mortified that I dressed up and had big plans of—"

"Yes?" Grinning, he looked her over appreciatively. "I'm sorry I missed out on getting a good look at you in heels and a short skirt—and receiving a kiss from you that would have made my day."

"Hud—"

"What? You looked cute."

"I wanted to flirt and be alone with my husband. Not to find another woman sitting beside you, touching your arm and making eyes at you."

"I moved away from her immediately. I told her she was never to act that way toward me again! That I'm a married man who loves his wife." He took a step closer to Trista. "The only woman I want to be alone with and close to is you."

"But I'm mad at you." She was still angry at him, right? Hud couldn't waltz in here with flowers and huskily-spoken words, and everything would be instantly fine.

"Do you have to be upset with me?"

"Yes." She pursed her lips and averted her gaze.

"I'm sorry this morning's plan got botched." He leaned his backside against the counter. "Honestly, it's not what you think, anyway. Melissa wants me to mentor her son."

"What?" The woman must be duping him into believing she wanted him to do something honorable like that just so she could be alone with him. The nerve of the woman!

"Her teenage son is in trouble at school. She wants me to hang out with him and act like a big brother." He shrugged. "I have some experience with that."

"And you believed her?"

"Why wouldn't I?" He peered down at her. "Oh, I see. You don't believe me, do you? You don't trust me."

"I don't trust her! I don't believe her!" Trista gripped the edge of the counter, not wanting to admit the whole truth to him. "She's flaunted herself around you since the first day she met you."

His face hued a wine color. "Doesn't matter. What matters is what you think of me. What do you want us to be as a couple?"

Heat coursed up her middle, but she wasn't ready to talk about him and her yet. She'd put herself out there by planning to play the flirt this morning. She'd left the office feeling humiliated and rejected—although the rejected part was mostly due to her own thoughts, not Hud's actions. "How she acts around you matters. What you allow her to do around you matters to me, too."

"Why didn't you just walk in and speak to me?" He lifted his chin. "You are my wife and business partner. You have a right to be in our office as much as I do. Why run away?"

She wanted to deny running. But she had left in a big rush. Even when he called her name, she fled. "For starters"—she let some irritation seep into her voice—"it looked like a private conversation or something romantic was going on, and I was intruding."

He gazed up at the ceiling, sighing. "Nothing romantic or remotely private was happening. I would have welcomed you to come in and talk with her. When I learned Melissa wanted help with her son, I wished you were there to discuss parenting with her. You know far more about kids than I do."

She released a breath of hot air and a tad of frustration. She may have overreacted a tiny bit—although admitting that even to herself was difficult and humiliating. Seeing Melissa touching Hud had driven her to instant, irrational thinking. Maybe, just maybe, she had falsely judged him about liking the woman's attention. "If I over-reacted or judged you wrongly, I apologize."

"*If* you judged me wrongly, Tris?" he said teasingly. In the next instant, he pulled her into an embrace, and she went willingly, even though she still felt disappointed about how things had turned out at the office. "I don't want to fight with you." He kissed her lightly.

"I don't want to fight with you either. Just stay away from that woman, okay?"

He pulled back, gazing at her. "I might run into her occasionally since I agreed to talk with her son."

"Hud!"

He tipped up her chin, meeting her gaze without any appearance of guile or evasiveness. "Is it okay with you if I try mentoring Greggory? I realize we should have discussed it before I committed to helping him. I'll back out if you feel strongly that I shouldn't get involved because of his mom's behavior." He stroked her cheek tenderly. "I mean that. It's you and me. How you feel about us means everything to me."

Trista huffed out a breath. "Are you sure she isn't drumming up a problem to get your sympathy? She is a huge flirt with you!"

"The only flirting I want to indulge in is with my wife."

He nuzzled his nose into her neck, distracting her. Warm feelings of marital affection filled her, nearly overriding all the chaotic thoughts and feelings she'd previously had. But she couldn't let herself get distracted from the issue yet. She moved away from Hud and dug under the sink for a vase. After filling a blue one partially full of water, she set the colorful flowers into the container and pondered Melissa's request. "What if Melissa and Greg went to counseling with Pastor Chad? Maybe she'd learn some parenting skills, too."

"I suggested she speak with him."

"You did?"

"I did. She said she'd think about it."

"That's good." His saying he'd call off his plan to help Melissa's son if she didn't want him to be involved sounded thoughtful and trustworthy. She was glad he'd also recommended that Melissa talk to their pastor.

"Do you want me to call and tell her I can't spend time with Greggory?"

Trista arranged a couple of the shorter flowers at the front of the arrangement. "Look. I'm proud of you for wanting to befriend and mentor this young man. We should be loving and caring to everyone."

"But?"

She wiped her hands on a towel, then stepped in front of him. "But I don't want you meeting with Melissa even to discuss her son."

"I won't." They stared into each other's eyes for several seconds. "You're sure this won't be a problem between us?" He tilted his head, gazing at her.

"I hope it won't be." Maybe she should have told him not to do it. But what if this was a way for him to care for a teenager needing a big-brother figure? What if God was opening a door for Hud to share the gospel with him? Who was she to stand in the way of that happening?

Hud clasped her hands and slowly leaned toward her. She lifted their linked hands to stop the kiss she anticipated from happening. "If Melissa needs to be present for anything, I will be there. Agreed?"

"Absolutely."

"All right. Then it's okay with me if you mentor Greggory."

"Thank you." He kissed her softly, and his gentle affection erased more of her doubts. She longed for things to improve between them—and she wanted to forget what transpired earlier. "I'm sorry everything got so fouled up." Hud smoothed his palms down her cheeks, gazing deeply into her eyes like he adored her. "When you came to the office, how were you planning to kiss your boss?"

So he was still thinking about that? She allowed a hint of a flirtatious smile to cross her lips. "You would not have believed the kiss I planned to give him."

He kissed her butterfly softly. "Something like that? Or more like—" He kissed her longer and more tenderly.

"Mmm. Maybe something more like this." She pressed her lips against his and kissed him passionately, smoothing her fingers through his hair and lingering over the kiss like she'd imagined doing last night. She slowly explored his lips with hers, hoping her kisses and affection told him without words just how much she still longed for romance and love with him.

Chapter Fifty-four

Later, they sat together on the couch, eating the pepperoni pizza Hud had ordered. Trista felt languid and relaxed as if they were having a lazy, carefree day on their honeymoon. She hadn't anticipated this kind of day when she'd dressed up to give her husband a flirty kiss at the office, especially not after finding him with Melissa. But she was glad she'd let her offense go. She wanted to believe the best in Hud. And the more time they spent together, the more comfortable she felt with him—and more trusting, too.

They ate pizza, drank coffee, and watched a romantic comedy. Not really watching it. More like looking at the movie occasionally and commenting on funny aspects as they might have done if they were on a date.

"This was a nice way to spend our day. Shall we do this more often?" She stroked Hud's scruffy cheek, enjoying touching his face and getting to know him better. She wanted to breathe in his scent. Breathe him in.

"I'd like that." He kissed her slowly, deliciously. "Every day with you is a dream come true. Baby, I can't wait until you always live here with me."

"Me too." She couldn't wait to start a real married life with him. "But we still have a certain problem to navigate." She hated bringing up a sore subject.

"How long do you think it will take for you and Layla to move in here?"

"We may need an intervention first." She held Hud's hand and circled her finger around his wedding band. The words she'd been wanting to tell him all afternoon thrummed in her mind. *I love you, Hud. I know beyond any doubt that I truly love you.*

"What kind of intervention are we talking about?"

"God's."

"Ah." He nodded solemnly. "I see."

"You know how we've been praying together about our marriage?"

"Yeah." He smiled softly, and she forced herself to concentrate on the topic instead of scooting onto his lap and kissing him some more.

"I'm going to start praying with Layla about us becoming a family, too. And about her accepting you as her dad."

"Sounds like a worthy plan."

"I've been tiptoeing around her feelings, hardly mentioning your becoming a father to her. I think that was a mistake. I'm going to change tactics and be more open about it." She focused on her thoughts, wanting to express herself well. "I'm going to try harder to help her become more accustomed to the idea of us. And encourage her to trust God about it herself."

"Hey, now. I've seen that intense look on your face before. Don't stress about this, okay?" He stroked some hair back from her cheeks. "We'll keep making our family a priority and a matter of prayer. But I'll wait patiently for you and Layla to move in. Don't get me wrong. I'm eager for that to happen. However, I rushed you into this marriage. Even though I've been impatient occasionally, I promise to do better." He brushed his lips against her forehead. "For now, I appreciate moments like we're having today. I thank God for them."

"Me too. But we are married, Hud."

"I know, sweetheart. I know." He took her in his arms, and his kisses were warm and inviting. "I love you. You are the only woman I want to spend the rest of my life with. It's you and me forever."

"Oh, Hud." She wrapped her arms around him. "I love you, too."

He leaned back, a look of wonder on his face. "You love me?"

"I do. I love you, Hud!" It felt so good to finally say the words and mean them.

A wide smile crossed his mouth. "Thank you for telling me, Tris."

"It only took me forty days since our wedding! But somewhere along the way I fell completely in love with you."

"That's amazing. Thank you for being my wife and joining me on this journey."

"It's an honor I will cherish for the rest of my life."

After more kisses, they settled back on the couch and watched more of the movie.

An hour later, Trista awoke with a start. Hud wasn't beside her, but she heard his voice coming from down the hall. He had to be talking on his phone. She rested her cheek against the pillow she'd been curled around and thought about how she'd told him she loved him. She loved Hud! And he loved her!

She'd also told him she would be calling on God's help to convince Layla of the benefits of having a dad and about moving into his apartment. But another idea was strumming through her thoughts. Maybe she should ask for Mom's help, too.

Chapter Fifty-five

Hud ended the phone call, wishing he hadn't picked up. When Melissa had railed on about her son being difficult and not listening to her, he empathized more with the kid than her. Being a teenager was rough. He'd been blessed to have Mom, Dad, and Gran take him and Aiden under their wings and love them through all the troublesome phases of youth.

Mom had always been such a great listener and encourager. She'd included him in everything Lake and Coe were doing, whether basketball, swimming lessons, or doing chores. He'd never felt ostracized because he wasn't born into the North family. Several times Gran had looked him in the eye and said, "Hudson, you are as much my grandboy as Lake and Coe. It's a matter of the heart. Not blood." Since Lake wasn't her grandson by blood either, Hud had believed her.

Through the years, even when he wasn't getting along with Dad, or Gran's meddling annoyed him, or his brothers' pranks got on his nerves, his big, noisy family had always been his own. Why couldn't Greggory and Melissa find a place of togetherness and love, even if they disagreed and drove each other nuts sometimes?

"Sorry about that." Hud walked up behind Trista, peering at herself in the hallway mirror and fingering her hair into place. Their gazes met in the mirror's reflection.

"I didn't want to leave without saying goodbye. But I need to pick Layla up from school." She turned around and hugged him.

"Today was amazing. Having time alone with you was great, even if we had to close the office." He'd loved waking up on the couch with his wife in his arms. And Trista saying she loved him? That was utterly delightful!

"Who called you?" Her cheeks darkened like she was embarrassed to ask. "By your softer tone, I surmised you weren't speaking to one of your brothers."

"It was Melissa." He hated mentioning the woman's name. "I cut it short, but she wanted to know if I'd thought of any ideas about reaching out to Greggory."

Trista smiled tightly. "Next time, include me, all right?"

"I will. Sorry. You were sleeping."

"Even so. I want to trust you completely, so help me out."

"If she calls again, I'll put it on speaker phone so you can hear and respond too." He kissed her softly. "Are we okay?" He didn't want anything jeopardizing the closeness they'd experienced today. He'd taken the call with Melissa, but only to again recommend that she seek a pastor's counsel.

"We're okay. But this stuff about Melissa is driving me up the wall."

"Makes you a little crazy, huh?"

"You'd better watch out!" She play-punched his arm. "Or I'll show up in another costume at your workplace."

"Promise? Because, seriously, I'd love for you to do that." She initiated some passionate kisses between them that set his temperature on fire.

"Now"—she stepped back—"I'd better get out of here, or I'll be late picking up my girl."

"See you tomorrow?"

"Count on it." She hurried to the door, then paused. "You could always sneak up to my room tonight."

"Why, Trista North!" He fake gasped. "What would your mom say about that?"

"She's usually in bed by nine." She winked and slipped out the door.

He wanted to go after her and kiss her again—or tug her back into the condo and beg her to stay a while longer. But she had parenting responsibilities that would have to come first sometimes, and he'd have to be okay with that. Their marriage and their love was worth whatever it took for them to make things work between them.

Glancing around, he noticed Trista had already thrown the pizza box in the trash and put their dirty dishes in the dishwasher. He appreciated her being neat like him. That was part of the reason why they got along so well as business partners.

He dug out the vacuum and ran it around the couch where some pizza crumbs had fallen. As he worked, he silently prayed about their marriage and family. He was doing that more often now, calling on God and having honest conversations with Him throughout the day. *And please help Layla accept me as a dad so we can start being a family.*

He shut off the vacuum and returned it to the hall closet, his thoughts turning to Greggory and his mom. He said a prayer for healing and reconciliation in their lives, too. Who would have thought anyone would consider him as a mentor for their kid? Wait until Lake heard about this! *Lake!* Oh, no. He'd forgotten all about returning his brother's call. He tapped Lake's name on his cell. "Hey, bro. Sorry I didn't get back to you sooner," he said as soon as Lake answered.

"No problem. You must have had your hands full."

"You could say that." Hud smiled at the thought of Trista being in his arms this afternoon.

"I called because Coe contacted me with an urgent request."

"Oh? What's happening?"

"You know how we talked about helping the brothers financially as needs arise?"

"Sure. Then we'd both chip in."

"Right. Coe asked me for some money." Lake cleared his throat. "He wants to bring someone back to the States."

"Someone as in—?"

"He wouldn't give specifics. But I assume it's a female friend by the tone of his voice. Remember how tight-lipped Coe can be?"

"Yeah. I do."

"She must be someone special to him, or he wouldn't be asking for the funds," Lake said with a wry tone. "Although, he seemed embarrassed about it."

"I'll split the cost with you. Just keep me in the loop."

"Will do. Oh. Coe wants this kept private for now."

"You mean not tell Mom and Gran?" Hud smirked. "That's more my style."

"No kidding. Mom and Dad are off on their cruise now, anyway."

"Good timing."

They talked about a few other things, including the financial contribution Lake and Irish were planning to make toward the artists' residencies on a yearly basis. After Hud thanked Lake for their generosity, he brought up the subject of Melissa asking him to mentor her son. Lake razzed him about not letting it go to his head, and the call ended on a jovial note.

However, Coe's situation troubled him. Why did he require money to bring someone to the States? Was there any chance he and this mystery person were more than acquaintances?

Chapter Fifty-six

Three days after the office fiasco Trista didn't want to think about anymore, she drew Mom aside for a quiet discussion before dinner. She had an idea that might resolve some of Layla's angst about them moving in with Hud, but she needed Mom's assistance.

"I understand why you want to be with that handsome husband of yours," Mom said with a wink. "Who wouldn't want to move in with a hunk like him?"

"Mom!"

"I have eyes, don't I? Just because my vision isn't perfect doesn't mean I don't recognize a nice set of abs and a cute smile when I see them."

"You think Hud's smile is cute?"

"Mmhmm." Mom smoothed her fingers over her short gray hair. "I've seen him looking you over, too."

"Shhhh." Trista gazed around the doorway into the living room, making sure Layla couldn't hear them over the television blaring a cartoon.

"He loves you, and you're both trusting the Lord for His help. That's what matters." Mom hugged her in a warm embrace. "I'm happy for you, honey bear."

"Thanks, Mom. I love him, too."

"How long did it take you to figure that out?" Stepping back from the hug, she grinned. "I've known since he started sleeping over here a few days ago."

"You know about that?" Trista's face flushed hot, and she cringed. "You don't mind, do you?"

"Why should I mind? He's your husband!"

"He sure is." Now, if only she could convince Layla that he'd make a great dad for her!

Mom scooped sweet potato fries off a cookie sheet and dropped them into a blue bowl. "He doesn't have to wait until after I retire for the night to come over, either."

Trista snorted. No doubt that's what Hud planned to do tonight.

"Layla, turn the TV off," Mom called in a lilting voice as she carried the bowl of fries into the dining room. "Supper's ready."

After Mom said grace and their plates were filled, Trista winked in her direction as a reminder of their plan. "So, Layla, Grammie and I have been talking." She eyed her daughter, who didn't appear to be listening. "Layla?"

"Huh? What?"

"Grammie needs to leave the house for a couple of days while the place is exterminated and aired out."

"Exterma-what?"

"I saw a huge brown spider in the bathroom." Trista cringed.

"Eeuw!"

"Exactly. We don't like spiders in the house, so some workers will get rid of them for us this weekend."

"I thought I'd have the rugs cleaned too." Mom buttered a piece of bread without looking up. "I'm going to stay with my friend, Lucille, for a few days."

"I like Lucille. She has a nice dog." Layla smiled and nodded like she thought she was also going to Lucille's. "Where are you going to stay, Mommy?"

"Sweet pea, you and I will be staying at Hud's."

"Huh-uh! I'm going with Grammie." Layla grabbed her grandmother's hand. "I'm coming with you, right?"

Mom sent Trista a desperate look as if she was tempted to cave already.

"You are coming with me." Trista kept her tone calm but firm. "Grammie is going to Lucille's. You and I are going to spend the weekend at Hud's apartment."

"I want to play with Jasper at Lucille's!" Layla crossed her arms. "I don't want to go to Hud's."

"Why not?" Even asking the question felt disloyal, but she wanted to get to the bottom of this. "Why don't you like Hud?"

"Because he's not my daddy."

"He could be if you'd let him."

"Huh-uh! Evan says he'll never be my real dad." She lifted her chin as if she knew Trista wouldn't like her comment but was going to say it anyway. "He has a mommy and a stepdad and a daddy and a stepmom. He knows all about family stuff."

"Who's Evan?" And why did he have such sway over her daughter?

"Only my best buddy in the whole world!" Since when did Evan rank higher than Layla's other friends? "He saw my family tree with Hud's name at the bottom. I told him Hud was my *maybe* dad, and he laughed! I like it when Evan laughs."

Trista groaned. "I wish you wouldn't call Hud that."

Layla ate a couple of fries. "Can I go to Lucille's with Grammie? Please?"

"Not this time."

"I want to go with her!"

"Honey bear, maybe—"

Trista sent Mom an exasperated look. One weekend at Hud's wouldn't kill Layla. She needed to find out how nice of a guy he was and give him a chance at being her dad. "You'll have a lovely bedroom there, which you helped paint."

"I hate that room! You can go to Hud's ugly house. Not me!" Layla shoved her plate and water sloshed out of her glass, flowing across the tablecloth.

"Layla!" Trista leaped backward to keep from getting soaked.

"Oh, dear," Mom said and started to stand up.

Trista cleared her throat loudly, and Mom eased back into her chair, cringing toward the wetness. "Layla is going to clean this mess herself. Layla, go get the towel off the oven door handle." Trista pointed toward the kitchen. "Then come back here and clean up the water."

"I don't want to." Layla scrunched up her face.

"Do as I say, now! Then you're going to apologize for your rude behavior."

Grumbling, Layla stomped into the kitchen. Goodness. What would she be like at thirteen if she had this sour attitude at five? *Lord, help us.*

Layla took her time cleaning up the water. Finally, she sat back down but still wore a pouty expression.

Trista scooted her chair in and resumed eating. "What do you have to say, young lady?" Layla pressed her lips together. "We all make mistakes. When we do, we apologize. If you get angry and say something rude or make a mistake, you say sorry."

"Sorry," Layla said through gritted teeth.

"Nicer, please."

"Sorry," she said with less hostility.

They ate in silence for several minutes. Dinnertime probably wasn't the best time to have discussed going to Hud's, anyway.

"I can't wait to see the wall you and Hud painted," Mom said quietly.

"Do you want to come over and see it?" Layla's eyes widened.

"Yes, in fact, I do."

"Mom—" If her mother went to Hud's, Layla would throw a gigantic tantrum when it came time for her to leave. No doubt she'd coax Mom into staying overnight! What would Hud say about that? The idea of getting an exterminator and cleaning the rugs this weekend was about Layla going to Hud's with Trista—without her grandmother.

"How about this?" Mom leaned toward Layla as if hatching a plan of her own. "How about if I go with you to see the painting you and Hud did? Then I can leave for Lucille's from there."

"May I go with you?" Layla asked in a wooing tone. "Please?"

"Layla, Grammie has her own plans," Trista said. "Sometimes you and I have different plans than hers."

"That's right." Mom's eyes moistened like she was close to tears. "You and Mommy are going to have fun at Hud's. However, I would like to see your beautiful wall. Is that okay?" Mom glanced at Trista as if asking her permission, and she nodded.

Layla sighed. "Maybe you can stay for a little while?"

"If Mommy says it's okay." Again, Mom met Trista's gaze.

"Sure." They were compromising and making small strides toward achieving peace in their newly formed family. She hoped and prayed that her marriage to Hud was worth all the trouble it was causing her family right here. While Layla ate her chicken nuggets, acting as if her angst had spent itself, Trista mouthed, "Thank you," to Mom.

"Of course." But a shadow darkened her face. Was the idea of Trista and Layla moving out of her house more emotional for Mom than she'd realized?

Chapter Fifty-seven

A few days had passed since Melissa asked Hud about mentoring her son, and he thought bringing Greggory to the jobsite might be a good ice-breaker. Pastor Chad had dropped by their office yesterday and mentioned having met Melissa and Greggory. So Hud assumed Melissa took his advice and called the pastor, which seemed like a positive step.

For the whole drive out to the development, the teenager sat hunched in the passenger seat of Hud's truck, barely speaking. He may have even dozed off for a few minutes. When they arrived at the project headquarters, Hud parked the truck. "We're here. Let's go." He hadn't brought the kid along just for him to sleep.

Scowling, Greggory shook his straggly, chin-length blond hair. "What if I stay here while you do whatever it is you do? Then you can take me home, and we'll call it even."

"Even? Hardly. I agreed to hang out with you because your mom is worried about you. That's what I plan to do."

"Whatever." Greggory lifted his chin toward the large equipment moving on the far side of the property. "What happened here?"

"A mudslide."

"I heard about that. Were you around when it happened?" Greggory met his gaze for a half-second as if he felt concerned, then resumed his bored slouch.

"I was in that shed over there." Hud pointed toward the small building.

"Must have been freaky. I saw a mudslide on TV. It's like oozing lava—only not hot."

"Something like that. Come on. I'll show you around." Hud hopped out of the truck, relieved when the teenager climbed out of the vehicle without any more balking. "Do you go by any name other than Greggory?"

"Kids at school call me Greg." He shrugged like he didn't care one way or the other.

"Okay, Greg, let's have a look around." As they strode along the perimeter of the development, Hud explained the layout of the art community and about providing housing and resources for artists in six-month residencies.

"Cool," the teenager muttered a few times.

Since the young man didn't ask questions, Hud shared the information he thought might be of interest to him. When they reached the roped-off area where the first community building would be, he decided to be more direct. "What's the deal with getting into trouble at school?"

"Who told you about that?" Greg squinted at him.

"Your mom. As I said, she's worried."

"What's it to you?"

"Honestly, I have no idea." What did he know about reaching a teenager? He thought of Aiden, alone in Denver, following his goal of being a found-object sculptor. Everyone had dreams, including Greg, right? Maybe that would be a better approach. "So what's your dream?"

"What dream?" Hands in his black leather jacket, Greg shuffled his shoulders. "What's there to look forward to on this island?"

"Do you like fishing?"

"No."

"Plan to go to college?"

"Nope."

"Enjoy sports?"

"Not since my mother signed me up for baseball, and I hated it!"

"Art?" Hud asked as a last resort.

"I like art. So what?"

"Wait. You like art?" Hud almost laughed at accidentally landing on one of the kid's interests. However, it was a good thing he didn't guffaw like he might have done with one of his brothers, since it would probably have made communicating with Greg more awkward.

"I sketch. No biggie." A long sigh filtered out of the teenager, who acted more like a boy of ten with his shoulders slumped, a frown furrowed on his face, and his gaze pinned on something in the distance.

"I didn't know." Did Melissa even realize her son liked sketching? "What do you hope to do with your artistic ability?"

"What ability? It's doodling."

"Yet it's the one thing you commented on positively." Hud lifted his gaze to the section of land marked off with stakes and rope for future houses. "Do you think artists would like to live here?"

"If you're providing free houses? Yeah."

"I mean with the community of artists sharing similar interests and resources. Talking about art all the time. That sort of thing."

"I guess."

"Can you picture yourself living in a place like this after you graduate?"

Greg's eyes widened just before a pinched expression covered any interest he'd momentarily revealed. "Might. Anything would be better than staying with my mom."

"Teenage angst is something to behold." Hud chuckled.

"Are you mocking me?" Greg turned abruptly toward the truck.

"Not really." Hud followed him, wishing he hadn't said that, even though he'd only meant it jokingly. "I come from a family of nine boys. I know all about teenage angst."

"Nine?" Greg wheeled around. "Are you kidding me?"

"I'm serious. My aunt and uncle adopted my brother and me into their family after our birth parents died."

"Bummer."

"I'll say. But my new family was a big loving group. Although our dad and grandmother had strong opinions about how we should live our lives."

"They'd get along fine with my mom, then."

"Perhaps. I didn't always get along with them." Hud resumed walking. "But if I survived the chaos of having so many parents and brothers, you'll survive one mom and get through your teenage years."

Greg's snort sounded like a deer huffing in the wild. "Mom's making me talk to some pastor dude."

Hud bit his lip, stopping another chuckle. "It'll be okay. Pastors are usually cool. My dad happens to be one."

"That so?"

"Yep. You will get through this," Hud reiterated strongly. "But if you ever want to talk, call me." He handed Greg a business card with his phone number on it.

"I don't talk with my dad much, but I don't need my mom setting me up with her idea of a role model, either." He tossed a scornful look at Hud as if doubting he'd make a good role model anyway.

"Still. If you'd like to chat, text me. We'll get coffee. Or lunch."

"Can we leave now?"

"Sure. One other thing. I'd like to see your sketchpad."

"No way!"

"I want you to come over to my place tomorrow night for some of the best homemade pizza you've ever tasted. And bring your drawings."

"I don't show them to anyone!" Greg stomped toward the truck.

"You'll come to dinner, right?" Hud persisted as he climbed in behind the steering wheel.

"Do I have a choice?" Greg cast him a pitiful expression.

"Not really."

"The pizza better be exceptional."

"It will be." Hud backed up the truck. "I'm serious about wanting to see your drawings."

Greg groaned, then muttered what seemed to be his favorite word, "Whatever."

Chapter Fifty-eight

"Oh, my! It's so beautiful!" Mom exclaimed on Friday night as she held Layla's hand and gazed admiringly at the paint-splattered wall at Hud's place. "I've never seen such a work of art!"

"I guess it's okay," Layla muttered.

"Okay?" Mom said dramatically. "It's fabulous! Fantastical!"

"You're silly, Grammie."

"Maybe so." Mom hugged Layla, and they both laughed.

Leaning against the doorframe, Trista observed their interactions with some trepidation about what was to come. She'd told Hud about her mom coming over to assist with Layla's transition—and how she hoped Mom could leave without Layla throwing a mega tantrum that might ruin his dinner plans.

Hud inviting Greggory *and* Melissa over for pizza tonight had taken Trista some getting used to. Even though he'd asked for her opinion and said he would invite only Greg if she preferred, how could she have said no when he was trying to do something honorable and helpful for the teenager and his mom? Then, after Pastor Chad praised them for encouraging a family in the community, how could she refuse to let Melissa come over?

Trista kept reminding herself that Melissa Mills was a single mom, so she should show her some extra grace and love. But she dreaded having to observe even one second of the woman's flirtatious behavior toward Hud. If that happened this evening, she wouldn't remain silent! Maybe a minute or two of quiet prayer before their arrival would help her prepare for the evening ahead. Trista focused back on Mom and Layla's conversation.

"What's your favorite part of the wall?" Mom asked.

"The blue part Hud painted." Layla pointed to a section of turquoise flecks.

"What part do you like best that you made?"

"The green sparkly paint."

"It is so pretty. You and Hud make a good team!" Mom turned and nodded once at Trista.

That was her cue. Mom had privately told her that she was going to have a little talk with Layla before she left tonight. Hoping for the best, Trista went to check on Hud, working in the kitchen. He'd prepared enough homemade pizza fixings to feed a whole church gathering. They might have to freeze the leftovers! But being married to a man who knew his way around a kitchen had some nice benefits. "Smells fantastic in here!"

"Thanks, baby. Things going okay with your mom and Layla?"

"Yeah. She's having a meaningful discussion with her. I pray it helps. We'll see when she tries to leave."

"Should I put my earplugs in?"

"Keep them handy." She sidled up to him and wrapped her arms around his waist. "I'm glad we're doing this."

"Hugging?"

"Yes. But I meant reaching out to Greg and Melissa."

"Really?" He set her back and peered into her eyes. "You're telling me you're glad we invited Melissa over? Since when?"

"Since I've been thinking of her as a single mom and how I might have been desperate for someone's help when Layla turned sixteen and I wasn't getting along with her." She shrugged. "Or maybe how I should have some grace for a fellow human enamored with Hudson North!"

Chuckling, he kissed her. "You are one special lady."

"As long as you keep thinking so, I'm good."

"I promise I will." He kissed her more fully. "Now, unless you're going to put on an apron and help me, you'd better skedaddle and stop distracting the cook—or there will be no dinner!"

"Yes, sir!" She ran her cheek down his scruffy chin. "But I like distracting you."

Groaning, he lifted her and set her on the kitchen counter, then kissed her like a man deeply in love with his wife. With every stroke of his fingers against her cheeks and his lips brushing hers, she succumbed to more loving feelings toward him.

A throat clearing broke them apart. "Oh, um. Mom?" Trista croaked. Hud helped her slide off the counter. Her face flaming hot, she dusted off her pants that had flour on them.

"Everything going okay, Beth?" Hud settled his arm over Trista's shoulder as if his mother-in-law hadn't just caught them kissing.

"Fine and dandy. Things are going fine in here, too, I see." Mom snickered. "Layla's in the bathroom. When she comes out, I'm going to say goodbye."

"How did it go?" Trista asked.

"As good as can be expected." Sighing, Mom set her purse strap over her shoulder.

"Thanks for everything." Trista hurried around the counter to where she stood. "I know this is hard on you, too. Thanks for helping us convince Layla that it's okay for her to be here for short spurts without you."

"Sure thing, honey bear." Mom kissed her cheek. "My home is always yours and Layla's." She pegged Hud with a mischievous gleam. "You're welcome there anytime too, son."

"Thanks, Mom. I appreciate that." He grinned.

"Now you won't have to sneak through the house at midnight." She gave him an exaggerated wink.

"No, ma'am." His cheeks hued an attractive wine color.

Trista chuckled at her blushing husband and walked with Mom to the front door. She tensed when the bathroom door opened, anticipating some screaming or wailing from Layla. But before she even uttered a sound, Hud dashed into the hallway and scooped her up. Layla gasped, staring wide-eyed at him.

"I need a special helper to spread cheese on the pizzas. Since you're so good at splattering paint, I think you'll make an excellent cheese spreader. Please, will you be my assistant?"

"I want to go with Grammie." Layla's lips trembled, and tears filled her eyes.

"Aww, sweet pea. It'll be okay," Trista cooed. "You'll see Grammie after the weekend."

"What do you say?" Hud asked. "Can you help me in the kitchen?"

"I guess," Layla said in a small voice. "Put me down first."

"Okay." He lowered her to the floor.

Layla lunged at her grandmother, wrapping her arms octopus-style around her. Mom hugged her. "You'll be fine, pumpkin. We'll be together in a couple of days." Layla didn't let go of her.

"Come on, Layla." Trista tugged on her arm. "Remember, Grammie's going over to Lucille's. We want her to have some fun too."

Sniffling and wiping her eyes, Layla stepped back. Then she fell into Trista's arms, crying. Trista held her and smoothed her hand over her back. "It's going to be okay."

"Bye, all." With her eyes tearing up, Mom slipped out the door.

Hud was still waiting in the hall, looking uncomfortable but not fleeing into the kitchen. Thankfully, he was willing to face this with her and even offered Layla the chance to assist with dinner preparations. "Do you want to help Hud make pizzas now?"

Layla shrugged.

Hud held out his hand toward her. "Come on, pizza princess. Let's make the most fabulous pizzas in the land your mom has ever tasted!" He winked at Trista.

Layla clasped his hand, and they walked down the short hallway together. A rush of emotion engulfed Trista. Maybe this weekend with the three of them hanging out here would be even better than she'd hoped.

Chapter Fifty-nine

"That's not the way you're supposed to do it!" Layla stood on a chair by the counter and squealed when Hud sprinkled grated cheese over her hair instead of on the pizza.

"Uh-huh." He used a childish tone like Layla's. "That's how my brothers and I used to do it."

"I bet your mommy got mad at you for wasting food." She flicked some cheese off her shoulders, hitting him with it.

"Hey, watch it!"

"No, you watch it!" Giggling, Layla grabbed a handful of grated cheese off the mound he'd made and held it up threateningly.

"No, you don't!" He held out his hands.

"Yes, I do!" She hurled the fistful of cheese at him. Flakes hit his face and hair. "I got you!"

"You got me, all right!" Hud flipped pieces of cheese off his face and onto the floor. He shook his hair, letting more flecks fall.

"What's going on in here?" Trista ran into the room and stopped. "Hud?"

"She did this." He pointed at Layla. "It's her fault."

"Huh-uh. He threw cheese on me first." Layla jabbed her finger at him. "It's his fault!"

"Our guests will be arriving any minute! What were you thinking making a mess like this?" Shaking her head at them, Trista planted her hands on her hips, but it looked like she was fighting laughter, too.

"Layla is the one who threw cheese all around the kitchen." More pieces of grated cheese fell to the floor from his hair and shoulders.

"No, I didn't! You aren't supposed to lie."

"Who says?"

"Mommy!"

"All right." He let out an exaggerated sigh. "I can't argue with her."

"God says so too—Grammie told me." Layla crossed her arms, peering at him from her chair like a miniature judge.

"Okay. I can't argue with God, or your mother, either." He shrugged sheepishly. "I confess it may have been some of my fault that my kitchen is now a disaster zone!"

"Get this cleaned up before Melissa and Greg arrive," Trista said sternly. "I mean it!"

Hud gazed at Layla, observing the grated cheese strewn through her hair. If he looked like she did, he was a mess. But the spontaneous fun between them had been worth it. Seeing her smiling had been worth it.

"Layla, finish helping Hud. Then hurry into the bathroom, and I'll get the cheese out of your hair." Trista strode around the corner.

"Who will help me get the cheese out of my hair?" Hud stuck out his lip like he'd seen Layla do a few times.

"Do I have to do everything?" She glared at him, and he nodded solemnly. "Squat down. Right here, mister!" She pointed at the space in front of the sink.

"Just a second." He stuck a pizza in the oven, then bent over in front of her like a servant bowing to a queen.

"Didn't your mommy tell you not to play with your food?" Layla plucked cheese and a few hairs out of his head.

"Ow! Yes, she did. Ouch! So did my grandmother. Be careful, will you?"

"Big baby." She snickered.

"You're the baby," he said mockingly.

"No, you are."

"Layla!" Trista called. "Come now! Let's get you cleaned up."

"Okay!" Layla climbed down from the chair and jabbed Hud's arm. "I like making pizza with you. Next time, let's have a bigger cheese fight!"

So she expected there to be a next time? Hud waited for her to leave the kitchen before he burst out laughing. It seemed he might have made a little headway in the father-daughter department.

Chapter Sixty

With five of them seated at the small dinette table in front of the window, Hud said grace. Since he and Trista had been praying together, he felt somewhat comfortable praying in front of the others.

"Who made the pizza?" Melissa's tone oozed with admiration as she gazed at the large pizza in the center of the table. Two more pizzas lined the countertop.

"I helped!" Layla chimed in.

"That she did." Hud messed up her hair like he would have done with his kid brother. Layla grinned at him. Pastor Chad was right—kids just wanted to have fun and to be loved and accepted. That wasn't a difficult concept, so why had it taken him so long to figure it out?

"It looks amazing." Trista used the pie server to slide a piece onto Layla's plate. "What do you think about it, Greg?"

"It's Greggory," Melissa corrected.

"Oh. Excuse me. What do you think about it, Greggory?"

"Whatever. It's pizza."

"Hey, no mocking my North secret recipe," Hud said with faux offense.

"Fine. It's okay." Greg sulked but still devoured several pieces.

"So, Greg—" Hud started after a lull.

Melissa cleared her throat. "Greggory."

"Right. I'm Hudson, but I prefer Hud." He was probably sticking his nose in where it didn't belong. But Melissa had asked him to intervene on Greg's behalf. Stepping on her toes might be a part of that process. He faced the teenager. "Do you prefer Greggory or Greg?"

"Greg," he muttered without glancing at his mom.

"So, Greg"—Hud ignored the riled look on Melissa's face—"did you bring the sketches I asked you to bring?"

"What's this about?" Melissa demanded.

Hud waited, hoping the teenager would explain, but he didn't. "I asked to see his drawings this evening."

"What drawings might that be?"

"I can draw." Layla lifted her chin toward Greg.

"Probably better than me."

"Want to see what I can draw?"

"Later, sweet pea." Trista tugged on Layla's hand.

"Why can't I show him now?"

"Hud is trying to talk with Greggory about what he likes to do."

"Doesn't matter, anyway." Greg grabbed another piece of pizza and stuffed half of it in his mouth.

"So he doodles." Melissa shrugged. "Even I can sketch. I could draw your portrait—dark eyes, square jaw, slightly puffy lips." She eyed Hud like she was envisioning sketching more than his face.

Trista cleared her throat loudly.

Hud clenched his jaw, stopping himself from saying something rude to Melissa. Her insensitive comments would make things only worse between her and Greg. It didn't take a parenting genius to figure that out! How could he tell her that she was part of the problem? She was so attention-seeking she didn't recognize her son's need for a bit of the spotlight. And her attempts at flattery toward Hud were shallow and pointless. "Melissa, I want to see Greg's sketches," he said firmly.

"But why?" Her voice rose.

Maybe he'd made a colossal mistake in inviting her to accompany Greg to this first meal with them, even though Trista had agreed to it. He'd thought he was being helpful by encouraging Melissa and Greg to do something together, but now he wondered. "How about if he shows us his sketches? Then we can all see them. What do you say, Greg?"

Groaning like Hud's request was a tremendous bother, the teenager trudged down the hall to the coat rack where he'd set a backpack earlier.

Hud glanced at Trista to make sure she was doing okay. She gave him an understanding smile, and he winked at her.

When Greg returned to the table, he pulled out a pristine-looking sketch pad—not a ratty drawing pad like Hud envisioned a teenager carrying. He handed it to Hud like he was passing him an object of immense value.

Layla climbed up on her knees and peered over Hud's arm. She seemed more comfortable with him now that they'd worked together on the pizzas—or because of their cheese fight. He'd have to remember to have more fun cooking with her in the future. He met Trista's gaze and found tears in her eyes. Tender emotions tugged on his heartstrings, too. Trista and Layla were his family now—*his family.* And God may have put Melissa and Greg in their lives for a reason, too.

A desire to do good for others and to show more grace urged him to press on with this gathering as planned tonight. He wanted to be helpful to Greg—a friend, at least. Would Gran say that was him listening to God's voice? Would Dad break into commentary on how Hud had a servant's heart like Hudson Taylor? Smiling, he felt warmed and humbled by those thoughts.

"Hurry up, Hud! I want to see it," Layla said.

Tempted to address her complaining tone, he opened the sketch pad and flipped through the pages filled with unbelievably realistic pencil sketches. Greg's ability to capture emotion and intricate details with a pencil was evident in each drawing. The wrinkles and fine lines around the older people's eyes, especially the ones of Native Americans in their traditional dance costumes, were stunning. Hud felt in awe of the teenager's artwork. "Man, Greg. These are fantastic! I'm impressed with your work!"

"Greggory?" Melissa's voice went softer than Hud had heard her speak. "Why didn't you tell me you could draw this well?"

"What—"

"Don't you dare say 'whatever!'"

Hud grinned at the red-faced teenager.

"So I like sketching and shading. Drawing makes me feel like I'm unraveling a mystery." It was as if the young man opened a small window of himself to let Hud and the others see inside.

"I would have put you in a special class. Paid for art lessons!" Melissa's voice escalated. "Sent you to New York!"

"Like I'd want any of that!" Greg hunched his shoulders. "I only agreed to let him see the drawings." He lifted his chin toward Hud.

Hud felt like he'd received a great honor. "Thank you for showing me your artwork. It's amazing." Carefully, he handed the sketch pad back to Greg. "You know what this means?"

The teenager shrugged like he didn't care and didn't want any more attention brought to himself.

"What does it mean? What are you talking about?" Eyeing Hud, Melissa clutched a ruby pendant on her necklace.

"He's an artist. When he graduates, he can apply to live in one of our project houses as an artist in residence, if he wants."

"I don't know about—"

"Really?" Greg cut into his mom's rebuttal. "Like you mean it?" His eyes widened expressively.

"I mean it." Hud nodded toward Trista. "My wife and I are making the artists' community because there's a need for it in Southeast Alaska. My kid brother will be moving here and living in one of the houses. He's a found-object sculptor."

"Wow."

"What is a found-object whatever?" Layla pushed away from Hud and settled back in her chair.

"Just what it sounds like," Greg answered.

"I can find stuff," Layla said in a petulant tone. "What's so big about that?" Greg rolled his eyes as an older brother might do to an annoying sibling.

"How about if we do a sculpture together?" Hud glanced around the table. "We could hunt for items here, then glue them together. Aiden used to search for stuff all over our house and make the weirdest-looking sculptures."

"That sounds like fun." Trista nodded toward Layla.

"Count me out." Greg stuffed his sketch pad back into his backpack. "Can we go now?" He gazed wearily at his mom like the evening was too taxing. He'd been interested in a possible artist's residency a few minutes ago. What had changed his attitude so quickly? Was it because of his mom's reaction? Or was he bored with everything?

"Sure, honey. We can go." Melissa stood and picked up her plate.

"Don't worry about that." Trista stood also. "Layla and I have clean-up duty tonight."

"Aww, Mommy!"

Hud grabbed a pizza plate with a couple of pieces left on it. "Hold up a sec, Greg. I'm going to give you some leftovers."

"Really, his name is Greggory." Melissa followed Hud into the kitchen. "I prefer it."

"But does he?"

"Who knows what he wants? Other than drawing. And I just found out about that." She rolled her eyes. "Thank you for dinner, though. I can't believe you cook like a chef. Your wife is a lucky lady."

"I couldn't agree more." Sidling up to Hud, Trista linked her hand in the crook of his elbow and pressed her warm cheek against his arm. He kissed the top of her head.

"Yes, well." Melissa cleared her throat like she was uncomfortable with their affectionate display. Even so, Hud and Trista shared a smile.

"My brothers and I learned to cook from our dad and grandmother." He glanced over his shoulder at Layla. "It's what I plan to do with my kids too." He handed Melissa the plate piled with pizza and covered with plastic wrap. "It's nice to find a common interest to focus on together. You and Greg both like sketching. Maybe you should try that for a family activity."

"What a unique idea! You may have helped us more than you know." She reached out as if to stroke his arm.

Trista stepped between Melissa and Hud and drew their guest toward the door. "I enjoyed visiting with you and Greggory tonight. I hope you'll come over again."

"Really?"

"Certainly."

Hud shook Greg's hand. "We'll meet up again soon."

"Whatever." The teenager started to leave, then turned back. "Thanks for, uh, looking at my sketches."

"Of course. You have talent. Keep doing what you enjoy." A softer look crossed Greg's face. He shrugged, then left.

As soon as the door closed, Hud exhaled a long breath. Hopefully their get-together had done some good for Greg—perhaps some good for all of them.

Chapter Sixty-one

"I have a different idea other than scrounging around the apartment for found objects," Trista said to Hud on Saturday morning.

They were sipping coffee and talking quietly before Layla woke up. She'd gone to bed last night without even fussing about being away from her grandmother. During her prayer time, Layla had been receptive to praying about the three of them becoming a family, too. Whatever Mom told her must have convinced her to be more agreeable. Or else Hud's cheese fight did the trick! Either way, Trista was immensely grateful.

"What's your idea?" Hud stroked his fingers across her jawline, momentarily distracting her.

"Let's drive out to Ward Lake and look for found objects there. That would give Layla a better idea of what Aiden does when he's making a sculpture. What do you say?"

"That it's wet and miserable outside."

"If we stopped doing things because of the rain in Ketchikan, we wouldn't go anywhere!" She nudged his arm. "Come on. It'll be fun. We'll bundle up, bring some plastic bags, and start collecting. We can haul our finds back here and sort through everything."

"You're serious?"

"Absolutely! I love being at the lake, even on cold, wet days. Besides, you'll keep me warm if I get cold, right?"

"You can count on that!"

"Then it's settled."

"What's settled?" Layla shuffled down the hall, tugging her sweater over her pajamas.

"Good morning, sleepyhead." Trista hurried over and kissed her cheek. "Did you sleep well?"

"I guess. What were you talking about?"

"You know how we were going to hunt for objects for an art project here?"

"Yeah." Layla peered suspiciously at Hud like he might have changed his mind.

"I thought hunting for stuff at Ward Lake would be fun."

Layla scowled. "It's too cold and wet out!"

"I'm with Layla!" Hud agreed.

"Oh, you guys. It's not that cold!"

"What's for breakfast?" Layla changed the subject.

Trista glanced at Hud. "Do you have anything in mind?"

"Leftover pizza or pancakes?"

"Blueberry pancakes?" Layla asked hopefully.

"Absolutely." Hud opened the freezer and hunted through some packages. He lifted out a bag of frozen berries, then pulled a whipped topping container out of the fridge door. "Give me fifteen minutes, and I'll have blueberry pancakes with whipped cream on the table that will tickle your tastebuds!"

Layla waved Trista down to her level and whispered, "He's a pretty good cook."

"I'll say! Maybe we should keep him."

"Maybe." Layla gazed over Trista's shoulder, watching Hud intently.

When Trista glanced back, he winked at her and smiled. It seemed like sparkling confetti dusted the room with happiness and hope for their future. She sighed, enjoying being this man's wife and the three of them becoming a family.

After a fantastic breakfast, they were finally on their way toward Ward Lake, and as Hud predicted, the rain was falling heavily.

"I don't want to get all wet," Layla whined.

"The trees will mostly protect us." Trista nodded, trying to convince her.

"Only if we go on the trail—which I don't want to do!"

"Okay. Okay." Hud pulled the truck over to the shoulder of the road.

"What are you doing?" Trista asked.

"Since it's raining so hard, don't you think we ought to head back?"

"I do," Layla grumbled.

"We have warm clothing on. Come on, Hud." Trista patted his shoulder. "We live in a rainy place. Let's just do this. It'll be fun."

"Please, can we go back to Hud's house?" Layla asked in a pleading tone. Hud's eyebrows rose. Her request must have surprised him, too.

"Layla, I want you to try this adventure," Trista appealed to her. "If it starts raining hard, we'll run back to the truck. But I think we'll have fun hunting for stuff outside!"

"It doesn't sound fun to me."

"Please?"

Hud and Layla glanced at each other with slight grimaces. Then, sighing, Hud pulled the truck back onto the road. At Ward Lake, he parked in the empty lot without commenting on the downpour.

The murky gray lake in front of the grassy beach was getting a good dousing of raindrops. The wet grass and trail didn't look inviting, but Trista didn't want them to leave without getting some objects for their sculpture. "Let's gather as many things as we can. We'll be fast!"

"It's too rainy, Mommy!" Layla said as soon as her feet hit the ground.

"You have warm clothes on." Trista adjusted her hat. "It'll be fine."

Hud glanced up at the dark, threatening clouds and frowned. "You sure about this?"

"Mostly." Maybe she should have agreed to return to the apartment. But they were here, so they might as well make the best of it. She handed Layla and Hud each a plastic grocery bag, then tucked one into her coat pocket and led the way across the soggy grass. "Collect anything that looks like something we can glue together. After the sculpture dries, we'll paint it."

"What color?" Layla jumped over a mud puddle.

"Lime green," Hud answered with a grin.

"At least you know that much about me." Layla made a smirky face at him.

"I know you like my blueberry pancakes with whipped cream."

"And your homemade pizza," Trista added.

"Doesn't mean he knows anything else about me." Layla sighed like she had teenage angst instead of five-year-old irritability. "Not like if he was my real daddy."

Hud huffed out a hoarse-sounding breath and stopped walking. Did Layla's snub hurt his feelings? Having a father was a new idea for her, but so was having a daughter for him.

"That's true, Layla," he said softly. "But I'd like the chance to be your real dad and become familiar with your likes and dislikes." He squinted at her with raindrops dripping down his cheeks. He lifted his chin in the defiant way she did sometimes. "But you don't know anything about me, either." Layla's jaw dropped. "If you were my kid, you'd already know some things about me. As it is, you don't know anything!"

Trista bit her lip to stop her chuckle from ruining the moment.

"I know you cook pizza and pancakes from *scat*."

Hud snorted like he was fighting laughter and resumed walking.

Trista prodded Layla forward. "It's scratch, sweet pea. From scratch."

"Whatever," she said like Greggory did last night.

"So I cook. What else do you know about me?" Hud asked over his shoulder.

"You like my mom. I saw you kissing her. That was disgusting!" He turned around, grinning. "And you were nice to that kid, even though his mom was annoying."

"What else?"

"You have twenty brothers."

"Eight, to be precise."

Layla pointed toward the trailhead, overshadowed by dripping evergreens. "I'm not walking around the lake in this yucky rain."

"No. But we are going to look for objects for our project," Trista said. "Hunt for anything pretty, funny, or cool."

"Whatever." Layla stomped toward the lake, away from the trail-head. Hud gave Trista a quick hug, then followed Layla.

Trista didn't mind searching for items by herself. But five minutes later, the rain came down in torrents as if the clouds were wringing themselves out overhead. The cover of trees didn't help much, either.

"We're heading for the truck!" Hud scooped up Layla and ran with her squealing.

"Be right there!" Trista picked up a few more items—a blue piece of fabric, a lipstick lid, and a small part of a gold chain. But when the rain came down in a drenching downpour, she sprinted for the truck. Hud opened the door, and she slid inside. "Now that's a gully washer!"

"It was fun, Mommy!" Layla shivered and giggled. "I found an old shoe for the sculpture." Trista was relieved to hear the positive tone in her daughter's voice. "We found a plastic soda bottle and some underwear!"

"What?"

"You said to find interesting things at the lake." Hud grinned. "So we did."

"Mommy, can we come back and do this another day?"

Trista forced her mouth not to drop open in shock. "Yes, of course, sweet pea."

"Maybe Greg would like to come with us too."

Trista whirled around. What had transformed Layla's attitude from being grumpy about the whole outing to happy in those five minutes she and Hud were hunting for items for the sculpture?

Chapter Sixty-two

After they changed out of their wet clothes, Hud worked with Trista and Layla at the table, sorting through all the pieces they'd collected. Damp cardboard went in one pile. Small sticks and twigs in another. One pile held miscellaneous items—gum wrapper, pacifier, doll shoe, lipstick lid, and cloth. Trista claimed veto power and tossed the underwear in the trash.

"When do we get to start gluing?" Layla asked with an impatient tone.

"It all has to dry first." Hud let a frown that rivaled hers cross his mouth. "You don't mind waiting until tomorrow to do the gluing, do you?"

"I'm going back to Grammie's house tomorrow."

"What if you didn't? What if you stayed here longer?"

"Why would I do that?"

"Hud's right." Trista met his gaze and smiled. "What if we stayed here for a few more days and worked on the sculpture together?"

Layla stared hard at Hud as if analyzing him.

"Will you give me a chance, Layla?"

"I want to be with Grammie!"

"Right. But you had a fun time today, didn't you?" He waited with bated breath. It felt like he stood on the precipice of a new beginning—of them truly becoming a family.

"That doesn't mean anything."

"Why can't it mean everything?" He gazed into Layla's green eyes. "I'd like to prove that I can be more than a *maybe* dad. How about a *real* dad who you enjoy doing activities with? Such as hunting for found objects. Or having cheese fights."

A small smile crossed Layla's mouth.

"What do you say?" Trista prompted her.

"If I stay, can we have blueberry pancakes tomorrow?"

"Yes," he said.

"And the next day?" Layla asked louder.

"And the day after that." He let his voice get louder too.

"Can I stay with Grammie on all the weekends?" Layla lifted her chin as if daring either of them to disagree. "That's what she said I could do."

Was that what Beth had talked to Layla about—staying with Hud and Trista during the week and with her on the weekends? God bless Beth!

"Of course, sweet pea." Trista clasped Layla's hand. "Any weekend Grammie is home, you may spend with her. She'll come here for dinner sometimes, too. What do you say?"

Would Layla throw a massive tantrum, yelling that she didn't want anything to do with moving into Hud's condo or having him for a dad? Had all their efforts to get her to want to stay here have been in vain? He held his breath.

"I'll think about it." She shrugged. "When will we paint the sculpture?"

Hud exhaled. "Tomorrow, if the pieces are dry. Or the next day."

"We're going to paint it lime green, right?"

"That's right."

Layla walked down the hallway, then paused and glanced back. "Oh, yeah. I like my room." She skipped into her bedroom and closed the door.

Trista clutched Hud's hand. "You did it!"

"What did I do?"

"She's accepted you—and us living here. You did it!" Cupping his cheeks between her hands, she kissed him thoroughly, which he enjoyed but he still didn't get it.

"Why do you think I did anything? Layla didn't agree to give me a chance."

Trista intertwined their fingers, her eyes glowing. "When she said she'd think about it and skipped happily into her room, that was her acquiescing to us staying here."

"It was?" He released a flabbergasted sigh.

"I'm not saying that was our last battle. But for now, it's something to be celebrated!"

He still felt baffled. "I don't understand girls any more than I did before this weekend of trying to win Layla over."

"You'll figure us out." Trista kissed his cheek.

"Does this mean you'll move your stuff over here?"

"Absolutely."

"That's amazing!" He kissed her and pulled her closer until she was almost in his lap. Remembering Layla might return at any moment, he ended their kiss and leaned his forehead against Trista's. "I love being married to you, baby."

"I love being married to you, my darling."

His phone buzzed, and he sat back and glanced at it. "Lake" crossed the screen. "I should take this."

"That's okay. I'll run and check on Layla." She got up quickly.

"You have the worst timing!" Hud said when he answered the call.

"Sorry, man. I wanted to let you know I sent Coe the funds. He and his friend will be arriving in Spokane in four days."

"Four days, huh?"

"Yeah. Something suspicious is going on." Lake made a disgruntled snort. "His secretive behavior is unlike our calm, cool, collected Coe. Is there any chance he married someone without telling us?"

"Coe would never do that!"

"No. I don't suppose he would. But why wouldn't he tell me her name? Why all the hush-hush stuff?"

"Maybe she's a dignitary—or someone he doesn't want us to recognize."

"Maybe. No doubt there's a good explanation." Lake sighed. "I wish you were going to be here for their arrival."

"I'll keep it in mind." Hud heard Trista coming back into the room. "Text me the ticket amount, and I'll transfer the money to you in a few minutes."

"Will do. Sorry for interrupting whatever, bro."

"No problem." Hud ended the call.

Trista sat on the couch beside him. "Layla's reading in her room."

"Okay. Where were we?" He tugged her into his arms.

"Whispering how much you love me?"

"I do love you, Trista North."

"And I love you, Hud North."

He kissed her a few times, so thankful for these moments alone to be together. Any second Layla could stomp into the room and demand to know why he was kissing her mom, but he was willing to take that risk. "You are the most important person in my life," he whispered in Trista's ear. "I want to spend all my waking hours with you."

"Since we work together, we do spend most of our waking hours together."

"But I want more. More time together. More love." He kissed her deeply, hungrily. They still had things to discuss—the money he would transfer to Lake, his adopting Layla, and if they needed a bigger house—but all he wanted to do was kiss and hold his wife for the rest of the day.

Chapter Sixty-three

On Tuesday morning, Layla asked Hud to drive her to school. Trista nodded eagerly at him over Layla's head as if a lot was riding on her request and his answer.

Everything about their long weekend had gone well. They went to church on Sunday, had a nice lunch afterward, and then worked on the sculpture together.

Their hours spent making the unusual three-foot creation from dozens of miscellaneous parts turned out to be more enjoyable than Hud had imagined. Even Greg came over on Sunday afternoon and offered pointers. He didn't know a lot about found-object sculptures, but he had an artistic eye and seemed to enjoy hanging out with their group. And he agreed to go to church with them the following week since he and his mom were already attending counseling sessions with Pastor Chad.

As they glued pieces together, then used a blow dryer to get it to dry faster, they laughed over the weird shape the sculpture had morphed into. It wasn't a masterpiece, but it was a fun collaboration. On Monday, they painted their creation green and gave it big black eyes. Layla called it a "Lime Monster" and begged Hud to take a picture of her with it and print a copy for her to show everyone at school.

Before Hud and Layla left the condo, Trista gave him a thumbs-up. Apparently, Layla asking him to drive her to kindergarten was a big deal—like she was the princess, and he was her chosen chauffeur. He chuckled at the idea, unable to grasp the concept of one child being doted on exclusively—especially when his upbringing included nine siblings sharing everything, including their parents' and grandmother's time.

"So, Hud," Layla said in a serious tone when he pulled to a stop beside the walkway leading to the elementary school. "What's it going to be?"

"What are we talking about?" He faced the five-year-old.

"Do you want to be my real dad or not?"

"Uh, yes!" Emotion clogged his throat. "Of course I want to be your real dad!"

"Then I accept." She stuck out her hand like they were about to shake on a business deal.

His heart pounding hard, he held his hand toward hers but didn't shake it. "What about you? Will you be my real daughter?" Moisture filled his eyes and he blinked rapidly.

"What about me getting a dog?"

So they were back to that?

"Well—" If this were a business negotiation, he would seek a compromise, right? "How about if I agree that someday you may have a dog?"

"Someday as in soon?" She moved her hand an inch closer to his.

"Someday as in eventually." Layla deserved to have a pet of her own while she was growing up. He would ensure that happened, but not right now.

She sighed melodramatically. "Okay, then. I will be your daughter."

"That's great! Thank you, Layla!" He shook her hand fervently.

"Whatever." She let go of his hand and tugged her backpack onto her shoulders.

He turned off the truck and came around to open her door, then helped her slide down from the seat. "Can I walk you into the building?"

"No, silly. Kids go in by themselves." She lifted her chin as if he'd insulted her.

"How about a kiss on the cheek?" He squatted beside her. "Does a real dad get to kiss his daughter?"

"I suppose."

He kissed her cheek, then said the words on his heart, "Have a wonderful day. I love you, Layla."

Her eyes widened and purple sparkles flickered in her irises like her mom's. Suddenly, she wrapped her arms around his shoulders and hugged him tightly. Then she let go and ran toward the stairs. Before entering the building, she turned back and waved. "Bye, Daddy!"

"Bye." He gulped and watched Layla enter the school. Just like that, she'd accepted him as her dad. She was his daughter! As tender emotions hit him again, he bowed his head and took a deep breath. *Thank You, Jesus, for what You're doing in my life. Help me to be a good dad to Layla like Smith was to me.*

Smith. Dad. A wave of gratitude toward the man who'd helped raise him rushed through Hud. Thinking of how Dad had been a loving and devoted parent to him and his brothers made him get even more choked up. He'd been lucky to have two great dads in his life—blessed, even. He'd never forget that again.

At the office, he walked straight to where Trista sat at their work table and kissed her softly. "Thank you for marrying me and letting me be a part of Layla's and your lives. Thank you for loving a guy like me."

"Ah, Hud. You're welcome. I love you so much." She kissed him, and the warmth and sweetness of their love filled his heart. He would rather spend the day kissing Trista than finding investors and ordering materials. He'd rather kiss his wife than do anything else. "Driving Layla to school must have been successful," she said with a smile.

"It was terrific. She might even like me a little."

"Of course she does! You're a nice guy. You're going to be a great dad."

"I hope so." He dropped into a chair, trying to focus on some printouts, but his eyes kept tearing up.

"What is it?" Trista clasped his hand across the layout of one of the artist's houses. "Are you okay?"

"Better than okay. Shall we call the attorney and get the adoption started?"

"Are you truly ready for that?" Her eyes filled with moisture, too.

"I am. I'm feeling so much about being a family man right now."

"What do you like best about being a family man?" She gave him a flirty smile.

"I like being your husband the best. Is there anything you like about being married to me?"

"I like your cooking." Slowly, she stood and strode around the table, her gaze fixed on his like a dancer crossing the dance floor to her partner. She settled on his lap and wrapped her arms around his neck. "And I like hearing you snoring in my ear in the mornings."

"Be serious."

"I am being serious. Your snoring reminds me that you are my husband, and we are close enough to hear each other snoring. I'm grateful for that." She took a breath. "I love you, Hud. And I thank God for bringing you into my life to be my husband—and my children's dad."

"Aww, baby, thanks. That means everything to me." With her gazing at him so lovingly, he felt like a better person for having known her and for what they'd already experienced as a couple. He kissed her again and again.

"I love you as I've never loved another person." She stroked his whiskered chin softly. "Trusting you to be mine was a giant leap for me. But I'm so glad I did."

"I'm glad you did, too. You are my heart. And I am yours."

Gran had said when the right woman came into his life, she would be perfect—and she was right! Trista was perfect for him in every way. An idea came to mind, and he scooted her off his lap and stood with her.

"What's wrong?"

"Not a single thing." Grinning, he grabbed her coat. "I have a question for you." He helped her put on her jacket. "Will you be my partner for life?"

"Yes, of course! But we already agreed about that. What's going on?"

He donned his jacket. "Let's close the office and go on a honeymoon."

"Walk away from all our tasks?" She glanced back toward the papers on the table.

"What's the benefit of owning our own business if we can't take time off when we want? If something comes up, we can work from our laptops. Let's go home, make plans, and dream together." He kissed her softly and then shut off the lights. "Are you okay with this?"

"If my husband wants to take a day off and dream with me, I'm taking a day off!"

"I'm thinking more like a week." He envisioned them sitting in a luxurious hot spring in Montana, spending time together in the bridal suite at the resort in Coeur d'Alene, and then stopping in

Thunder Ridge to see Coe. "Will you take some time off with your new husband?" He kissed her a couple more times.

"I have a question for you. Are you going to cook something delicious for me?"

Leaning back slightly, he grinned. "I'll cook anything you want, whenever you want it."

"That's a promise I'll hold you to."

"Good."

Their lips met once more. And once more.

Then Hud clasped Trista's hand and led her out of their office. In his heart, he was leading his wife into a deeper, closer, enduring relationship. And while their marriage had started out as one of convenience, they were now enjoying a sweet, loving marriage that would last a lifetime. And he thanked God for such a precious gift.

Epilogue

"Dear Mom," Coe wrote in an email he'd been debating whether to write for the last half hour. Should he write Mom? Or just show up in Thunder Ridge with Skye?

He'd come to India to follow the Lord's leading with a heart to serve others in desperate circumstances. He'd fulfilled that goal. But what of the disturbing situation he was in now? Was everything that had happened to him a part of God's plan?

Coe was usually so careful in a foreign country, avoiding any appearance of wrongdoing. When he'd offered to escort Skye home after church on Sunday night, he'd thought he was doing the gentlemanly thing by walking with her and ensuring she got home safely.

But he hadn't anticipated the consequences of kissing her good night. He didn't mean for their first kiss to turn so passionate. And he couldn't have foreseen how upset Skye's strict ex-military father—and Coe's host for the humanitarian aid group he worked with in India—would be when he saw them embracing.

"You will leave the country at once and never see my daughter again!" Liam Tamarack shook with rage, his face beet red and his fists clenched.

Coe didn't resist the man's security team when they roughly dragged him off the property, despite the anger and humiliation coursing through him.

Then, in the middle of the night, Skye knocked on his door—another situation that could have had dire consequences. "Father says I must marry Edmund Lung, supposedly for my protection. How can he think I'd go along with such a scheme? He's gone too far this time! Please, take me away with you?" Her dark gaze met his with a look of pleading or longing. "I really want to be with you, Coe."

Every tender emotion he possessed begged him to say he would do as she asked—and what she hadn't asked. She was implying marriage, wasn't she? Their kissing proved they had passion. Was that enough to build a relationship on?

"I have news I don't want to explain via email," he typed quickly. "When I get to Thunder Ridge, I will tell you everything. Pray for my safe return. Love, Coe."

Thank you for reading *Hud*, Book 2 in The Preacher's Sons series!

Look for Coe's story coming in 2024.

The Preacher's Sons series is a spin-off from *Liv & the Preacher*. If you haven't read Liv and Smith's story yet, try it today

Special acknowledgements:

Paula McGrew, thank you for your help and encouragement with *Hud*. I appreciate your editorial assistance and your heart for my stories so much!

Mary Acuff, Kellie Griffin, Joanna Brown, Beth McDonald, and Jason Hanks, thank you for being beta readers for my projects. I'm thankful for the positive things you have to say *and* the deeper critiques that make my stories better. Thank you for saying "yes" to helping me again!

Suzanne Williams, thank you for another sweet cover. I appreciate all the work you've put into making my covers beautiful.

Jason, thank you for always being positive about my writing and encouraging me to continue with my stories. You are a blessing to me!

Kyle Quinn, thank you for taking time to chat with me about business stuff. I am proud of your entrepreneurial spirit!

Readers, thank you so much for giving my stories a chance! I appreciate you!

This is a work of fiction. Any mistakes are my own. ~meh

Christian fiction by Mary Hanks:

Liv & the Preacher

The Preacher's Sons:

Lake, Hud

Restored Series:

Ocean of Regret, Sea of Rescue, Bay of Refuge, Tide of Resolve, Waves of Reason, Port of Return, Sound of Rejoicing, Shores of Resilience

Basalt Bay Series:

Callie's Time

Second Chance Series:

Winter's Past, April's Storm, Summer's Dream, Autumn's Break, Season's Flame

About Mary Hanks:

When Mary isn't exploring the world through her characters' eyes, she is singing toddler songs and playing with her grandchildren. Vanilla lattes, gardening, and taking walks with Jason, her husband of 40+ years, rank high on her list of favorites. Telling stories is a huge part of Mary's life, and she hopes to continue writing heart-warming tales of grace, mercy, and love for a long time.

www.maryehanks.com